THE DEAD ARE BLIND

THE DEAD ARE BLIND

by

Max Afford

RAMBLE HOUSE

It seems scarcely necessary for me to point out that the B.B.C. subsidiary station at Wigmore Street, together with the various heroes and villains in this chronicle, exist only in imagination.

ISBN 13 978-1-60543-004-1

ISBN 10 1-60543-004-8

First published: 1937
Reprinted: 2007 Ramble House
Cover Art: Gavin L. O'Keefe
Preparation: Fender Tucker

THE last phrase written . . . a neat line drawn under it and the sheet of manuscript blotted carefully. Laying down the pen, I turned to where Jeffery sat smoking by the fire.

"It's finished," I told him. "Finished—all except for the title."

Blackburn tossed his cigarette among the coals and stood up. "Why not," he suggested, "call it the Extraordinary Case of Sound without Sight and Sight Without Sound—because that's just what it was, you know."

Book One

SOUND WITHOUT SIGHT

"Everyone who has anything to do with a radio-play subconsciously makes a great act of faith before it begins. He privately asserts his belief that the sounds he is about to make will be carried to other places, and there heard, in private, by a number of people forever unknown and invisible to him."

THE STUFF OF RADIO
(Lance Sieveking).

I

GENERAL NEWS SESSION

"What if it be a poison, which the friar
Subtly hath minister'd to have me dead?"
Romeo and Juliet. Act IV.

TO JEFFERY BLACKBURN, it is *the* case.

Knowing Blackburn so well, I have the unshakable conviction that no matter what future adventures the Fates may have in store for him, the Extraordinary Case of Sound without Sight and Sight without Sound will always remain very close to his heart. Long after he brought to a successful close this dark misalliance of inspired cunning and ruthless ambition, he would dwell lovingly over the remarkable details that even now cause it to be discussed as a criminological *tour de force* wherever the subject of murder sets tongues babbling.

"The criminal anticipated everything—with one exception," Jeffery remarked once in speaking of this case. "He weighed, measured, and calculated in all laws, forgetting only the Law of Possibility." And if that statement is sententious, it is none the less true. Blackburn's entry into the queer business of the broadcasting studio was so indeterminately casual as to arouse a plethora of suppositions. If the Chief Inspector had not received that invitation . . .? If Jeffery had refused to accompany him to the opening . . .? If Miles Conroy had not remembered a certain association of ideas . . .? But why continue when a separate volume might be written on the subject of the postulative and the hypothetical as applied to this astonishing case.

Recalling the abrupt manner in which Blackburn was pitchforked into the murder of Judge Sheldon, and the foreboding events that preceded the raising of the curtain on the frightful business of the Dolls of Death, there is a certain irony in the fact that his chances of being connected with the case under discussion were, in the ordinary course of events, exceptionally remote. He stepped into the business merely as a spectator, a rather reluctant witness who paused momentarily to scoff and remained to ensnare his hands in a net of crime that was to enmesh innocent and guilty alike.

Spring came early to London that year. But the city was not caught unaware. There was entertainment and amusement for all classes in the varied programme of attractions that spread through a thawing muddy March and well into leafy June. The Royal Automobile Club held an international rally at Eastbourne; the *Daily Mail* Ideal Homes Exhibition attracted an army of admiring provincials to Olympia, while the British Industries Fair brought the home counties to shoulder each other in the Manchester streets. The opening of the Shakespeare Dramatic Festival season, the Royal Academy and the Russian Art Exhibitions, drew the artistic; the Derby, the Grand National, and the Cup Final at Wembley gathered in the sporting multitudes. Yet with these and a hundred other diversions to capture his wandering fancy, William Jamieson Read, Chief Detective-Inspector of the Criminal Investigation Department, Scotland Yard, must turn his inquisitive mind to the business of broadcasting.

Jeffery Blackburn, however, shared none of his companion's enthusiasm for the science. The young man considered radio a wholly inadequate means of recreation, and his chief objection, apart from a vilification of the quality of the programmes presented, was to the medium's lack of depth. He compared it to a surrealist one-dimensional portrait which may hold the eye for a few minutes out of curiosity and then inspire nothing save a sense of absurdity. Perhaps this was unfair, but Jeffery, whose love of the dramatic caused him to translate everything into terms of movement and colour, would grow very restless over the "mechanical anaemia" of the reproduction. He openly scoffed at the idea that the radio could possibly replace the manifest emotion of the stage or the concentrated arresting melodrama of the newspaper headline. It was true that a large and expensive wireless set augmented the furnishings of the service flat in Victoria which he shared with the Chief Inspector. Jeffery, however, never lost an opportunity to point out that the inclusion of the polished cabinet was merely another indication of his good-natured tolerance toward the eccentricities of his friend.

"A well-drawing pipe, a good brand of whisky, and the voice of the ether are the Chief's only vices," Blackburn would explain deprecatingly when he ushered his friends into the flat, to find the Chief Inspector slippered before the fire and the radio bellowing triumphantly. "There are times when I suspect that it is really nothing more than an affectation—like Holmes and the cocaine, you know."

Whereupon Read would cock a fierce eyebrow at the visitors and, reaching forward, twist the ebonite knobs of the machine until the clamour reverberated through the rooms.

Radio plays—"execrations of the ether" to Jeffery—had an unfailing fascination for Read. He insisted upon entering wholeheartedly into the spirit of the entertainment, turning out the lights and sitting back with closed eyes during their recital. Meanwhile, an unsympathetic Jeffery fumbled his way about the room, bruising himself on protuberances which made surprising appearance in the gloom or throwing himself down in a chair and holding martyred peace until the drama had run its course. Occasionally these intervals would be enlivened by the young man's sense of humour and he would contribute remarks that turned serious dialogue into facetious burlesque, in spite of Read's irritable plea to "give the players a chance, son!" It was at such times as these that the radio might easily have become an instrument of disruption, but Jeffery had long since realized the truth of the adage regarding one man's meat and another's poison. Thus he compromised, and at length the bare announcement of a radio play was sufficient to send him hurrying to another room and shutting the door tightly behind him.

On this particular Monday night an early dinner had been served at the flat. The two men sat with coffee and cigarettes over the faint sternutation of the gas-fire. The conversation had turned to radio plays in general. A commercial station at Luxembourg had made a feature of the broadcasting of "dinner-hour thrillers", presented to the listening world by courtesy of the Widdis Wonder Wash-cloth, and, as far as the Chief Inspector was concerned, no evening meal was complete without this accompaniment of mystery and mayhem. Since Mr. Blackburn's appetite was stronger than his prejudices, he was forced to lend an unwilling ear to these presentations and so their post-prandial conversation centred about the theme of the play heard on that evening.

"A very fair production," announced Read, pushing back his coffee-cup and reaching for his pipe. In the background, tuned down to a barely audible whisper, the radio hissed in a defeated monotone.

"A very stupid production," commented Jeffery. "Wash-cloths and obscure toxicology! *O tempora! O mores!*"

Read cocked a bushy eyebrow over his half-lit pipe. His tone was acid. "The trouble with you, lad, is that you're too damned highbrow!"

"Possibly," Jeffery agreed amiably. "Yet even the lowest of brows may be excused for sneering at a play with the theme built around a mysterious Indian poison, unknown to modern science, which kills instantly, is tasteless and odourless, and impossible to detect in the victim's body! 'Pon my suffering soul, Chief, there ought to be a law against foisting that kind of nonsense on the public!"

The Chief Inspector shrugged. "Of course—if you're going to pick holes . . ." He paused and levelled an accusing pipe-stem at the young man. "Anyway, son—how d'you know that there isn't such a poison?"

"And that remark," said Jeffery reproachfully, "comes from a Chief Detective-Inspector of Scotland Yard!"

"Well?" barked Read.

Blackburn hitched his chair forward. "What a question! My dear Chief, how do I know that the earth is round? If such a poison does exist, why didn't Dr. Pritchard use it instead of antimony? Why didn't Thomas Wainwright discover it? Take all the notorious poisoners! William Palmer used strychnine, Henry Seddon was suspected of having used arsenic. Hawley Crippen sought to fool the police when he poisoned his wife with hyoscin hydrobromide. And in every case, an autopsy of the bodies revealed the poison! If an undetectable toxin does exist, wouldn't those monsters have tried it? Particularly criminals like Neil Cream and Dr. Lamson, who made a living out of poisoning until they were arrested!"

"You're talking about twenty-year-old crimes," Read objected. "What about the modern developments in chemistry?"

Jeffery flicked an ash from his cigarette. "I'll grant you that chemists are discovering new poisons every month," he admitted. "But that fact only serves to weaken your argument, Chief. Once a poison is discovered and tabulated, obviously it can no longer be termed undetectable!" He leaned back in his chair. "As for methods of poisoning—well, you know that there's nothing new under the sun. Take the example of the Thompson-Bywaters case in 1922. Mrs. Thompson is believed to have used powdered glass in an attempt to poison her husband. Lucrezia Borgia used the same little trick somewhere around 1540."

"What about this new stuff Conroy was telling us of—tetra ethyl lead, the basis of motor spirit?"

"My dear Chief, that's no argument! The foolish can poison with practically anything from disinfectant to weed-killer. Drinking virgin petrol is merely a modernized version of the hemlock of Socrates. And might I point out that tetra ethyl is a *known* poison—"

The big man snapped like a baited terrier. "Of course it's known! But there may be others of a similar nature as yet undiscovered!"

Jeffery yawned. "Outside of those bedtime stories for adults that constitute your present mental pabulum, have you ever heard of such a poison?"

"Talk sense, son!" Thunder rumbled in the Chief Inspector's tone. "Of course we haven't heard of it! If it's undiscovered, naturally it's unknown!" He quietened and hunched his broad shoulders uncomfortably. "I only hope that you're right, lad. If such a poison did exist, it could become a terrible instrument in the hands of the wrong person!"

The young man grinned. "Not in radio plays, Chief. *Veritas omnia vincit* is the simple motto emblazoned across the typewriter of every radio dramatist. Truth always comes out, no matter how obscure the circumstances. That's just why they're all so illogical!"

Read gave a dry chuckle. He was teasing the tobacco in his pipe with a match-end. "You can save your breath by addressing such constructive criticism to the fountain-head," he announced. As Jeffery stared at him, he continued: "D'you remember Nickerson, the young man who was programme director at the B.B.C.? He approached you a few months ago to do a series of talks over the air on the subject of criminology—"

"Which I refused," interrupted Blackburn. "Yes, I remember George Nickerson. What about him?"

"He's appointed manager of the new subsidiary station built near Portland Place—somewhere in Wigmore Street, I understand. It's the official opening tonight." Read paused and bent to fiddle with the tap of the gas-fire. "He's sent along an invitation for two," he concluded rather lamely.

"Oh . . .!" Jeffery wrinkled his face mischievously. "So that's the reason for the early dinner tonight! Alice wants to climb through the looking-glass?"

Read straightened. Like a cornered squid emitting its inky screen, he enveloped himself in a cloud of tobacco smoke. "Of course I'm going," he snapped. "There's a radio play *Darkness is Danger* going on at ten-thirty and I want to see it!" And as the other regarded him in amused silence, Read literally thrust his head through the smoke coils. "Any objections?" he grated.

Jeffery crushed out his cigarette. "None at all," he returned mildly. "You can have your busman's holiday with my complete sanction."

"I suppose"—each word was smeared with a sneer—"I suppose that you would consider it quite beneath your dignity to come with me?"

Jeffery clasped his hands behind his head and stared at the ceiling. "Touch gently upon a man's hobby-horse as you would upon his vices, for are they not one and the same?" he murmured. "How well Alexander knew—" He broke off and sat up as Read's chair rasped on the floor. The big man was on his feet.

"I've more to do than sit and listen to your blasted quotations," he snarled. Jeffery leaned forward and pushed him gently back into his chair. He shook a reproachful head. "Where's the iron self-control, Chief? Where is the old poker face, the masterly restraint? I declare that idleness is playing havoc with your inhibitions—"

"Ach—!"

"As a matter of fact," continued Jeffery calmly, "I'd rather like to come with you. Since criminology has completely absorbed my time and talents, I have relinquished all ambitions regarding that epochal treatise on the binomial theorem." He sighed. "Consequently I find the evenings rather dull since all the super-criminals appear to have turned their nefarious attentions to dinner-hour radio thrillers. Yes, Chief, I'll come along with you."

The sudden buzz of the house telephone cut into Read's sour rejoinder. He heaved himself from the low chair and moved across to the instrument. Jeffery heard him bark a gruff "hello" into the mouthpiece and there were curious guttural sounds. The grimness faded from the Chief Inspector's face as he listened. Then he nodded. "That's very good of you," he said with surprising amiability. "Yes—come right up." He replaced the receiver and turned.

"Is the Commissioner calling on us?" queried Jeffery brightly.

Read's lips tightened, then he decided to ignore the remark. "It's Nickerson." His voice was controlled. "He's calling on his way to the studio—wants to know if we're going. He'll be up here in a moment. And," said the Chief Inspector heavily, "if you frighten him off with any of that Oxford-and-Cambridge stuff, I'll break your damn' neck!

At that moment the door-bell shrilled, announcing the new arrival. Jeffery rose to meet the guest.

George Nickerson was not unlike an electrical impulse himself. He spoke in short staccato barks and such was his energy that he was rarely in the same position for more than a few minutes at a time. Jeffery, however, was interested and not a little amused by the attitude of Read. The Chief Inspector had pulled a third chair to the fire and was busy with the whisky tantalus. Blackburn, who knew from experience how rarely it was that his companion troubled to be even amiable to strangers, speculated wonderingly on the change. Having greeted the newcomer, he sat back to listen. The first remark, however, was addressed to him. Nickerson leaned over the back of his chair.

"About those talks, Mr. Blackburn—haven't changed your mind? Good opportunity! Wonderful publicity! Imagine it—your voice reaching tens of thousands of listeners!"

"I'd rather not imagine it, thanks," Jeffery said dryly. He smiled. "It's very good of you to offer, but honestly, I had enough publicity over the Mannikin Murders to last me for the rest of my life."

Nickerson shrugged his shoulders. "As you like." He turned to take a glass from the Chief Inspector. "I suppose we couldn't interest you, sir?"

Read's expression was wistful. "Couldn't do it—official capacity—never allow it," he mumbled. "But there's nothing to stop the young chap from doing it, except silly prejudice."

Jeffery looked hurt. "At least I've sunk my prejudices to the point of accompanying you to this opening tonight, Chief. You might give me credit—"

"Sssh—!" Read silenced him fiercely. He was standing with one ear cocked alertly, then his eyes dropped to his wrist-watch. Abruptly he turned. "The news session," he announced, jerking his head toward the radio. "We've already missed half of it! Never miss the general news session," he explained to Nickerson as he crossed and twisted the tuning dials.

A cheerful disinterested voice floated into the room, retailing tabloid descriptions of the outstanding news events. The three men listened in silence. There came a rustle of paper as the voice paused. A few moments later, the precise clipped tones were heard again:

> "We are in receipt of the latest news concerning the condition of Miss Agatha Boycott-Smith, well-known philanthropist, who lies seriously ill at her home at Royston Towers, Hertfordshire. We are pleased to announce that her condition has improved slightly. She has been forbidden to see friends and her sole relative, a nephew, has been recalled to the Towers. . . .

"That completes our first news bul—"

The voice was choked into silence as the Chief Inspector clicked the master-switch and returned to the fire-place. "Who is this woman?" he demanded. "They've been giving out bulletins regarding her illness over the past week! I've never heard of her."

Jeffery grinned. "Shows your laudable single-mindedness of purpose, Chief. Certainly the lady has never appeared in your *Illustrated Circular* or been featured in *Informations.* But if you took the trouble to emerge from your official shell occasionally, you couldn't help but encounter the name!"

Read was settling in his chair. He glanced up. "Why is that?"

"There's a Boycott-Smith wing in half a dozen country hospitals, a Boycott-Smith Free Library in the East End, and a Boycott-Smith scholarship in at least three of our universities. Only last year, the lady gave an immense sum to the unemployment relief." Jeffery smoked for a moment. "And they say she is still worth a cool million!"

The Chief Inspector grunted. "She must have bought a half-interest in the wireless stations by the way they keep harping on her condition!"

George Nickerson, who had been following this conversation with nervous birdlike movements, shook his head. He grinned. "I don't think you'll find Miss Boycott-Smith putting any more money into entertainment. Not since her disastrous venture with that film company!"

"What was that?" asked Jeffery.

"Didn't you hear about it?" asked Nickerson. "It happened about six months ago. Andrew Newland, her nephew, was partly to blame. He's a friend of mine and a good sort of chap—but a perfect bonehead when it comes to business—"

"Newland?" repeated the Chief Inspector. "There was an Andrew Newland played rugger for England against Australia—"

"That's the lad," their guest cut in. "It was following his success in that game this film company offered him a contract. Of course, his aunt's money was the attraction, but the novelty of the stunt appealed to Andrew. They were going to make a series of sporting films, wild and woolly adventures that would appeal to the kiddies, with Newland as a kind of sporting Buffalo Bill! Newland persuaded his aunt to sink a packet of money in the company and I believe they made about three films with Andy playing lead."

"And what happened?"

Nickerson grinned. "They were so bad that they were never shown. Then the aunt's attorney got to hear of the business and told her that she'd been stung. She stopped paying out money and the company went broke the following week. It seems that she hadn't been too favourably impressed with the business from the start. She'd only considered it for Newland's sake. Miss Boycott-Smith is rather proud of the family name and considers the public eye definitely *infra dignitatum.* There was the very deuce of a row about two years ago when Newland tried for the middle-weight championship of England. He did it on a bet and was, incidentally, battered to blazes! His aunt came to hear of it and almost disinherited him on the spot!"

"Mr. Newland must be a singularly foolish young man to quarrel with a million pounds," remarked Jeffery.

"Oh, the trouble soon blew over," the manager assured him. "They're terribly fond of each other, really. Newland's a decent, straight-shooting sort, not particularly brainy, perhaps, but thoroughly genuine. He realizes that Miss Boycott-Smith has been a mother to him since he was ten years old. I understand that his father was an invalid and died in a hospital. The shock of it killed his mother some months afterwards. His aunt adopted him and gave him everything. He thinks the world of her"—and here Mr. Nickerson's grin flashed out again—"that is, next to a certain young lady playing in the show tonight."

"Ah!" exclaimed Jeffery. "Romance in radio-land?"

The manager nodded. "I don't know much about the girl—her name's Marlowe. Mary Marlowe. But she seems a nice quiet type of young lady. It's generally understood that their engagement will be announced as soon as his aunt's illness clears one way or the other." Somewhat irrelevantly, Nickerson added: "I hope that girl makes good tonight. I put her in the cast at Newland's request and there was some unpleasantness at the change."

"Change?"

"Yes." A slight uneasiness crept into the manager's tone. He finished his drink and sat down. "Originally, it was arranged that the author should play Marlowe's part. Tonight's production of *Darkness is Danger* was written by Katharine Knowles."

"The detective novelist?" asked Blackburn interestedly,

"That's right." George Nickerson grinned. "She's a queer stick. Wears extraordinary hats perched on mounds of hair. Favours gold ornaments on long chains, and high collars. I always think of Knowles as a cross between the popular conception of Mrs. Pankhurst and Charlie's Aunt! But there's no doubt that Knowles is supreme in her particular line. Her plots are ingenious to the point of brilliance! You'll realize that when you hear *Darkness is Danger."*

"And she was to play a part in her own drama?"

Nickerson nodded. "I understand that she's working on a new novel that has a background of a radio station," he explained. "She was keen to get actual experience. She asked me if she could play this part in her show. I told her yes—provided she pleased the producer." The manager shrugged. "She didn't! We put her through two rehearsals and she was terrible! The producer came to me and protested—said she'd ruin the play! Newland happened to be in my office at the time and he pleaded with me to give Marlowe a trial."

He paused and glanced at each man in turn. "Naturally I was chary about the proposition. Marlowe had never appeared before a microphone—her sole experience was in amateur theatricals. It seemed like taking too great a chance. But Newland was so insistent that she could do the part that I decided to speak to the producer. Anyhow, to cut the story short, Marlowe got the part and she seems to be making quite a presentable job of it."

Read stroked his moustache. "And how did the Knowles woman take the change?"

Nickerson rubbed his jaw. His tone was rueful. "Not very well, I'm afraid. She bounced out of the studio and declared she was finished with radio work for ever! She'd never set foot in a studio again!" The manager gave a wry smile. "Still, we get used to scenes like that. They're more or less part of our day's work."

"Did you hear from Miss Knowles again?"

"We received a curt note from the lady about two days later. It demanded that we omit all reference to her name in connection with the play—that she wished to have nothing whatever to do with the production. So you can guess how she feels about the business."

Jeffery's tone was amused. "Then I take it the lady won't be among those present tonight?"

Nickerson shook his head. "I very much doubt it. I sent her an invitation, merely as a polite gesture. I hear she was most incensed over what she called my unwarranted impudence! Apparently the old dear is still riding the high horse and the opening will have to stagger along without her patronage."

Blackburn clicked his tongue. "How disappointing! I've always wanted to meet a radio playwright." His grey eyes twinkled. "Until this moment, I was inclined to consider them to be of the genus illusionary—rather like the unicorn or the manticora."

"Jeffery . . .!" rumbled the Chief Inspector warningly. His switching of the subject was obvious. "I suppose young Newland will be on board tonight to witness the debut of his lady-love?"

The manager shook his head. "I understand he's gone up to the Towers to be with his aunt in case the end comes. She was very low this morning. Of course, he'll listen in at the Towers. But I don't anticipate that the girl will flop. She's being produced by our best man—Carl von Bethke. He's a former talkie director who came to us from the Kinofilm people. Apart from that, Newland's attended some of the rehearsals with the girl and she's shown up quite well."

He paused, and on his last words the clock on the mantel chimed seven-thirty. Nickerson glanced at his wrist-watch and rose with a quick movement. "I must fly," he announced. "By the way, I'd like to show you over the studio before the play commences, so it would be as well to be early on the scene."

Read knocked the ashes from his pipe into the tray. "Black or white tie?" he asked.

"Black," returned Nickerson. "It's a semi-formal turn-out. Don't trouble to come down," he added as the Chief Inspector straightened. "I can let myself out. I'll see you both at the studio." With a wave of his hand, he was gone.

The Chief Inspector glanced down at the recumbent Jeffery and rubbed his hands briskly. His brick-red face glowed. "Come along, son! Stir yourself from that fire. Can't keep the B.B.C. waiting!"

Jeffery stretched himself and yawned prodigiously. "Vast pity we haven't perfected television," he murmured as he rose. "I always appear so extremely *distingue* in a black tie."

II

APPOINTMENT WITH ECHO

For the bird of the air shall carry the voice, and that which hath wings shall tell the matter.

Eccles. X, 20.

1

AFTER the tumult of Piccadilly and the surging traffic about Oxford Circus, the hush of Wigmore Street gave the impression of turning into some shuttered thoroughfare, long forgotten by clamorous crowds. To Jeffery, as he guided the long nose of the sports Bentley into the street, it was something of a paradox that this silent approach should harbour the Autolycusian ear that symbolized the modern radio station. He murmured some such observation to the Chief Inspector who sat beside him, but that gentleman was not impressed with flights of fancy. "Rats!" he said curtly. "Keep your mind on your driving."

The censure was not altogether unnecessary. Outside the studio there was a constant volutation of movement. Motor-cars crawled, halted, and backed, discharging couples and parties. This portion of the street was alive with a febrile agitation, vibrant with subdued chatter and an occasional laugh or high greeting that overlay the background of traffic sounds. Mr. Blackburn suffered faint misgivings regarding the sartorial influence of his dark tie as he watched the prim neon sign flicker on tall black hats and powdered shoulders. His companion, of tougher fibre where social niceties were concerned, experienced no such qualms. Read's eyes were glued on the tall modernistic building and the glass and chromium facade which gleamed like the palace of the Ice Princess when the moving headlights danced upon it.

A uniformed attendant took charge of their car as they stepped out. A polite commissionaire ushered them into the foyer. As they moved through the heavy glass doors, the many-sided personality of an opening night swept down upon them. The atmosphere was heavy with expensive perfumes from flowered bouquets and dressing-table phial, and shot through with shrill comment and excited laughter. Flashlights exploded in their faces and the frank scrutiny of press cameras peered from every corner. The Chief Inspector drummed an impatient heel on the thick fawn carpet and gnawed his clipped moustache. Even Jeffery seemed rather overwhelmed by this concentrated spotlight.

"If this is semi-official," Read grunted, his eyes flickering over jewelled throats rising from the richest furs, "I'd hate to see them turn on the works properly!"

With restrained use of shoulders and elbows, the two men moved slowly across the crowded foyer until their progress was halted by a tightly fitting double door bearing the notice in twisted glass letters, "Entrance to Studios". Here they were forced to pause. Read set a massive back against the door and peered over heads that grew more numerous with every passing minute. The air was filmed with richly aromatic smoke from perfumed cigarettes and fragrant cigars. The Chief Inspector, watching over the crowd, gave a sudden vicious grunt of surprise and Jeffery saw his eyes narrow in quick recognition. Without a word, the big man dived into the throng, to reappear a few moments later grasping a young man by the arm. A very slim, very sleek young man whose black eyes glittered like a cornered serpent's in his pale, powdered face. There was something very snakelike in his whole appearance as he twisted his black-coated body sinuously in the other's grip. The Chief Inspector glanced around. Directly opposite was a door marked "Cloakrooms". Read, with a glance at Jeffery, jerked his head in this direction and began to pilot his unwilling companion toward the door. Arriving, he thrust it open, found it empty and almost dragged the slim young man inside. The captive jerked himself free with a convulsive movement.

"Take your damn' paws off me!" he hissed. "Who the devil are you, anyway?"

"Now then, Mr. Steinie Rodda—" began Read when the young man's eyes blazed afresh. He snarled.

"That's not my name! You're making a mistake! Let me get out of here!"

The Chief Inspector, his back to the door, balanced himself firmly, feet apart. He measured the panting young man with cold grey eyes.

"So—your name isn't Steinie Rodda and you don't know me, eh?" His tone was dangerously quiet. "Well, my lad, I don't know what alias you're working under now—but I'll warrant you've never forgotten the time I rounded you up with the Yashukichi Miyagawa dope gang back in 1932!" Under the grey moustache his lips twisted grimly. "Perhaps you can recall that morning in Old Bailey when Justice Travers Humphreys sentenced you—"

"All right, Mr. Read, all right!" A pink tongue nicked across the young man's lips and his eyes glistened with hatred. "I'll come clean! I am Steinie Rodda. But I'm going straight now—honest I am! I was invited here tonight—"

"By the Ancient and Associated Order of Pocket-Dippers and Snatchers, I suppose?" grated Read.

"Certainly not by the B.B.C.!"

He reached forward and grasped the other's arm. "Come on, Steinie—out with the truth! Why are you here?"

"I got an invite," hissed Steinie. "And take your hand off my arm. You don't know who might be looking at us!"

"People look at you every week in the *Police Gazette,*" retorted the Chief Inspector grimly. "Oh yes—we're keeping our eye on you, Steinie! We've had your dabs out for inspection half a dozen times in the past couple of years, in connection with cases that seemed to bear your trademark." He released the trembling young man and stepped back. Steinie retreated a pace. He thrust a hand into his pocket and pulled out what appeared to be a small automatic. The Chief Inspector, under the impression that it was a weapon, tensed his big frame for a spring and even Jeffery was momentarily startled. Then the young man pressed the trigger and from the barrel a cigarette appeared. Steinie took it with one hand, with the other he returned the trick cigarette-case to his pocket. He seemed to be thoroughly enjoying his companions' discomfiture. An evil leer hovered about his thin lips as he lit up.

Read's eyebrows were like a black bar across his forehead. "If you ever pull a trick like that on me again, Steinie," he said slowly, "I'll break you across my knee!" He stood aside from the door and his voice quickened. "Now, get the hell out of here! And if you pull anything after this chance, God help you, my powdered beauty!"

The sleek Mr. Rodda needed no second bidding. He gave a swift twist to his body and slithered out of the door like a black streak. The Chief Inspector watched him go, then turned to Jeffery. "That's one of the nastiest pieces of work that ever suckled mothers' milk," he grunted. "You could no more expect Steinie to be honest than you could train a crab to walk straight!"

They were outside in the thronged foyer again. Blackburn shook his head. "After hearing you quote Aristophanes, albeit quite unconsciously, nothing in the world would surprise me," he said with suspicious gravity. "I am only waiting to be told that there is no such person as Mr. Nickerson and that this is all a very bad nightmare!" He glanced around. "And talking of Mr. Nickerson—where is he?"

"How should I know?" demanded Read. "You heard what he said—that he'd meet us at the studio."

Jeffery eyed the crowd with faint disfavour. "Isn't it about time we took the law into our own hands and did something, Chief? This is beginning to look like a Covent Garden opening!"

The Chief Inspector nodded. Turning, he surveyed the double doors barring entrance to the studios. Squaring his shoulders defiantly, he placed a massive hand upon the nearest and was about to push, when the door flew open and George Nickerson himself emerged. A changed Mr. Nickerson. Gone was his air of smooth self-confidence. Now his face was grey and worried, his manner nervously abstracted. He came face to face with the Chief Inspector and his companion, to pause abruptly in the entrance.

"Hello! So you got along all right?" His tone was polite but vague, that of a man whose mind runs on more important and urgent matters. He came forward and touched Read on the arm. "Look here, sir—I won't be able to show you around tonight. I'll have to turn you over to our studio director. All sorts of unforeseen things have occurred!"

"Anything seriously wrong?" inquired Read.

"Serious enough! We've had a breakdown between studios. It was discovered late this afternoon and our engineers have been working like niggers to get the line fixed in time for the play tonight." He twitched his head toward the electric clock on the wall. "They'll never do it—they haven't even found it yet!" The manager hunched despairing shoulders. "It would happen on the opening night, when everything should be at the highest point of efficiency!"

The Chief Inspector was perturbed. "Does that mean that the station is off the air?"

In spite of his anxiety, Nickerson was able to summon a feeble grin. "It's not as bad as that, fortunately. The break-down occurred between our effects rooms in the basement and the dramatic studio, where the radio plays are produced. It will mean that all the effects used in the play tonight will have to be worked over the one microphone—they'll have to be in the same studio as the artistes. Just as it was in the early days of broadcasting before effects rooms were used. It will be a makeshift and a damned inconvenient one at that, but under the circumstances—" He broke off to signal to a young man who was pushing his way through the crowd. "Here is Charles Finlay now—he's our studio director."

Finlay was a tall, spectacled young man with a prematurely aged face. He came forward, and being buttonholed by Nickerson acknowledged the introductions with a grave bow. The manager, whose attention was distributed between the clock and the crowd, apologized for this deputizing and was about to hurry off when the studio director stopped him. Reaching in his pocket, Finlay brought out a telegram. "Came for you a few minutes ago, sir," he explained, proffering it. "That's why I was looking for you."

"More trouble, I suppose," Nickerson grunted. He slit the envelope, extracted the message, and as he read, his face twisted wryly. "All the way from Hertfordshire," he said with bitter amusement, "just packed full of irony!" He raised his eyes and held out the message. "Newland's wired his blessing on the opening and his regrets that he can't be among the delighted visitors! Personally, I should say he's very fortunate to be out of it all!" With this observation, the manager nodded, moved forward and was swallowed by the crowd.

"I'd no impression that Society gathered so eagerly at Echo's shrine," remarked Jeffery, watching the throng that thickened and swarmed between the glass and chromium walls. "Did you actually issue invitations to all these people?"

Finlay shrugged. "That's what I've been asking myself all the evening," he confessed. "Even Mr. Nickerson appears rather surprised at the crowd. Naturally, there's a good percentage of gate-crashers—it's impossible to keep them out! We've done everything we can to prevent it, but you can't walk up to every person and demand to see their invitation." He made a gesture as though dismissing the subject. "Anyhow, that's not my worry." He stepped forward and pushed open one of the doors. "We'll make a start on the rounds, I think. Come this way."

They passed through the doors. Both frames swung into place behind them, leaving a silence that tingled the eardrums. The studio director led them across deep carpets and through a winding corridor lit by thin, pale tubes set high in the walls. So pronounced was the hush that the Chief Inspector remarked upon it. Finlay nodded. The place was sound-proof, he explained. Every wall was insulated with special fibre that absorbed echo and prevented a reverberation that gave an edge to the transmission. When he concluded, the pause had that abrupt and pronounced quality as though a hand had been clapped across his lips. To Jeffery, always sharply sensitive to surroundings, the silence had a dead muteness that was totally unlike the hush of everyday things, and he had all the sensations of treading some winding catacomb deep in the bowels of the earth. It was almost a relief when their progress was barred by another door above which, protruding like a warning forefinger, a small light glowed luridly. Even as they halted, it flickered out.

"This," explained Finlay, gesturing toward the door, "is the entrance to our main, or Number One, studio. The pilot light above the door, which is connected to the microphone key on the panel inside, glows as a warning when the microphone is thrown open. It stops people from blundering in and creating a disturbance. Microphone closed, out goes the light. Consequently, we can go through." He pushed open the door. "Go inside."

Jeffery was staring about him. At the opposite end of the studio, near the stage, a mound of flowers scented the air, and across the centre of the dais itself, a broad band of ribbon was looped. The studio director caught Jeffery's glance and nodded.

"The opening ceremony is to be performed in here," he said. "We're going to broadcast the addresses and then give a short recorded programme from our emergency studio on the next floor while the feature drama *Darkness is Danger* is prepared."

Read, hands in pockets, nodded. "Will the play go on in here?" he asked.

Finlay shook his head. "No. We have a special studio for our dramatic productions. It gives a different acoustic from this one. This studio is acoustically planned for massed work, such as choirs, orchestras, bands, musical comedy, or operatic work. Its size enables it to 'take' massed sounds. In dialogue, when every word must be heard clearly, a smaller studio capable of concentrating the sound is necessary."

The Chief Inspector grinned. "It's a case of all hands to the pump in a radio station, I guess."

The studio director was leading them across the studio. "Of course, it's all carefully rehearsed," he said. "Perfect synchronization is obtained by a code of light signals. Tonight, however, we're only using the one studio—there's been some trouble with the wiring, I understand."

They paused again at a square glass window set a few feet above the floor in the wall of the studio. The visitors glanced through. They had a confused impression of a huge switchboard, studded with myriad keys and buttons, meshed here and there with rubber cables. A hundred tiny lights of different colours, set like jewels in the black iron-work of the board, winked and blinked at them. Three seats were screwed into the floor opposite this imposing erection and two were occupied by young men in sweaters. Jeffery saw that the nearest operator was handling a large ebonite knob, turning it delicately backward and forward. Above his head, the black mouth of a loud speaker yawned cavernously, and half a dozen clocks looked down with bland indifference from the rear wall.

"This is the control room," explained Finlay. "In this room, the sound output from each studio is 'controlled'—perhaps 'modulated' would be the better word. The loud speaker gives the boys a 'playback' of the reproduction. That speaker is blazing away now, but you can't hear it through the sound-proof glass of this window." He turned and smiled. "Tonight's lesson is almost over. I'll take you through to the dramatic studio."

2

Through another tight-fitting door, down dimly-lit, carpeted corridors they passed, following closely on the heels of their guide. "Through caverns measureless to Man," murmured the irrepressible Jeffery as they trod soundlessly. This time their tour ended at a door bearing the stern warning—"Absolutely No Admittance" beneath the twisted glass letters, "Studio Number Two. Production". Finlay thrust open the door and gestured his companions forward. Read, followed by Jeffery, entered and the studio director clicked the door shut behind them.

They looked about. The studio was smaller than the one they had previously seen, but infinitely less chilling. It resembled more than anything a pleasant and well-furnished sitting-room. There were three "windows". The largest of these was set in the far wall and looked out into the main studio almost in line with the announcer's desk. The other two were set in the same wall as the door by which they had entered. (See plan.) The nearest of these smaller panes gave visual communication with a small, cupboard-like room which Finlay explained was later to be used as a "talks" studio, while the farthest window pierced the wall of the control room.

Each of these apertures was fitted with valance and curtains, while a centre curtain of heavy velvet, suspended from rings, made it possible to block the window at a moment's notice. These window curtains harmonized in toning with the carpet and the wall shading. Concealed lighting bathed the studio in an amber glow and set off several excellent water-colours hung here and there. Amid an imitation fire-place, a radiator gleamed ruddily. There was an air of comfortable intimacy about the room which drew a delighted grunt from the Chief Inspector.

"Dashed if they shouldn't pay money to act in here," he commented. "I wouldn't mind having a shot at *The Wreck of the Hesperus* myself under these conditions!" He glanced around. "Where's the microphone?"

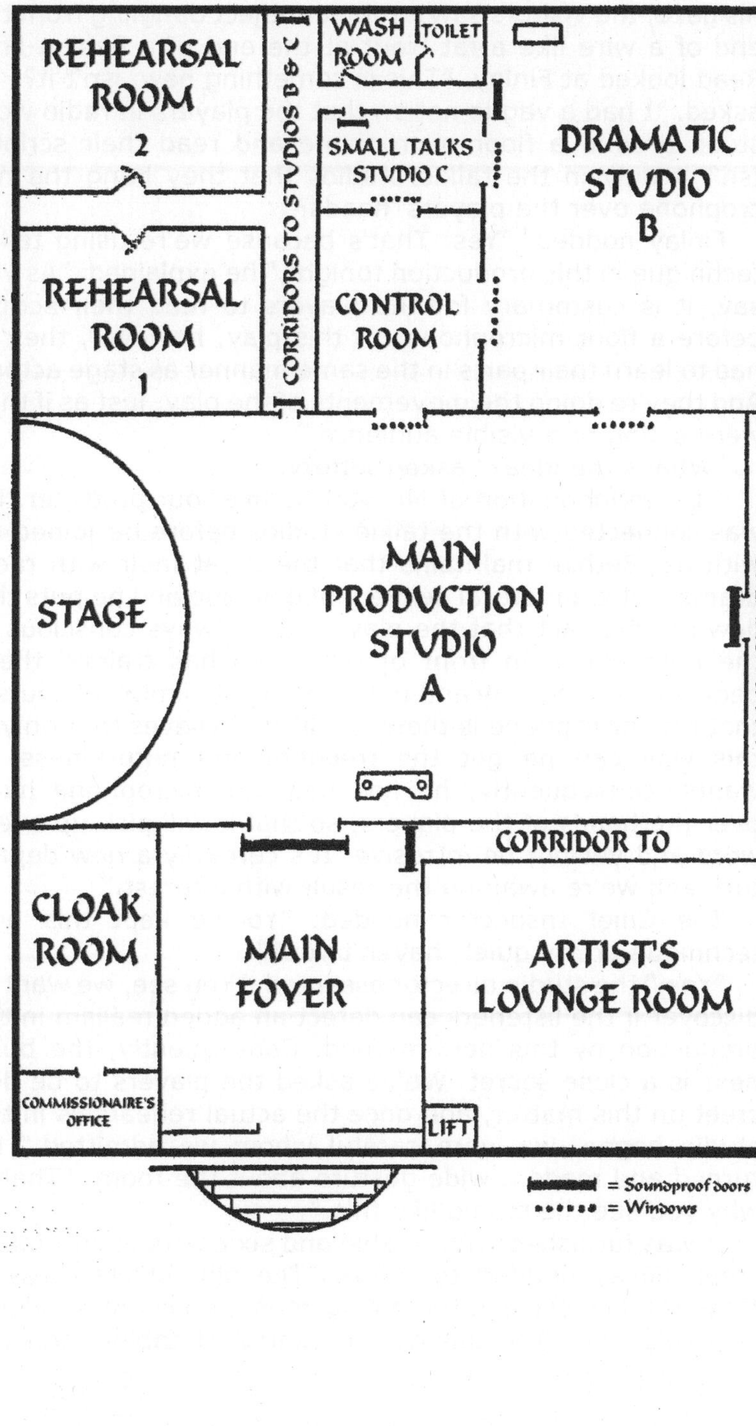
REHEARSAL ROOM 2
CORRIDORS TO STUDIOS B & C
WASH ROOM
TOILET
SMALL TALKS STUDIO C
DRAMATIC STUDIO B
REHEARSAL ROOM 1
CONTROL ROOM
STAGE
MAIN PRODUCTION STUDIO A
MAIN STUDIO
CORRIDOR TO
CLOAK ROOM
MAIN FOYER
ARTIST'S LOUNGE ROOM
COMMISSIONAIRE'S OFFICE
LIFT
= Soundproof doors
= Windows

The studio director raised his eyes to the ceiling. Following his gaze, the visitors saw a tubular object dangling from the end of a wire like a fat trout at the end of a fishing-line. Read looked at Finlay. "This is something new, isn't it?" he asked. "I had a vague notion that the players in radio work stood around a floor microphone and read their scripts. Isn't it only in the talkie studios that they hang the microphone over the players' heads?"

Finlay nodded. "Yes. That's because we're using talkie technique in this production tonight," he explained. "As you say, it is customary for the players to read their scripts before a floor microphone. In this play, however, they've had to learn their parts in the same manner as stage actors. And they're doing the movements of the play, just as if they were acting to a visible audience."

"What's the idea?" asked Jeffery.

"It's an innovation of Mr. von Bethke, our producer. He was connected with the talkie studios before he joined up with us. Bethke maintains that the great fault with radio drama is the unnatural delivery of dialogue and he puts this down to the fact that the players are always conscious of the microphone in front of them. He has trained these people to act the play and to forget, within limits, of course, that the microphone is there at all! He believes that only in this way can he get the freedom and naturalness he wants—consequently, he has had the microphone hung over the heads of the players, so that it will pick up every word and yet not be intrusive. It's certainly a new departure and we're awaiting the result with interest."

The Chief Inspector nodded. "You've kept this new technique pretty quiet, haven't you?"

"Yes," the studio director assented. "You see, we want to discover if the listeners can detect an added realism in the production by this new method. Consequently, the business is a close secret. We've asked the players to be discreet on this matter, and once the actual rehearsals in the studio began, we were careful whom we admitted." He turned and made a wide gesture about the room. "That is why you see the studio like this."

It was furnished with a table and six chairs of chromium steel. Finlay nodded to these. "The plot of *Darkness is Danger* takes place in the dining-room of a country lodge," he explained. "The guests are seated at table when the mysterious events occur. Thus the players will sit down and speak their dialogue just as they would on the stage."

"And just what," asked Mr. Blackburn, "is the reason for that extraordinary collection of objects?"

He jerked his head to the far side of the room. Against the wall stood a long, wooden bench covered with a bewildering assemblage of articles. There were boxes and cubes of all shapes and sizes, some with small coils of electric wire twisting from them, others with funnel-like mouths and studded with tiny push-buttons. There were megaphones like gargantuan fools' caps, two tiny but complicated machines resembling portable phonographs, an instrument like a blacksmith's blower and a small but perfect model door, complete with bolts, lock, and key. Jeffery crossed and stared down at this strange variety. Read was by his side. Without raising his eyes, the big man spoke.

"What's this? Holding a jumble sale after the opening?"

Finlay's grave face lit in a smile. "Rather looks like it, I suppose." He walked across to the table and moved behind it, facing them. "These are the sound effects for the play tonight. They look weird, I admit, but then they do weird things! Some of these gadgets cost close on fifty pounds to buy—in fact, you couldn't buy them! They're specially made for us." He waved a hand at the collection. "You might not believe it, but we can get every noise from a crying baby to an elephant stampede or an avalanche with these things. And the model door explains itself. It's used for the exit and entry of different characters. If you slammed an ordinary door, the detonation would blast the microphone. With this model, placed at a correctly rehearsed distance, you get just the right effect."

Jeffery was moving about the bench, peering down with inquisitive eyes. "And what in the name of fortune does this represent?" he asked.

The object of his curiosity was a long hatpin with a small ebonite knob at the blunted end. It was lying on a square of oiled silk stretched tightly across a wooden frame. Finlay glanced down. "That gives us an effect of dripping water," he explained. "The microphone is a queer contraption—it distorts natural sounds to an almost unrecognizable degree. Ordinary water dripping sounds like Niagara in flood time.

But the gentle tapping of that ebonite knob on the oiled silk gives a most realistic effect."

The Chief Inspector was following his words closely. "It's rather unusual to work with the effects in the same studio as the players, I believe?"

A slight frown shadowed the studio director's face. He nodded. "Our effects studios are in the basement and there is a special staff of men to operate them. In those rooms, the larger and more elaborate effects are permanently installed, bathtubs, gravel troughs, thunder-sheets, and a dozen and one queer contrivances. The effects studios are 'lined up' with the ground-floor studios. Usually the dialogue is spoken in this studio while the effects are worked below. The men follow their scripts and synchronization is made possible by 'flick-lights', tiny lights on the microphone which glow when an effect is needed. Thus, although players and effects men are invisible to each other sound and dialogue work in perfectly."

Jeffery, one eye on that fascinating bench, asked quickly: "But wouldn't it be possible to work these effects from some other studio?"

Finlay shook his head. "Because of the rush of opening, our engineers have installed flick-lights only on the microphones in the effects rooms and in the main studio. Naturally we couldn't clutter up Number One with this collection on the opening night, so we've been forced to put them in here." He shrugged. "Anyhow, we can only hope for the best. When it was realized this afternoon that the line could not be fixed in time, von Bethke called a late rehearsal in this studio and spent some time with Ted Martin, the head effects man, getting the distances right for tonight."

Blackburn had crossed to the window looking into the tiny "talks" studio. "What's to prevent the effects from being worked in there?" he queried. "You'd have perfect visual control of your players through this glass."

"But you'd have no microphone," returned Finlay. "We're really opening before the studio is properly equipped. Everything will be ready before the end of the week, but at the moment there's a speaker in that small room but no microphone." He shook his head. "No. We wouldn't have put the effects in here if we could have possibly avoided it! But it was either doing that—or calling off the play altogether!" Again that half-smile played about his lips. "So we took the lesser of the two evils."

A silence fell upon the trio. The Chief Inspector was moving about, his blue eyes taking in every detail. He paused by the large window which looked out into the main studio. "What's the idea of all the glassware? Is it just to make the place more homely?"

"By no means!" Finlay came across and drummed his fingers on the glass. "These windows give what we call 'visual control'. You have probably heard the announcements that precede and follow our main features—such as the reading of the scene of the play and the names of the players in the cast," he continued. And as they nodded—"These are put over by an announcer in a separate studio, which prevents any interference with the actual production. Customarily, the announcer sits in Number One studio directly opposite this window. He has perfect vision of the players in here, and they of him. Thus he can follow their movements and his voice comes to them through a loud speaker in the wall. In this way, both players and announcer are in actual communication with each other although separated by sound-proof walls."

Jeffery was peering through, so close to the glass that his breath fogged it as he spoke. "But won't that studio be jammed with people? Surely your announcer could never make himself heard above the din?"

"Naturally we can't use both studios tonight," Finlay returned. "The opening has made a certain amount of rearrangement necessary. Stewart—he's our feature announcer—will be in this studio with the players."

Read was swivelling his head from side to side. "And the other windows?"

"As you see, the window on your right looks into the control room. Vision of what's going on is absolutely necessary to the operators. And the window farther down in the wall communicates with the tiny 'talks' studio. I understand that Mr. Nickerson is putting you gentlemen in there to watch the play being produced tonight."

Finlay reached up a hand and was about to pull the velvet curtain across the window, masking the view, when something chained his arm in mid-air. Jeffery and the Chief Inspector, following his eyes, saw that the doors of the main studio had been opened and the crowds were pushing inside, a tumbling wave of people, frothed with white fur, satin, and shirt-front, that was already spreading widely across the carpeted floor of the larger studio. There must have been mild babel in that room, yet not the faintest echo reached the trio watching through the glass. It was like viewing a badly directed mob scene from a silent film, and Jeffery was impressed with the unnaturalness of complete silence as he stared at this throng of excited mutes who jostled, gesticulated, and mouthed in apparent dumb-show. George Nickerson came into view through the doors, the centre of a small but important-looking group being very obsequious to a withered, horse-faced old gentleman who appeared to have dressed in a hurry. The manager was gesturing to various parts of the studio and his elderly companion nodded vaguely from time to time. As they passed from the range of the window:

"Sir Tallis Morgan," Finlay announced. He swept the heavy curtain across the glass, blocking the view. "Must be getting close to the deadline! Shall we go along?"

"Must we?" murmured Jeffery. He fingered his tie dubiously. "I've rather a horror of celebrities in the mass. The startled fawn—the timid doe, y'know."

Finlay smiled. "Naturally you don't have to go inside unless you want to," he said. "But I understood that was why you came along."

"I'd much rather just poke about," confessed Jeffery. "The ingenious alchemy of this place intrigues me beyond words. There's something almost Hyrcynian about this place which presents sound without sight and sight without sound by the throwing of a key. Y'know, it reminds me—"

"Never mind the simile," grunted Read. He turned to Finlay. "Could we meet the cast? And this von Bethke?"

"Certainly. They're in the rehearsal room running through their—" The studio director broke off as a knock sounded at the door. As the three men wheeled, it swung open and a stranger walked in.

Or rather, he shambled inside. The newcomer was a loose-limbed, stoop-shouldered young man whose gangling frame seemed held together by the grey slacks and sweater that he wore. He had a yellow skin and his drooping mouth emphasized a puckered, receding chin. This quaint, goblin face was redeemed by two remarkable eyes, brown, clear, soft, and drenched in melancholy, the eyes of a whipped spaniel. The man paused awkwardly just inside the door and surveyed the group lugubriously. Then he nodded to Finlay and his pendulous jaw began to chew rhythmically. A nasal tone revealed his origin as he spoke.

"Say, Mis-ter Finlay," he drawled his words. "Mr. Von wants t' see you right urgent. That there pole-cat's playing up again! She's lettin' loose hell an' high water in that there rehearsal room."

The studio director frowned. "Miss Lusinska?"

"Uh-ha!" The young man nodded gloomily and moved his loose frame into the room. "That dame mus' think she's Garbo or somethin'. Now she says she won't act so long as th' noises are here!" Indignation momentarily washed the dolour from his expression, and he waved a lanky arm at the effects table. "I almos' ups an' says my noises can't work too good while you're in th' room, either!"

Finlay turned to his companions, a half-smile on his face. "This is Ted Martin, chief of our effects department." He introduced Jeffery and the Chief Inspector. The lugubrious one nodded glumly as he grasped their hands.

"Call me Happy," invited Mr. Martin, a ghost of a grin on his slack lips. "That's what th' gang here call me. An' all because I got more worries than a one-armed paper-hanger with hives. Th' trouble with me," confided Ted with a slow drawl, "is that I tries to please all an' finishes up pleasin' no one!"

"A truly Aesopian philosophy," murmured Jeffery, but Finlay cut in on his words:

"What's wrong with the sound effects being in here?"

Martin shrugged. "She jus' don't like them, as I said." He chewed, his brown eyes alight with reminiscence. "I wuz in th' rehearsal room with th' gang—they're goin' through their little pieces f'r tonight—an' all at once th' door bursts open an' Madam Pole-cat comes in like a bat outa hell! 'Get that rubbish outa that studio,' she says, mild as a tiger smellin' blood. 'Not till I gets orders from th' producer,' I says. Then she comes up t' me, her fingers crookin' at my face like she wuz goin' to have my eyes. 'Lady,' I says, quiet-like. 'Lady—one o' these days someone will learn you!' " Again that engaging grin shadowed his saffron face. "An' then I turns an' walks out on her!"

Finlay shook a reproving head. "You shouldn't have spoken like that to Lusinska, Ted. After all, she's a splendid artiste in her own line."

Martin's face set. "I can't see it," he said doggedly. "That dame does her best work away from th' mike."

"What happened after you walked out?"

"Madam turns on Mis-ter Von an' starts t' give him red hell. That's why you'd better get along. She's gotten him jittery as an expectant father!"

The studio director was running nervous fingers over his clothes and something hesitant in his attitude gave them the impression that he was postponing this interview as long as possible. Then he cleared his throat and glanced up at the clock on the wall. "You'd better get your stuff ready, Ted," he said abruptly. "You're on the air in twenty minutes."

The effects man nodded. "That's what I come for," he drawled. Pulling a folded script from his pocket, he shambled across to the table and began to arrange the objects with practised fingers, glancing occasionally at the open script. Jeffery and the Chief Inspector, watching him, were attracted by Finlay's voice addressing them.

"If you gentlemen would care to meet the cast, this seems as good an opportunity as any." There was an underlying grimness in his tone. Read looked rather doubtful and Jeffery was on the point of a hasty negative. The big man plucked at his moustache.

"I should say we'd be butting in at rather an awkward moment," he began, but Finlay stopped him with a gesture. He strode across the room and opened the door. "When you meet Lusinska, you'll appreciate the fact that the support of a Chief Inspector of Scotland Yard is just the thing I want." His tone was lighter, but the stern set of his face was unchanged.

Read gave a half-glance at Jeffery, who shrugged. After a moment's hesitation, the two men moved toward the door. As they passed through, the Chief Inspector muttered:

"Proper League of Nations you've got here! Yankee effects man—German producer—British studio director—and this Lusinska woman." His tone became an interrogative. "What's she?"

"Tartar!"

The word was as precise and as emphatic as the click of the studio door which Finlay shut behind them.

3

Jeffery said dryly: "By nationality or by nature?"

"Both," their guide assured him. He walked in silence for a while, then burst out almost peevishly: "It's sickening! Olga Lusinska has turned the place upside down ever since the first rehearsals for this show began! It's going to be her first and last part with us!"

The trio turned a corner. "Why was she chosen?" Read asked. "Aren't the talkies her medium?"

"It was von Bethke's idea," Finlay explained sombrely. "She's a kind of protegee of his. Working with this new technique he wanted a star who knew the business thoroughly. He engaged Lusinska at some staggering sum, quite outside ordinary artistes' fees. This, together with her tantrums, has so upset the rest of the cast that Mr. Nickerson has made the solemn vow never to use her again!"

"The B.B.C. doesn't stand for temperament?" asked Jeffery quizzically.

"It doesn't stand for anything that upsets its routine," returned Finlay stolidly. A note of finality in his voice checked the conversation. Jeffery shrugged. The world behind the microphone, he reflected, appeared as complicated and as full of tea-cup storms as life behind the stage-curtain. He was about to make some trite remark on this to bridge the awkward silence when the hush was shattered in the most unexpected manner. From somewhere down the corridor, a throaty contralto voice that held the purring snarl of a baited animal reached them.

"You hate me—all of you! You've hated me from the very moment I came here! And why? Because you're jealous of Lusinska! Lusinska who can make fools of you all—just like that!" A vicious snap of fingers was a contemptuous period to the diatribe.

A man's voice, fawning, oleaginous, followed timorously. A voice with a guttural undertone that revealed the speaker's identity at once.

"Now—now, Olga *liebling*—"

"It's your fault—fat fool!" Like flame through smoke, venom flickered in the husky tone. "You bring me here—to what? To a half-finished rubbish heap! To a madhouse, peopled by imbeciles! I must act among brooms and buckets and mops! Ah! The devil take you all!"

The advancing trio had reached the half-open door. Jeffery had only time to read the lettering, "Rehearsal Room Number One", when the studio director, his face pale, thrust it open. The visitors stood aside to let him enter, but their eyes were busy.

The atmosphere of the room was hazy with smoke and quivering with dangerous cross-currents. They recognized Olga Lusinska at once from her photographs. She faced them, fingers clenched into small, hard bunches, her slim body tense with rage. A lock of dark hair snaked down across a face pallid with fury, so that the make-up that flushed the sullen, Slavonic cheek-bones stood out grotesquely.

Plainly this unexpected intrusion had disconcerted her. A bitter retort snapped on her lips, which remained open, while her eyes, slightly oval, glittered as they flew from face to face. So alive, so vibrant was her personality that she completely overshadowed the half-dozen other people in the room. It was Lusinska herself who broke the swollen, bursting silence that fell so abruptly. Her fingers unclenched, crawled slowly to her hips, and her lips set in a thin hard line.

"So . . .?" It was a long-drawn sibilant. "You have come at last, Mr. Finlay!"

The studio director said curtly: "Yes. Now what's all this trouble?" He blinked through the smoke. "Mr. von Bethke!"

A pot-bellied little Humpty-Dumpty of a man came forward. He was fat to the point of grossness, a stunted Falstaff with pendulous belly and corpulent thighs. His head, almost bald and absurdly small for that swollen body, nodded like a child's toy. There was something infinitely puckish about Carl von Bethke's whole appearance, Jeffery decided, until he raised his eyes to the man's face. Then he received a shock. The face had once been as lumpish as the body; now the skin was puckered into a dozen hanging folds that became myriad crinkles about the eyes and the mouth. Like sapphires set amid ruching, the eyes peered forth, china blue, hard, immeasurably wise and experienced, eyes without soul or compassion. . . . Jeffery realized that he was staring, and at the same moment von

Bethke noticed the appraisal. Those pale orbs lit with sudden fierce suspicion, the next moment heavy, sensual lids veiled them. He faced the studio director, his expression bland.

"It is nothing, Mr. Finlay. Nothing at all! Lusinska—she is nervous before the play starts. Always she is like this—then she gives magnificent performance! You will see!" He turned to where the woman stood motionless, watching him, and spread fat hands. "Is not that so, Olga *liebste?*"

Olga Lusinska ignored him. Her eyes burned into Finlay's face. "I demand that you have those effects shifted from that studio," she said slowly. She clasped her elbows across her breast, a gesture of finality. "Otherwise, I do not play!"

Finlay snapped his fingers irritably. "For heaven's sake, be reasonable, Miss Lusinska," he cried. "You know we can't put those effects anywhere else! They wouldn't have been put there at all if any other arrangement had been possible!"

The actress shrugged. One small foot tapped the floor measuredly. "That is your affair! I do not argue!" Deliberately she turned her back upon the studio director.

There was a heavy, frustrated pause. Finlay, scarlet with rage and humiliation, clenched his fists and unclenched them. Jeffery stole a side-glance at Read. The Chief Inspector's ruddy face was almost as crimson as the studio director's and his clipped grey moustache bristled in a manner that Blackburn knew only too well. Then an interruption came from the far corner of the room. A tall dark man with the face of a clean-shaven Mephistopheles rose to his feet, his thin, mobile lips twisted.

"I think," he said to no one in particular, "that there's a particularly bad smell in this room. I'm going along to the studio." He crossed the room, and with a muttered word of apology passed the two by the door and went out into the corridor.

Lusinska wheeled like a cat. She flung out her arms. "See—see!" she cried. "That's what it has been all the time! That's what I must tolerate! And why? Because I have courage to speak out, while the others whisper always in corners—afraid!"

"That's not true!" A plump, middle-aged woman with an ugly, good-natured face entered the fray. She was sitting in one of the lounge chairs knitting a varicoloured article and her nimble fingers did not pause nor did she raise her head from her work. "We've never complained! It's you who have made the trouble all along!" She jerked a greying head. "The others will bear me out."

"The others" were a young girl and two lads barely out of their teens, one boy a smooth tow-head, his companion a curly carrot-top. All three looked abashed at being thrust so abruptly into the disturbance. The red-headed youth mumbled something, avoiding Lusinska's ophidian eye. The remaining couple concentrated on their scripts, ignoring the invitation to participate. Lusinska stood panting a little, the tiny valley between her breasts widening and narrowing as she breathed. Then Finlay squared his shoulders and drew a long breath like a man about to plunge into cold water. His tone was icy, cutting.

"I've been very patient with you, Miss Lusinska." He stared at her with cold, hostile eyes. "But there is a limit to everything! You must realize that this is a most important occasion—the opening night! Already we've encountered enough difficulties and setbacks without your adding to them." His voice rose, gathered fire. "I was given to understand that you were a genuine trouper, a person who would pull together with the rest of the cast! Instead, you've done your level best to upset everything and make everyone's life as unpleasant as possible—"

"Atta boy!" muttered Read audibly. Von Bethke was making awkward napping gestures of protest. Lusinska stood frozen with surprise, mouth open, slanted eyes wide. The blood flushed her cheeks, then drained away leaving them paler than before. "How—how dare you?" she whispered thickly.

The studio director's gaunt face was pale, but behind his spectacles his eyes glinted with the faintest spark of red. "It's quite time we had an understanding," he said steadily. "You've made more trouble and put the studio to more inconvenience than has ever occurred before. And because we've overlooked these tantrums, don't imagine that we haven't noticed them—"

"Stop!" The woman's face was fiendish, a hideous Gorgon mask of narrowed eyes, jutting cheek-bones, vicious twisted lips. Something in her throat choked the words so that they grated horribly. "Insults! Insults! I demand to see Mr. Nickerson—I demand—" The sentence

splintered unexpectedly and her hand flew to her throat. Her thin body began to tremble and she swayed drunkenly. Von Bethke and Finlay sprang forward, but she twisted like a wildcat. "Don't touch me!" she panted and almost flung herself out of the room. As she squirmed through the door, Jeffery could hear her teeth chattering.

With that sudden dramatic passing, the tension in the room slackened like a tight band released. The snub-nosed actress laid down her knitting and rose. The two young men and the girl raised their eyes and the fair-haired boy tossed his well-thumbed script on to a chair. Finlay raised a slightly trembling hand, removed his glasses, wiped them with his handkerchief and hooked them back across his ears. "Now," he said, "you gentlemen might as well meet the cast—or what's left of them."

He beckoned them forward. "Chief Inspector Read of Scotland Yard," he announced. "And Mr. Blackburn. They're guests of Mr. Nickerson tonight." He glanced around. "Mr. von Bethke you have already met—informally."

The tubby producer raised a plump hand. Behind those heavy lids his eyes were cold and hard as ice pellets. He nodded vigorously so that the paps of his face quivered. "I must apologize for Miss Lusinska," he murmured. "She is—is *teufelsweib!*" And as Jeffery made a deprecating gesture, von Bethke reached out his hand. "This is a pleasure. You are to see the play tonight—yes? It is an honour, indeed,"—and his shrill tones had all the bland insincerity of a mechanical bird twittering.

"Thank you," said Jeffery gravely. He released the soft, fat hand as the homely-faced actress stepped forward, poking fingers into her whitening hair. "Miss Martha Rockwell," Finlay introduced.

A sly grin spread across the woman's ugly-humorous face. "Don't you know better than to give my right name to the cops?" she mimicked, her broad inflections harmonizing well with that wide mouth and snub nose. She nodded cheerfully to the visitors. "You can't pin anything suspicious on poor old Martha Rockwell. I'm an honest working girl. Couldn't be anything else with a face like this, worse luck!"

Her buxom geniality and a quality of genuine earthiness in her personality had an exhilarating effect that cleared the last vestiges of that strained atmosphere. For the first time since entering the rehearsal room, Finlay smiled.

"Good old Martha," he said fondly. He spoke over his shoulder to the visitors. "We're all terribly fond of Miss Rockwell. She's been with us ever since the days of carbon microphones. And she can still speak her piece better than most!"

Miss Rockwell seated herself and picked up her knitting. "I've yet to hear a more satisfying piece spoken than the one you let loose a few minutes ago," she remarked matter-of-factly. "I've been aching to say all that a lot less politely ever since that woman came into the cast!" She gave a gratified little wag of her head. "That was certainly flannel to these creaking joints!"

"And now for the newest acquisition to our ranks," said Finlay. "Miss Mary Marlowe."

The girl standing between the two lads stepped forward and acknowledged their greeting with a grave inclination of her head. Jeffery, recalling what Nickerson had said regarding this girl, studied her covertly. There was about her an impression of experience. It was not so much in her features, which were a little too chiselled for beauty, as in the determined set of her mouth and the firm chin-line. Here was a young woman who had been forced to make her way in the world unaided, Jeffery guessed. Yet there was something else, some queer, intangible impression that he could not place.

"And the pups," the studio director was saying. "On my right, Mr. Vance Garnett,"—the fair-headed lad nodded sheepishly—"on my left, Mr. Robert Hammond." Beneath his curly poll, the freckled face of young Mr. Hammond puckered in an engaging grin. He eyed the Chief Inspector hesitantly, then produced a slim book from his pocket. "Er—could I have your autograph, sir?" he asked politely. Then with delightful naïveté, "I'm collecting names of celebrities."

Read, grimly amused, nodded and took the proffered book. The lad was fumbling eagerly with his fountain-pen. Jeffery, wryly musing on the unfairness of publicity, turned to Martha Rockwell. "And what part might you be playing in tonight's show?" he asked.

"The housekeeper," the actress replied. "One of the sinister variety with a penchant for ouija boards and crystal gazing. I sneak about quoting scripture and foretelling doom. As a matter of fact, I'm suspected of all the dirty doing from the start."

"Katharine Knowles wrote the dialogue, I believe?"

"That's so—and she's a much better author than she is an actress!" The knitting-needles kept up a clicking obbligato to her words. "It's really quite a clever thing, this piece. Lusinska plays a woman who unconsciously comes into possession of valuable papers. A gang of crooks are after them. She takes a house in the country, miles from anywhere, and the gang attempt to frighten her away. One night there's a storm. She becomes terrified and invites three friends down. The storm floods the country and the house is surrounded by water."

The Chief Inspector, his obligation to notoriety through, was listening carefully. "Who are the friends?"

"Gordon Finniss—he's the dark lad that went out after taking that crack at Lusinska—plays one," explained Martha. "The pups"—she jerked her head toward the lads—"play the other two. Miss Marlowe is Lusinska's French companion. The five sit down to supper, and in the middle of the meal the lights go out! Lusinska, who's locked the door, believes she hears footsteps outside and she sends Marlowe to the door to listen. Then," continued Martha, with ghoulish delight, "there's a whopping great scream—the lights are put on and Lusinska is found dead across the table. It turns out that she's been poisoned."

"Poisoned!" It was an ejaculation from Blackburn.

"Of course!" Miss Rockwell raised surprised eyes. "It has to be poison, because Marlowe does the trick. And nobody suspects her of the murder because she's supposed to be listening at the door all the time."

Vance Garnett said warmly: "What a spoil-sport you are, Martha! Why did you have to tell the end? Why couldn't you have let them guess?"

"Nonsense," said Miss Rockwell firmly. "That just shows your extreme youth, young man!" Her needles oscillated like mechanical shuttles. "That business of guessing the criminal is hopelessly old-fashioned. Nowadays, the thrill comes not so much from seeking the identity of the murderer as *knowing it beforehand . . .* and watching the battle of wits to prove his guilt! It's much better fun when you know the murderer and can stand off and watch him covering his tracks, destroying his traces, checkmating the police at every move. That's the thrill of modern crime!" Almost warily, she glanced up and her deep-set eyes were gleaming. "It's much more satisfactory than blundering about in the dark trying to guess *who!* That's why I always read the end of a detective novel first to get the most enjoyment out of it!"

Jeffery was looking at the matronly actress with renewed interest. "There's something intriguingly Oriental in your suggestion that appeals to me," he murmured. "And I agree with you that detective fiction definitely needs some new ideas. Although your idea is hardly original. Austin Freeman used that method some years ago."

It was von Bethke who broke the silence that had fallen. He had been standing at one side of the room, watching every movement with those hard eyes. Now he gave a short cough and glanced ostentatiously at his wrist-watch.

"All this is no doubt of interest to a student of crime," he said with a faint sneering hiss of sibilants. "But we are here to do a production." Again he glanced at his watch. "The play is to go on the air in five minutes." He flashed a glance at his players and there was a concerted movement from them. "I am sure that the gentlemen will excuse us." His eyes rested upon the elder actress. "After the production, Miss Rockwell, we would be delighted to listen to your interesting theories. But now—to work!" He snapped his fingers authoritatively and shepherded his people out of the room.

There was a pause. Suddenly, unaccountably, Blackburn gave a little shudder. The Chief Inspector stared at him. "What's the matter, son?" he inquired. "Someone walking over your grave?"

Jeffery said quietly: "Mine—or some other unfortunate's." Without another word, he turned and left the rehearsal room.

III

THE RIDDLE OF THE WRONG BODY

"It all came different," repeated the Mock-turtle thoughtfully.

Alice in Wonderland.

1

LIKE heavy pebbles tossed one by one on to the quiet surface of a shadowed lake, the chimes of ten-thirty sounded. Inside the small "talks" studio, dark except for the subdued light from the control room that filtered through the window, Mr. Jeffery Blackburn, with Chief Inspector Read and George Nickerson, stood watching through the glass partition giving uninterrupted vision of the dramatic studio next door. From a small speaker built into the wall above their heads, a carefully accented voice spoke.

"The time of ten-thirty brings us to Unit Three of our Inaugural Programme. This is a radio drama, *Darkness is Danger,* produced by Carl von Bethke at the new subsidiary studio of the B.B.C. The scene of this play is . . ."

And in tens of thousands of homes, listeners sat back in their chairs with ears attuned to the instrument bringing them the modern entertainment of sound without sight.

Blackburn, in the fortunate position of being able to use both senses, was relying upon his eyes rather than his ears. He was more interested in the scene on the other side of the plate-glass panel than the words which came tripping from the elevated speaker. As for the Chief Inspector, he was unfolding like some large and ruddy flower, his moustache almost brushing the window, his eyes missing no single detail. Jeffery, noticing this, marvelled again at the protean quality of human nature. For the simple truth was that William Read, the hard-lipped, square-jawed, experienced man-hunter, the nightmare bogy of a hundred criminals, the grizzled veteran of a dozen unforgettable experiences, was as thrilled as a child at the circus.

Stewart, the feature announcer, having read the scene of the drama, backed soundlessly into a corner. A chord of music swelled, dropped to an eerie movement of woodwind and strings, and meantime the hanging microphone moved to a position directly over the table, poised above the heads of Lusinska, who occupied the centre position, of Mary Marlowe, Finniss, Garnett, and Hammond, seated about. Martha Rockwell, awaiting her "entrance", stood off at one side. Farther away, partly hidden by the angle of the wall, the lugubrious Martin hovered by his effects table. And presiding over all this, like some stunted high priest in a temple of black art, was Carl von Bethke—von Bethke, script in hand and a pair of earphones clapped on his bullet-head.

Now the producer waved a plump hand, the music faded and they saw Olga Lusinska swallow something in her throat. One hand, resting on the table, trembled violently. Von Bethke waited a second, then stabbed a finger in her direction. Lusinska raised her head. . . .

And then . . .

"Hannah. Are you there, Hannah? Ah! Yes, would you serve the cocktails in here?" The actress' husky tone raised a quick curtain on *Darkness is Danger,* and, by their side, George Nickerson heaved a sigh of relief.

"Well, it's on the air," he announced.

Jeffery glanced at him. "Did you anticipate that it wouldn't go over?"

"You never know!" The manager shrugged. "Do you realize that we've never worked under such obsolete conditions as this since the early days at Savoy Hill?" He stared through the window and his tone was reminiscent. "It reminds me of the times when we used moving coil microphones—slung on a rubber band and supported by clumsy great stands on wheels—"

"Sssh . . ." cautioned Read fiercely.

Jeffery grimaced at Nickerson. "Mustn't spoil an old man's pleasure," he murmured. Once again their attention was focused on the business of the play.

The minutes ticked by.

For all his patronizing attitude toward this form of entertainment, Jeffery Blackburn found his interest deepening. His eyes rarely moved from that glass panel and the fascinating masquerade inside. With the microphone poised like some mechanical Recording Angel above their heads, the players went through their dialogue and movements with the automatic smoothness of long practice. It was like watching a rehearsal of a stage-drama in which the actors were word-perfect and at ease. Von Bethke had retired to one side and was listening with closed eyes as the play ran its course. It was only when some character unwittingly strolled out of microphone range and his voice lost normal level that the producer came to life, urging the player back into position with curt, admonishing gestures.

The illusion of the drama was astonishingly real. Robbed of the evidence of vision, it was impossible to believe that this smooth, effortless dialogue emanated from a small room cluttered with people and mechanical effects. Jeffery proved this by closing his eyes. Immediately the walls fell away and he was transported to this lonely, rain-drenched house on the moors; he was actually inside that shadowy, curtained dining-room with its flickering candles, actually sharing in the emotions that coloured the voices of the players. Lusinska, in particular, was superbly real. Always she underplayed, the sensations transformed into her tones were repressed but infinitely disturbing. The other players, inspired by her performance, worked in keeping. Jeffery found himself making mental genuflection to the production of Carl von Bethke. That the tubby Teuton knew his business was apparent by the manner in which the play gripped and thrilled.

In his corner, Ted Martin toiled like a machine. It was difficult to conceive that the dozen and one effects which gave depth and background to the drama had their genesis in the labours of this single individual. The sullen booming of rain over the house, the eerie fluted wail of the wind, the creak and rattle of buffeted windows, the soft put-put of water dripping from a leaky ceiling—all these and others were timed and produced with amazing skill and accuracy.

And then the drama moved to its first climax.

Lusinska, her husky tones dark with fear, was retailing to her guests the story of her persecution. Her voice, controlled, held a trembling note of terror. "They have given me until twelve o'clock to leave this house. But I will not be driven out like a dog into this storm!"

Mary Marlowe, her companion, said quietly: "You're very foolish, madam. For your own safety, you must go! These men will stop at nothing!"

"At nothing?" It was Gordon Finniss, his resonant voice repressed to suavity. "They have threatened you, Miss Holmes?"

"Yes!" It was a whisper.

"In what way?"

"If I am not out of this house by midnight, I am to die!"

Incredulity tinged Finniss' tones. "But surely you don't take that seriously? This is England, Miss Holmes—police-protected, law-abiding England! No possible harm—" (Ted Martin's fingers flew to something on his bench and clear, bell-like, a clock began to chime the hour of twelve.) "See, it is midnight now and you are still unharmed!"

Lusinska said tensely: "It serves only to make this horror more real, more tangible, when—"

(Von Bethke had slipped to the studio door as she started to speak. His hand flew to the light-switch; there was an audible *click* and the room was plunged in darkness. Except for a splash of pale radiance reflected from the control room window, the studio was a place of Stygian gloom.)

"Who put out those lights?" It was Lusinska, still speaking in character, and terror and hysteria struggled in her tones. "They said they would put out the lights . . . before they struck!"

"Nonsense!" There came the scrape of a chair as Finniss rose. "I'll go and see. . . ." The watching trio saw him move back, a dim-seen, shadowy figure, into the reflected light of the control room. He alone was visible and he halted as a sudden scream from Lusinska rasped the nerves.

"Don't move!"

A silence. Now her voice had shrunk to a sick whisper. "Listen! Can't you hear? Footsteps . . . coming up the stairs . . . closer . . . closer . . .!"

"I tell you, Miss Holmes—!"

"Louise! Louise—where are you?"

"*Oui, madame!* I am here—by your side!"

"Louise—go to the door. Silently—don't make a sound—and listen—"

"*Pourquoi, madame—?*"

"Go, I tell you! Go at once . . . to the door . . .!"

They heard her cross the room. Then silence, blackness, mental oblivion, when ears and eyes were strained almost painfully. Ten clogging, dragging seconds passed. Abruptly, the hush was broken by a sudden pain-choked, agonizing gasp; there was mild concentrated pandemonium of a body threshing wildly, then a soft thud as of a bag of wash dropped. Again that black, yawning silence swallowed every other sound. The three men in the small ante-room were motionless as statues. Something stickily wet dripped into Jeffery's eyes. Almost with a jerk, he raised his hand to find his forehead dewed with perspiration. Then, as though from the other side of the world, George Nickerson gave a fat chuckle, and that shell of suspense cast about them cracked and split.

"That's acting for you," the manager was saying. "Great idea of Von's to switch out the studio lights and give added realism to the scene. And if that death-rattle of Lusinska's hasn't got the customers looking over their shoulders, I'm a Chinaman's jade god!"

So unexpected was this leaping transition from grim drama to the prosaic, that their minds floundered momentarily between masquerade and reality, groping blindly in a mental fog as they struggled for sane readjustment. Thus it was that the disassociated chain of sound that followed made little or no impression on such chaos. Yet these sounds actually occurred, although, despite that tumultuous hush, only one impinged sufficiently on their reeling consciousness to be recognizable. Through the half-open door of the small room, muffled by distance, there came the throb of an electric starter and the rising hum of a motor-car engine. Then for the third time, that unbroken stillness enveloped them.

George Nickerson broke the hush after what seemed an age. Gone was the high note of satisfaction, now his voice held something of that dark frenzy that had animated Lusinska's tones. He turned a puzzled, paling face toward Read and Jeffery. "What's wrong?" he asked. "Why don't they go on with the play?"

His query was answered. With almost blinding violence, the lights in the dramatic studio flashed on. Von Bethke stood revealed with trembling sausage-fingers crooked about the switch. Behind that glass panel, the people inside the studio stood chained in an attitude of frozen horror like hapless souls stricken by Medusa's eye. Every face was drained of colour—turned toward the centre of the floor.

"God in heaven!" Nickerson's voice grated like a rusty pump. "Look!"

The injunction was needless. Blackburn and Read were already clawing at the window. On the carpet lay the body of a woman, a body twisted and convulsed. One leg was drawn up beneath her in a flurry of disordered clothing. She lay on her back, arms outflung, hands clenched. The light shone pitilessly down on her contorted face. Their minds, still in the grip of that dark masquerade, were ready to place the sullen mask of Lusinska on that fallen twisted body. But the Russian actress was standing, white and rigid as a pillar of marble, some feet away. Jeffery swallowed something that jerked and ticked in his throat. "What—?" he stammered.

"Who—?" By his side, George Nickerson gave a little retching sound.

"It's—it's Mary Marlowe!"

At the same moment, Olga Lusinska swayed as she stood, thrust out one hand to claw at empty air, sagged like a rag doll and dropped soundlessly to the studio floor.

2

It was as though that involuntary movement loosed the invisible strings that bound them in their attitudes. The people in the dramatic studio came to life with the exaggerated speed of a quick motion film. Von Bethke was the centre of the group that flew to the side of the sprawled body. The others crowded about him as he knelt, staring down with glazed eyes. The producer laid his hand on the girl's heart, then staggered to his feet, his face ashen. "Get a doctor," he croaked. "Get a doctor, quickly!"

Into the tiny studio those ominous words came, sending Read, Jeffery, and Nickerson flying out into the corridor. At the door of the dramatic studio was Charles Finlay and a sweatered young man from the control room. The studio director was furiously shaking the handle of the door. As the trio rushed up, he turned a strained white face to the manager.

"I can't open it, sir. They must have locked it on the inside!"

Nickerson pushed him aside almost roughly and peered through the keyhole. "There's no key in the lock," he panted. "I can see clear through! Just a moment!" He stepped back as the knob rattled. "They're dragging on it from the other side. They can't know it's locked!"

"What can we do—?" began Finlay, when the manager wheeled on him. "Get the master-keys from the commissionaire in the front office," he snapped. "And tell him to see if there's a doctor among that crowd in Number One—and send him in here!" As Finlay raced away, Nickerson turned back, to glance up at the door. The tiny pilot light was aglow. He almost wrung his hands in horror. "Why don't they turn off that microphone?" he wailed. "They're telling all Britain that there's been an accident!"

The young man in the sweater shook his head. "That's all right, sir. We cut the studio off the air as soon as we saw what had happened when the lights flashed up." His tone was unsteady. "There's not a sound gone through ever since!"

"Thank God someone managed to keep their head," grunted Nickerson. He hunched his shoulders and peered through the keyhole again. "Who the devil locked this door?" he demanded. "And where's the key now?"

"Is it customary to lock this door during productions?" Read barked.

The manager shook an anxious head. "It's the first time I've ever known it done. Perhaps Von was afraid of that crowd in Number One—thought they'd blunder in while the play was on."

The arrival of Finlay with keys diverted his attention. "Here you are, sir. And Chaston's making inquiries about that doctor. There'll be one along in a minute."

Nickerson almost snatched the bunch of keys from his hand and selected one with fingers that trembled. He fitted it into the lock, and silently the door swung back. For one moment, as Nickerson stood in the entrance, there was a shocked, stunned pause. Then it was as though the entire studio gave tongue, in the trembling spate of sound that whirled about his head, carrying questions, explanations, and denials eddying and twisting like straws in a flooded gutter. For some seconds the manager listened in dazed bewilderment, then he raised his hand.

"Quiet!" he bellowed. "All of you—be quiet!" The babel died as suddenly as it was born. He ran sadly harassed eyes over the studio, then wheeled and began to fire staccato orders.

"Finlay—get into Studio C, and put an explanation over the air! Indisposition of member of cast—play will be repeated later. And the usual regrets! Not a word about this business! Martin, you turn off that microphone and push those chairs and that table out of the way! You"—he turned to the young man from the control room—"carry Miss Lusinska into the rehearsal room and get the night-nurse to attend to her! Miss Rockwell, you go with her!" He raised his voice. "Where's Mr. Stewart?"

"Here, sir!" The feature announcer came forward from his corner.

"Get up to C and lay your hands on all the records for the early morning session! Shoot them over straight away and keep the programme bright! None of your heavy stuff. Give 'em light orchestral, foxtrots and populars! We've got to wipe the taste of this thing out of their mouths!"

Stewart started off at the double. "Yes, sir!"

"Just a moment!" Nickerson was like an electric spark. "Tell Finlay to get down into A and keep the crowd from drifting in here! There's been a slight accident—that's all anybody's got to know about this business! That goes for the girls on the switch-board, too. Every line in the place'll be plugged in a few minutes. And keep those damned reporters out of here if you have to chloroform them!" Stewart nodded and raced away.

Nickerson kicked the door shut after him and ran a handkerchief across his pale face. His eyes dropped to the body on the floor and he made a little gesture of distaste. "Mr. Hammond and Mr. Garnett—would you lift Miss Marlowe's body on to the chesterfield? Thank you." He turned to where von Bethke stood, his pendulous cheeks the colour of wet ashes. "How did that door come to be locked?"

The producer stared at him, a look of imbecile vacuity on his face. "I thought you had locked it—you opened it—" he stuttered. "You had the keys—"

The manager's nerves, strung to breaking-point, gave an edge to his tone. "Of course I opened the door, but these are the master-keys!" he snapped, shaking the bunch before the other's eyes. "Has that door been locked all through the show?"

Von Bethke's fingers went to his lips. "I cannot say. I—I tried to open it. I thought you had locked it on the outside." His mind seemed crawling sluggishly about this enigma. "The door was open when the play began. I can swear to that. No one in here locked it."

"Well, it was locked when we tried to get in," rapped Nickerson. "And the door couldn't have locked itself." He wheeled on the others. "Did any of you people lock this door?"

Heads were shaken blankly. Denials quivered on white lips.

"But this is absurd," the manager's tone was raw with irritation. "Somebody must have locked this door! Who was last to come in here?"

A silence. Eyes searched faces blank as the walls behind them. Feet shuffled, hands were uneasy. A sudden exclamation was wrenched from Ted Martin's lips and every eye flew in his direction. The lanky effects man was pointing to the wall telephone. The amber light set below the mouthpiece of the instrument was blinking furiously.

"Who the devil can that be?" snapped Nickerson. "See who it is!"

Martin shambled across and lifted the receiver. A moment later, he turned.

"Mis-ter Newland on the wire for you, sir. Wants t' speak to you urgent." He held out the receiver, but the manager waved it aside.

"Heaven knows what I'll say to him," he muttered, and made an irresolute step toward the instrument. Then he shook his head. "I'll take the call in my office. I can talk better there. The rest of you wait here!" He almost ran from the studio.

The two young men, who had been interrupted in their moving of the body by Nickerson's questions, bent to their unhappy task. Very gently, they carried the dead clay that had been Mary Marlowe across the studio and laid it carefully on the divan pushed against the wall. As they arranged it, one arm slipped free and trailed limply upon the floor. Von Bethke, who had been watching the operation from under lowered lids, gave a sudden guttural ejaculation.

"What's that? In her hand?"

Heads jerked. Eyes flew to the member. Between the tightly bunched fingers something gleamed in the light that bathed the studio. Gordon Finniss, after a quick inquiring glance around, dropped on his knees and, very tenderly, began to unclasp the dead fingers. So difficult was his task it was obvious that *rigor* was already stiffening the dead limbs. The reluctant digits were strained apart one by one, and with their loosening a small metal object dropped soundlessly to the carpeted floor.

"It's a key!" Hammond exclaimed.

It was Ted Martin who supplemented this information. Slow wonder drawled his tone. "It's th' key of this studio!"

A faint prescience of something unnamable prickled Jeffery's skin. He spoke sharply from his position near the door. "Are you sure?"

Finniss was on his feet, key in hand. "We can soon prove it," he said shortly. He crossed to the door, fitted the key in the lock and turned it. The key fitted exactly, and as he worked it the metal slugs of the lock flew backward and forward. "It's the key all right," he added redundantly.

Von Bethke, those queer hard eyes on the door, said slowly, almost broodingly: "Then Marlowe locked the door herself—locked herself in here." It was not so much a question as a statement, and no one answered. He teased the loose skin of his face thoughtfully. "Yes, that is so! I remember she was last to come in here." His bullet-head jerked up and down. "Yes, that is so," he repeated, with weighty emphasis. "She locked herself in here."

Gordon Finniss turned on him, his lean face shadowed. "Why on earth should she want to do that?"

The producer shrugged his fat shoulders and both hands described a vague arc. Young Garnett, his eyes averted from that still figure on the chesterfield, said with a certain trembling simplicity: "If Miss Marlowe *did* lock that door, she could have done it easily without anybody knowing. That key is always left in the lock on the inside of the door. She'd merely have to turn the key as she came in and slip it out."

Gordon Finniss repeated helplessly: "But why should she—?"

Hands moved in bewildered negation. Eyes were vacant. By the door, the Chief Inspector worried his moustache.

Jeffery drummed restless fingers. Gone was his air of condescending tolerance. Above narrowed grey eyes, his forehead was puckered in a worried frown. The silence became heavier, more dampening with the passing of every minute. It was as though the insulating fibre of the walls sucked all animation from the room. It was almost a relief when Nickerson returned. His face was more composed, but his movements were still jerky and uncertain. He spoke as he entered.

"I had to tell Newland the truth," he said quietly. "He heard everything through his speaker. So much so that he's leaving the Towers right away in his car. He'll probably get down first thing in the morning."

He was pacing the room, hands linked behind his back. "We set the programme running again," he announced moodily, "but there's the devil to pay outside. Half London must be on the telephone! Thank God Sir Tallis left before this thing happened! I've managed to stave off the reporters with some sort of a story, but they're hanging round like vultures waiting for the doctor's verdict—" He broke off and stared round irritably.

"By the way, where is the doctor?"

As though awaiting its cue, a voice sounded in the corridor, a full rich resonance that contrasted acutely with the manager's bleak tones.

"Of course I can go in! I was sent for! Let me pass, sir! I am Dr. Townsend!"

3

A pre-war generation of parents would have called Dr. Arthur Townsend a "well-preserved" man. They probably did so, for he brought into the dramatic studio a presence contemporaneous with a past era, a brass-knobbed, four-posted bedside manner redolent of cabomel, sal volatile, and Seidlitz powder. His heavy florid face was set amid impressive grey sideburns, and if the doctor held his head high it gave the impression not so much of confidence as a habit acquired through balancing a stethoscope inside his tall hat.

He advanced into the room under his own steam, as it were, nodded patronizingly to the groups and listened absently to Nickerson's explanations. Then he cleared his throat portentously. "Sounds very much like heart trouble," he announced. "Did the young lady suffer that way at all? Shortness of breath? Blood-pressure?"

George Nickerson shook his head. "I couldn't say." His tone was weary. "We know practically nothing about the young lady. This was her first part with us."

"Hmm!" With lips pursed and hands clasped behind his back, Dr. Townsend moved across to the chesterfield and stared down at the body, wagging a grave head. "Convulsions, eh? Slightly cyanosed features. Hmm! Looks like too much excitement. Too many cigarettes and too many cocktails!" Somewhat clumsily, he lowered himself beside the body. "However, we'll soon find out."

The people in the studio watched his examination without comment. Jeffery and the Chief Inspector had not moved from their position by the door. Gordon Finniss, with Hammond and Garnett, formed a restless trio under the suspended microphone. Nickerson paced the room. Von Bethke had moved to Martin's side near the effects table. Their eyes followed every motion of the doctor's fingers.

Leadenly the hands of the electric clock on the wall crept onward. The silence was almost hypnotizing. Jeffery had the curious impression that the walls were closing in on them. Over their heads the hanging microphone swung gently . . . backward . . . forward . . . backward. With a suddenness that caught at their hearts, Dr. Townsend cleared his throat. He leaned heavily on the chesterfield as he rose. He marched to the centre of the studio, tapping his finger-points daintily.

"Well?" cried George Nickerson, his voice shrill.

Dr. Townsend puffed out his cheeks. "One of the best authenticated cases of heart failure I have ever seen," he announced.

His words fell upon silence, a tensing concentrated silence that burst abruptly like an over-inflated balloon. The dead air of the room became alive and quivering with surprised exclamations, half-formed sentences, questions that dried on startled lips. The clamour eased and Nickerson said thinly:

"Heart failure? You're sure of that?"

The doctor's head went back. Out came his jaw. "I am, sir, a qualified practitioner—"

The manager made a little gesture of apology. "I'm not doubting your word, Doctor. But it was so sudden—so unexpected—"

"Abrupt demise is the outstanding characteristic of heart failure," said Dr. Townsend, with a curl of his lips.

Nickerson ran a hand through his thinning hair. "Of course, of course," he muttered vaguely. He did not appear to have noticed the snub in the other's reply. He turned slowly and looked at the body. "Is that convulsed attitude natural in cases of heart weakness?"

"Certainly!" The doctor's tone was cold. "The unfortunate sufferer struggles for breath and convulses the entire body in the effort of respiration. I have known cases in which the patient has actually flung himself out of bed in the struggles against suffocation!"

Something inside Jeffery contracted in a sudden spasm of pity. He asked gravely: "Doctor, what could have brought on such an attack? I understood that heart failure is usually caused by some physical strain—"

"Or mental strain!" Townsend's resonance overlapped his hushed tone. The doctor's manner became heavy, pedantic. "To the cardiac sufferer, any outstanding mental stimulus such as excitement, anxiety, or tense emotion, is sufficient to bring about a collapse." He swung on the manager. "You say that this poor woman was stricken down at a dramatic moment in the production? That would be quite sufficient. The intense nervous reaction of the darkened studio, the emotional strain of pouring her personality into the character, the mounting excitement of the drama—all these things would naturally put an added stress upon a heart probably weakened by hereditary cardiac trouble!" Again he addressed Nickerson directly: "You say that you do not know if this young woman inherited any such weaknesses?"

"We know very little about the girl at all," the manager repeated.

Gordon Finniss had been eying the body curiously. He took a half-step forward. "Doctor . . .?" His manner was as hesitant as his words.

"Well, young man?"

Finniss' hands moved uneasily, to settle in his pockets. "Doctor, I've had some experience in pathology—went through the war with the R.A.M.C." His voice slowed. "And we were taught that a body struck down with cardiac disease usually remains in a flaccid condition for some time after death." He paused and seemed to fumble for words. "Yet—well—in this case, *rigor* seems to have set in almost immediately."

A rising tide of colour stained Dr. Townsend's heavy face a rich magenta. He surveyed the actor fiercely from under bushy eyebrows, so that Jeffery was reminded of an affronted Papa Barrett rebuking a rebellious Henrietta. He boomed like a struck gong:

"And, young man, were you ever taught in the R.A.M.C. that *rigor* is the most peculiar and unreliable feature of a post-mortem examination? Were you not taught that it can be governed by a dozen irrelevant details—the sugar content of the blood, by violent exercise before death, by the temperature of the room in which the patient dies?" Head flung back, eyelids drooped insolently, he barked the question: "Were you not taught that?"

Scarlet-faced, the unfortunate Finniss stammered: "Of course, Doctor! But I merely wished—"

"You merely wished to show your ignorance," snapped Townsend. He dismissed the young man with a lofty wave of his hand and addressed the manager. "I am quite satisfied that the death is due to cardiac weakness, Mr.—Mr.—?"

"Nickerson is my name."

"Quite satisfied, Mr. Nickerson. There are half a dozen unequivocal symptoms that convince me beyond all doubt! There is no need for me to elaborate on them now. Sufficient to say that I am willing to sign the death certificate to this end." A chill crept into his tone. "If, on the other hand, you would rather have a consultation . . .?" He paused with thick eyebrows arched aggressively.

"Certainly not, Doctor." Again that weariness was apparent in Nickerson's voice. "If you are satisfied, I am sure we have no reason to doubt you."

Dr. Townsend inclined a dignified head. "As you will. I will arrange for the removal of the body. I do not think an inquest will be necessary. You, of course, must inform the police and take steps to communicate with the deceased's people. There will, no doubt, be a certain amount of unpleasant publicity, although"—and here his lips curled again—"in these days, nobody appears to worry much about that!"

And with this trenchant reflection on an age that had left him so far behind, Dr. Arthur Townsend moved serenely from Number Two studio, leaving behind him a silence that was more eloquent than the voice of Stentor on the Trojan battlefields.

4

The traffic light at Oxford Circus blinked a warning eye and Mr. Blackburn manipulated clutch, gears, and brake. The Bentley slowed, stopped, and was immediately engulfed in purring engines. The Chief Inspector, settled comfortably in his seat, stifled a prodigious yawn with the back of his hand.

"Well, son," he mused sleepily. "You seem to attract sensation as a monkey attracts fleas! Only once in the history of the B.B.C. an accident like this—and you have a box-seat for the show!"

"Ummm," muttered Jeffery absently. His eyes were turned toward that baleful scarlet orb, eyes that were vague and shadowed. Read, long accustomed to his companion's moods, was continuing a murmured conversation with himself.

"Pretty rough on Nickerson, though! The opening night, of all times! I like that chap—fellow after my own heart—gets things done!" Drowsily his thoughts ran on, moving off at a tangent. "No wonder that Russian dame fainted—it all looked pretty ghastly when those lights showed up. Guess that lad—what's his name?—Newland—will be upset. That's another job for Nickerson in the morning." He grunted. "Looks like a hopeless dawn for—" He shot abruptly from his seat, wide awake, and jerked his companion's arm.

"For Pete's sake, lad, get a move on! You're holding up all the traffic in the Circus!"

"Er—what—?" Jeffery came to life with a start.

"Sorry," he grunted. He slipped in the clutch with a jerk and the car jumped forward, sending the Chief Inspector bouncing in his seat. The powerful single-seater swung in and out of the traffic like a startled eel. Read flinched as they slithered past a long-snouted Rolls, their fenders kissing. He was opening his mouth to bellow a warning when Jeffery spoke.

"Chief!" His tone was brooding. "Do you remember, just after that girl dropped in the studio, hearing any other sounds?"

The big man stared at him. "Why, I—" he began, then paused. "Yes," he said slowly, "I do remember. There was the sound of a motor-car being started somewhere and driven away."

Jeffery shook his head almost irritably. "I know *that!* But did you hear any other noise?"

Read stared at him curiously. "What's biting you now, son? I didn't hear any other sound. There was too much else to think about."

Jeffery swung the wheel and the Bentley shot down New Bond Street. "There was another sound," he said quietly, "It's been worrying me all the evening. And I've just remembered what it was! It was the muffled click of a door shutting somewhere close by!"

IV

JIGSAW

1

Nothing's so hard but search will find it out.

ROBERT HERRICK.

MR. JEFFERY BLACKBURN had long considered the matutinal rising of the lark to be merely another example of the limited brain capacity of the feathered *genus.* "When you cannot find repose in yourself, it is useless to look for it elsewhere," he would quote, distorting de Rochefoucauld shamelessly in an effort to justify his inability to rise before nine o'clock. It had taken the Chief Inspector, reared on Spartan habits, some time to accustom himself to his companion's sluggishness. Eventually, after threats, pleas, and ridicule failed to move Jeffery's recumbent form at a respectable hour, he had given up in disgust and was now almost reconciled to the business of sitting down to a solitary breakfast.

Judge, then, Read's amazement when, moving drowsily showerwards a few minutes after seven o'clock on the following morning, he encountered an astonishing spectacle in the sitting-room. Jeffery, a black-and-white check dressing-gown over his pyjamas, was lying back in front of the fire, hands clasped behind tousled head and the inevitable cigarette between his lips. The Chief Inspector halted, gasped, knuckled one eye under the momentary impression that this was some phantasm of his sleepy brain, then, as the vision remained as solid as ever, he exploded.

"Jeffery! What the devil are you doing up at this hour?"

The cigarette between the young man's lips quivered. He did not move. "Good morning, sire," he said amiably. "I couldn't sleep."

Read stared incredulously. "You couldn't—*what?"*

"Sleep," repeated the imperturbable Jeffery. "You've heard of it, I suppose? 'The innocent sleep; sleep, that knits up the ravell'd sleeve of care, the death of each day's life, sore labour's bath, balm of hurt minds, great nature's second course'." He rolled his head. "Oh, great Thane of Cawdor, what a whale of a lie!"

The Chief Inspector crossed the room and stood over him. "Are you aware, young man, that it's only seven o'clock?"

Jeffery was not impressed. "Indeed," he murmured. "I've been sitting here since five o'clock!"

Read frowned. "What's the matter?" he inquired grimly. "Indigestion?"

"That's it!" Blackburn sat up and turned red-rimmed eyes on his companion. "Yes—indigestion! Mental indigestion!" His tone was animated. "A bubbling, churning, regurgitating flux of thoughts that positively kicked me out of bed!" He jumped to his feet, crushed out his cigarette and faced the elder man.

"Chief! I'm not at all satisfied about that girl's death last night!"

"Great Land o' Goshen, son!" Read stared at the other's grey face. "What's biting you over that?"

"Oh, there's half a dozen things that don't cog!" Jeffery moved restless hands. "And yet, for the life of me, I can't understand why they should cog. It's just that my sensitive nostrils detect a fish-like odour, but hang me if I can tell from which direction it comes!"

The Chief Inspector jerked at the strings of his dressing-gown. "Well?" he demanded. "What am I supposed to do about it?"

Blackburn said slowly: "You can ask Miles Conroy to have a look at that girl's body."

The elder man stared, his expression a mixture of scorn and amazement. "Son—you're just plumb crazy!"

"Yes," returned Jeffery grimly. "Just crazy enough to feel sure that Mary Marlowe didn't die of heart failure!"

"But that doctor's diagnosis—?"

The young man cut him short. "You, Chief, of all people, should know that doctors aren't infallible! Doctors diagnosed James Maybrick's illness as chronic dyspepsia. They called Eliza Barrow's complaint congestion of the liver, and the slow wasting sickness of Pierre L'Anglier acute gastritis!" His voice slowed. "Yet an autopsy of these bodies proved beyond all doubt that these people had been poisoned!"

"*Poison!*" Read's face set like stone. "Lad—you surely don't suspect . . .?" His voice trailed away. He stared at his companion from under black brows. Jeffery shrugged, a little helpless movement.

"I don't know, Chief! All I can say is that I'm far from satisfied. That's why I want Conroy to see that body." He grasped the big man's knotted arm. "Do it for me, Chief! And if the Chief Medical Officer of the C.I.D. says it's heart failure, I'll never mention the subject again!"

The Chief Inspector moved to the fire and spread huge hands to the glow. He spoke without turning. "But you don't realize what you're asking, son! Remember, this thing concerns the B.B.C.! If there is anything in your suspicions—if there has been foul play, why, the sensation would tear London wide open! On the other hand, if it is all the clean potato, I stand to look the biggest fool in the Department!"

And Jeffery said miserably: "I know, Chief. But all the same . . ."

Read's expression softened as he turned. "Give me your reasons, lad. You can't expect me to bring the Department into this business just because you've had too much supper! What makes you think something is wrong?" He dragged a chair under him and sat down.

Jeffery took a cigarette from the box on the mantel and lit it. "All right! I'll enumerate the outstanding points, leaving the more problematical details such as the cause of the death, for a later occasion." He blew a long feather of smoke.

"The first agitating consideration centres about those sounds we heard directly after Miss Marlowe collapsed in the studio. I heard them—as you probably did—more or less subconsciously, and it wasn't until I began to concentrate on their actual sound quality that I recognized them as having any significance at all! Driving back from the studio last night, I successfully identified two of the noises—the soft click of a door closing and the noise of a starting motor-car. But there was a third sound, a commonplace, familiar echo that hovered just outside my consciousness. It wasn't until early this morning when I was pacing the floor that I identified that third noise." He paused and looked down at his companion. "Chief—it was the soft movement of footsteps walking cautiously along a carpeted surface!"

Read was watching him closely. "Well, lad," he said stolidly, "I'll need something more convincing than that! There's no law forbidding people to walk along a corridor. As a matter of fact, we know that two people *did* come along that passage after Marlowe's collapse! Remember? We found that studio director and another young chap dragging at the locked door as we ran from the small studio! What you heard was probably their movements!"

Something of the elation in Blackburn's face died.

He shook a wrinkled head. "Oh, if I could only explain what I feel," he said. "If I could only bring you to my conviction that the steps I heard weren't the blundering movements of good honest panic. They were cautious, furtive steps—"

"Stick to facts, son," interrupted Read curtly. "Go on!"

Blackburn gave a little shiver and pulled his dressing-gown tighter about him. "Then," he said quietly, "there's the intriguing problem of the wrong victim."

The Chief Inspector started. "The wrong . . .?"

"Victim," Jeffery repeated firmly. "Don't you see that if we were to follow the lead of probability, Olga Lusinska appears as the only person in that studio to whom trouble might occur? I'm not referring to her part in the play, although that," continued Blackburn meditatively, "presents another peculiar angle. I'm alluding to the fact that she was unpopular with the rest of the cast and her bitter tongue had made more than one enemy. Why, then, was Mary Marlowe, a harmless, unknown personality, struck down?"

Read leaned back and crossed his legs. "The most obvious reply to that is the fact that Marlowe suffered from a weak heart and Lusinska didn't! Don't go imagining obstacles where none exist, son. Anyone of those people in the studio might have gone floppo if they suffered from Marlowe's complaint. That stands to reason!"

"Nothing stands to reason until it is proved," returned the young man. "If foul play had been planned for last night, it seems only logical to assume that it was directed against Lusinska. In that case, why was Mary Marlowe killed? Was it a mistake?" He broke off suddenly. "Now that's—"

"That's a large slice of what our American friends call first-grade boloney," snorted Read. "What's set you off like this? Here you go spinning out elaborate, cross-eyed theories without the slightest foundation! There's not one of your so-called problems that I haven't been able to answer sensibly!"

Deliberately Jeffery sat down in his chair. He leaned forward. "Then answer this one, my bulky Oedipus," he said grimly. *"Why did Mary Marlowe lock herself in that studio?"*

The Chief Inspector opened his mouth for a quick retort, then closed it again. He stared at the young man with narrowed eyes. "What do you mean by that?"

"Don't stall!" snapped Jeffery. "Where's your ready answer?" And as Read remained silent, he went on: "The reply should leap to your lips! Marlowe locked herself in that studio and kept the key in her hand obviously to prevent someone inside going out . . . or someone outside *coming in!"*

Read shifted uncomfortably. "Now, just a minute, Jeff—"

"Sixty of them if you wish, Chief! But you can't get away from the fact that no other person in that studio knew that the door was locked!"

"So far as we know! But one of them may have been lying—"

"Ah!" Blackburn pounced. "Exactly! One, perhaps several, of the people in that studio may have known that the door was locked! Then why should they deny it? What is the motive behind their lying? Immediately we ask ourselves that question, we strike a tangle! Why should one or several persons perjure themselves over such a simple thing as a locked door? Doesn't that throw a new and rather sinister light on the whole business?"

"God Almighty, boy!" The Chief Inspector threw his hands in the air. "We don't know if they were lying! They were all probably in complete ignorance of the door being locked!"

Jeffery grinned. "You're twisting again! It was your suggestion that they might have been lying! Well, let's say that they didn't know the door was locked. That brings me back to my original line of argument. Now, stop interrupting for a moment and I'll develop my premise!"

He leaned back, cigarette between lips, and fixed his eyes on the fencing foils crossed above the mantel.

"It seems highly improbable to me that Marlowe locked that door to prevent any person *going out* of that studio. The people inside were *known!* Now—and this is purely hypothetical—if Marlowe feared that an attack was to be made on her life while she was in that studio, an attack, that is, from some person who was in the room with her, her action in locking the door to protect herself is so insane that we can discard it altogether! Then, did she lock the door to prevent the guilty party from escaping? Again, I think not. Remember, all the people in that room were well-known, and had any individual been missing when the lights flashed up, his or her absence would have been noticed at once and consequent suspicion aroused. No. I think we can forget that possibility."

He paused. Read nodded without speaking.

"Now," continued Jeffery, "if we consider that the door may have been locked to prevent an outsider—an unknown outsider—*entering* the studio, the idea at once becomes more feasible. Let us imagine that among the crowd invited to the opening of the studio is a person with a grudge against Marlowe. What better opportunity would this individual have than during that darkened sequence of the play? It would be quite possible for our hypothetical murderer to slip in and out, naturally risking the chance of being seen during his action.

"Marlowe may have anticipated this. Hence the locking of the studio door. Now, see where this brings us." Jeffery held up his hand and began to tick off the points on his fingers. "Marlowe locked the door because she feared an attack on her life. Now she is dead. Ergo—she was attacked! Ergo—she was murdered! Ergo—the pompous Dr. Townsend's diagnosis is ridiculous!"

"Ergo my Aunt Fanny!" The Chief Inspector made a contemptuous noise in his throat, something between a snort and a grunt. "You've got it all cock-eyed, son! Your hypothetical construction falls down on its most important point! You say that the girl locked the door because she feared that someone outside would enter and attack her? Well, we know she was struck down, but if it was foul play, how in Solomon's Folly did the murderer get in? *That door was locked all the time!"*

"I know—I know!" Jeffery sprang to his feet and ran irritable fingers through his tousled hair. "That's why there's something wrong with the whole damn' thing! It's got no sequence—no sensible design! It's—it's like trying to work out a jigsaw puzzle with only half the pieces!" He swung round on Read. "And do you know why, Chief? Because we've got only half the story! That's the reason it's all so lop-sided!"

The Chief Inspector shook his head and rose. His voice was kindly. "No, son. I'll tell you why it looks lop-sided to you. It's because you've got a perfectly legitimate case of two and two—and you're trying to add it up to thirteen. A girl dies of heart failure—and you want to make a complicated mystery out of it! It won't work, my lad,"

He crossed and placed a hand on the young man's shoulder. "I'm willing to bet the back buttons on my trousers that you're making a mountain out of a molehill, Jeff. Now, go and get yourself a soothing nerve draught and swallow some bacon and eggs. Forget about—"

The determined buzz of the telephone cut into his faintly amused adhortation. He turned on his heel. "Who's the early bird?" he demanded.

Jeffery was already at the instrument. Read saw an expression of mingled surprise and gratification cross his lean worried face as he answered the unseen caller. A few moments later, he replaced the receiver and turned to his companion. Gone was the harassed air, his anxious manner. He hummed the tail-end of a tune as he approached the Chief Inspector, and cocked a quizzical eye at him.

"Better hurry and brush the teeth, doughty Cerberus," he chuckled. "We have a caller after breakfast." He was untying the strings of his dressing-gown as he spoke. "That was Mr. Andrew Newland on the 'phone. He's been around to see Nickerson and he's paying us an early call." He surveyed Read, head on one side, expression droll. "I don't think Mr. Newland is at all satisfied about Miss Marlowe's abrupt attack of heart failure!"

2

Andrew Newland, arriving punctually at nine o'clock, fitted Nickerson's description so completely that Jeffery experienced a fleeting disappointment. Just what he had expected of their visitor he could not say, but it was something rather different from the reality. There was about this broad-shouldered young gentleman no trace of the pampered heir of riches, rather it was an aura of cold baths, early morning gallops, and the concentrated activity of squash courts that he brought into the room. There was about his whole appearance a sturdiness, a stolidness, that bordered dangerously on the phlegmatic; he gave the impression that having once formed an opinion, he would be reluctant to the point of obstinacy in changing those views.

Newland stood, feet apart, glancing from one man to the other. The Chief Inspector came forward, murmured introductions and proffered cigarettes. Newland shook his head. He leaned over the back of a chair and began pulling off his driving gloves.

"You'll have to excuse me butting in on you like this." His voice was deep, masculine. "Matter of fact, I've had a nasty slap in the eye this morning and I'm not too sure whether I'm on my head or my heels. I've been talking to George this morning—Mr. Nickerson, you know. He told me the truth about"—his voice faltered then steadied—"about Miss Marlowe's death."

Read nodded politely. "We quite realize that you must be upset about the tragedy, Mr. Newland." His tone was purposely soft. "But frankly, how can we help you?"

"By finding out the truth!"

The Chief Inspector raised his eyebrows. "The truth?"

Deep in Andrew Newland's dark eyes something flickered. Slowly he walked round his chair and sat down. He said weightily: "Mr. Read, I know that you're often troubled with crazy people who have strange ideas about things. I can imagine that you've schooled yourself to be polite to them—just as you're being polite to me. I can understand—"

"My dear Mr. Newland," began Read, but the young man waved him aside with a fierce gesture.

"I can understand your point of view exactly," he continued as if no interruption had occurred. "But this, sir, is a different matter—a vastly different matter." His deep voice was curiously repressed. "I don't know what happened in that studio last night. I was coming down to be with Mary—I wish to God I had now—but there were family matters. So I can't say what really happened last night. But I do know this: That girl did not die of heart failure! Her heart was as strong as mine!" He thumped his broad chest with a clenched paw as he spoke.

There was a silence. Read, under the steady scrutiny of Newland's dark eyes, picked up his pipe and turned it over in his fingers. "We had a doctor examine Miss Marlowe immediately after her seizure," he pointed out. "He is a thoroughly competent man and is quite satisfied that the death was due to heart weakness."

"And I say it wasn't!" Newland thrust out his jaw. He stood up, his solid wrestler's build towering over them. "Look here, sir! A heart just doesn't conk out on a person! People with weak hearts complain of all sorts of things—things like blood pressure, dizziness, and shortness of breath. Oh, I know"—as Read started to speak. "After I left George Nickerson I had a talk with a friend of mine from Harley Street. He told me all about this heart-failure business. Quite enough to convince me that there's some mighty funny doings somewhere!"

Jeffery, in his chair, maintained thoughtful silence. Newland, hands thrust in his pockets, was still standing. Read filled his pipe with slow deliberation, lit it and tossed the match into the ash-tray. "Sit down, Mr. Newland," he invited.

Reluctantly the young man lowered his bulk into the chair. He shook a moody head. "Guess I'm making a damn' fool of myself," he muttered. Up came his eyes. "But if the police won't believe me, who will? Because I'm willing to wager every penny I have, that Mary—Miss Marlowe didn't die because of heart weakness!"

From his chair Jeffery spoke. "You noticed no such symptoms during your friendship with Miss Marlowe?"

Eagerly Newland turned to him. "Certainly not! The opposite was the case. Sport was an absolute fetish with that girl! She was simply tireless at tennis! She could play me out. And she excelled at swimming, riding, and hiking." He made a gesture of deprecation. "It's absurd to think about it! If her heart had been at all weak, she could never have stood up to those exercises!"

"Ummm." Read was noncommittal. He puffed at his pipe. "I suppose there was no chance of the weakness being hereditary and lying dormant? Did you know her people at all?"

Newland shook his head. "Her parents, I understood, were dead," he said quietly. "She never mentioned others in her family. I gathered that she was very much alone in the world." His voice rose. "That poor kid was just the sort whose death would go unquestioned, simply because there was no one to make a fuss!"

"How did she live?" inquired Jeffery.

"Like a cat—odds and ends!" The young man's tone was moody. "She earned a few guineas at free-lance journalism, interviewing screen and radio personalities for the womens' papers. She eked this out with other jobs. Heaven only knows what they were! By the look of her hands, I should say she scrubbed floors! That was why I was so keen for Nickerson to give her that wireless engagement last night. She needed every penny she could get to keep body and soul together!" Newland's big hands clenched and relaxed slowly.

"That's rather peculiar," Blackburn said slowly. He tossed aside his cigarette end and rose to select another.

Newland's head jerked up. "Peculiar? What is peculiar?"

Jeffery did not answer at once. He sat down and lit his cigarette. Over the match-flame his eyes sought the visitor's face. "I think you ought to know, Mr. Newland," he said quietly, "that, like yourself, I am not at all satisfied with the explanation given about Miss Marlowe's death. There are several points which are curious, to say the least.

"Here is one of them. When Mr. Nickerson reported Miss Marlowe's death late last night, an officer was sent to her address. She had a flat in Bayswater. That officer's duty was to break the sad news to her family or her friends. Imagine his surprise when he discovered that the girl was completely alone. According to her landlady, she had no close friends and very few acquaintances. Sometimes Miss Marlowe would be absent from her flat for weeks at a time, returning unexpectedly and without explanation of her truancy. Yet"—and Jeffery's voice slowed—"she appeared to live quite comfortably and her flat was adequately if not almost luxuriously furnished. Yet you tell us that she gave you the impression of poverty."

Andrew Newland was staring at Jeffery with black eyes that slowly hardened. As the young man finished, the blood rushed hotly into Newland's face. He clenched his hands and jerked to his feet. "Say—listen," he said heavily, "you're not suggesting—"

"I'm suggesting nothing," Blackburn snapped. He pushed the young man gently back into his seat. "I'm merely trying to convey to you that Miss Marlowe is a singularly vague figure against a vaguer background!" He twirled a burnt match in his long fingers. "I believe that if we can delve far enough into that background we may discover something that will throw an added light on her death. You, Mr. Newland, appear to have known Miss Marlowe as well as anyone. It is to you that we look for enlightenment. What can you tell us?"

The angry flush on the young man's face faded to an embarrassed pink. He sat down, eyes on his clasped fingers. "I'm sorry," he muttered. "Shouldn't have said that. . . ." His voice trailed awkwardly.

The Chief Inspector said crisply: "Forget it, lad! We're looking to you for help. What do you know about this young lady?"

Newland raised his head. "I can't tell you much at all," he said simply. "I was very fond of Mary and I didn't see her nearly often enough. As you say, there were occasions when she would disappear for a week at a time. But when I questioned her, she put me off with some lame excuse about being absent on a journalistic assignment. But of course that wasn't true. When I pressed her for an explanation, she would fly into the most horrible rages. She had the very devil of a temper," he added with a sombre plaintiveness.

"Did she ever tell you anything of her life?"

The young man shook his head. "Never. Whenever we talked, it was about commonplace matters—things that happened to us during the day. As soon as the conversation veered in the direction of anything personal, she would deflect it. There was always a kind of shuttered reticence about her that puzzled me." He lowered his eyes. "But I didn't care—it didn't worry me that much."

"Were you ever inside her flat?"

"Never. She wouldn't allow it. I would drive her home sometimes and drop her at the house. It's one of those old-fashioned places. But she'd never let me come inside. I often wondered why." His voice faltered. "I—I seem to suspect the reason now."

Read put the question. "Where did you meet Miss Marlowe?"

"It was at a literary party down Chelsea way," New-land replied. "Rather a dreadful crowd there—grubby, unshaven lot, I thought. And a couple of the hand-on-hip type—proper nancies!" His voice was a growl. "Mary stood out from that crowd. I was passing down Bayswater Road on my way home and our hostess asked me to drop Mary. We had a long talk that night and—and I came to like her."

"How long ago was this?"

"About four months ago."

"And have you seen her very often since that night?"

"Whenever she'd let me." There was a sad eagerness in his tone. "But she was a curious girl—always kept me at arm's length." He gave a nodding movement of his head. "I'm sure there was something funny about her life—something not quite open. Yes, the more I think about it, the more I'm convinced of that."

Jeffery pressed a point. "Did she give you the impression of being afraid of anything—or anybody?"

Newland's dark brow wrinkled. "Not exactly that." He fumbled for words to express his meaning. "I'm sorry to be so dashed vague, but—well—I don't know. The further we go, the queerer this thing seems to get!"

"But surely," persisted Jeffery, "surely you couldn't be in the company of this girl on and off for nearly four months without discovering something about her life or her friends?"

"She didn't have many friends," the young man said quietly. "Mostly, we went about with people whom she'd met through me. She didn't make friends very easily herself. For one thing, she was terribly shy and nervous. Had an absolute horror of meeting people! We didn't go about much in public. I'd take her for long runs in my car. She liked that! Several times we went up to the Towers. Then we'd go to the pictures or else take tea in some quiet café."

"And what did you talk about?"

"We didn't talk much at all," said the other naïvely. "We just used to sit there."

Read stood up. "It would seem that Miss Marlowe's life had you almost as worried as her death now has," he said dryly.

Newland was on his feet. "Well, sir—can you wonder I'm suspicious? Does everything seem above-board to you?"

The Chief Inspector tugged at his moustache, ruminating. Then he clasped his hands behind his back and nodded. "All right," he announced. "If it will ease your mind, I'll put the Chief Medical Officer on to the business."

Newland reached forward and grasped his hand. "Thanks," he said earnestly. "I only want to know—to be sure! It's—it's the least I can do for that girl."

"You'd better ring Mac straight away," suggested Jeffery.

Read nodded. "I suppose he'll be down at headquarters—what's the time now?"

Newland pulled back the cuff of his coat, then grunted at his bare wrist. "Keep forgetting," he muttered. "Smashed my watch three days ago and it's in the jeweller's. Haven't got another." But Jeffery supplied the information.

"I'll get him right away," Read promised.

Their visitor was pulling on his driving gloves. "I'll be staying at the Winchester for the next few days," he said. "If you discover anything, would you get in touch with me, sir?"

Read grunted. "Remember," he said, "not a word of this to a soul! If this thing turns out to be a frost, I'll get hell's delight from the Chief Commissioner. As it is, I'm doing this thing against my better judgment!"

"I understand." Andrew Newland nodded to his hosts and, turning, walked from the room. As the door closed behind him . . .

"There walks the world's typical Romeo," groaned Jeffery, pushing back his chair. "He is the closest friend of this mysterious young lady . . . the one person who was in the best position to discover something about the girl. And he spends his time sitting in cafés, staring at her!"

3

The death in the radio studio was good red meat for the morning papers. There were headlines in every sheet. *"Darkness was Danger for Mary Marlowe"* screamed one particularly sensational rag. But their letter-press contained nothing that Jeffery did not already know. After ploughing thoroughly through the reports, he screwed the papers into a bundle and kicked them into a corner.

Ill-at-ease and restless, he wandered about the flat, lighting a cigarette and tossing it away after the first few puffs, making ado about mixing a drink, and leaving it untasted. Then he crossed to the window and stared out with unseeing eyes. He recognized the symptoms only too well. His mind was actively disturbed; the cold, incisive reasoning machine that was his brain was vibrating and pulsing, and without the counterweight of balancing material it throbbed like some over-accelerated high-power engine in neutral gear. The subtle intuition that had never failed him whispered that chance had, all unwittingly, guided his feet to the entrance of some dark and devious maze, the more sinister since it appeared on the surface so straightforward.

"Oh, curse it," he growled, prowling the room. "Why couldn't I leave Melpomene and Thalia to cut their oral capers unaided? This is what comes of being led by the nose!"

He flung himself irritably into a chair, and picking up a book flicked aimlessly through the pages. Then he tossed it aside, leaned back in his favourite attitude, hands clasped behind head, and closed his eyes. The clock on the mantel struck noon. Jeffery sat up.

"I'll take a chance!" he muttered. "At least it will give me something to occupy my time." He rose and, crossing to the telephone, put through a call to headquarters where he inquired the address of Mary Marlowe's flat. Half an hour later, he was steering the Bentley through the ordered terraces of Bayswater.

He turned off from the main thoroughfares, glittering with the plate-glass of the sprawling department stores and tumultuous with the bustle of the noonday shoppers, down green avenues and through mathematically planned gardens. Uncertain of the locality, he turned his car into a terrace, drew it to a standstill and jumped out. From a group of children playing on the pavement, he inquired the whereabouts of Byam Place and learned that it bisected the terrace some hundred yards along. Jeffery deliberated between driving and walking, then, persuaded by the sunshine and the breeze that carried the scent of spring from the adjacent gardens, decided on the latter course. He sauntered on, musing. He had no fixed plan in mind; indeed, his resolution to look through Mary Marlowe's dwelling was not so much in the hope of unearthing anything definite as to give himself the satisfaction of doing *something,* no matter how trivial, in this perplexing case. He had almost reached Byam Place and was about to turn the corner when he saw something that tensed his lean body and brought him to a sudden halt.

Byam Place extended only a short way and its further progress was impeded by a towering grey stone block of buildings. About half-way down, an open scarlet sports car was drawn up. A woman was seated in this car, a woman whose shoulders were swathed in a fur-collared driving coat. Dark shoulder-length hair fell from an absurd little hat clinging to one side of her head. She was obviously ill at ease and cast nervous flashing glances over her shoulder. In one of these apprehensive backward movements of her head, Jeffery recognized slanting eyes and high cheek-bones.

The woman in the car was Olga Lusinska!

Scarcely had the identification flashed across his mind than the woman leaned forward. At that moment, the door of the house opposite opened and a dark, slim figure, a camel-hair overcoat turned up about his ears, emerged. Jeffery's mouth twisted grimly. Here was enigma! He remembered the last occasion he had looked upon that willowy figure, those black eyes glittering in that pale face. The young man in the overcoat was Mr. Steinie Rodda.

But if Mr. Rodda had been perturbed at their last meeting, he looked positively ill at the moment. His eyes were shadowed by dark rims emphasized by the greenish pallor of his face. Jeffery watched him draw that trick cigarette-gun from his pocket, shoot a cigarette dexterously between his lips, and his trembling fingers wasting three matches before he succeeded in lighting it. A much less astute person than Jeffery could have perceived the plain truth—that Steinie Rodda was afraid to the point of sickening panic.

The woman in the car made some urgent whispered remark. The watcher saw the young man shake his head irritably. He tossed his cigarette away and almost flung himself into the car, treading the self-starter viciously. With the engine's rising hum, Jeffery frowned. He had heard that noise before—last night, in the breathless hush that followed the pain-choked gasp of the stricken girl. His mind was still wrestling with possibilities when the engine accelerated and Rodda swung the wheel. The car shot out of the narrow street like a startled tanager and tore into the terrace, its siren screaming derision at traffic rules.

Blackburn watched them go, his grey eyes thoughtful. "Now," he murmured, "that raises in my inquisitive mind three intriguing questions. What possible connection can there be between the elegant Steinie and Miss Marlowe? How long have Lusinska and Steinie been on such intimate terms? And just what was it that brought Mr. Rodda to Mary Marlowe's flat?" He shrugged. "Or am I building bricks without straw and on the wrong track altogether? In which case, abide by the prosy Beecher's counsel, remembering that activity with mistakes is better than indolence without mistakes!" He thrust his hands into his pockets. *"Allans, mon ami!"*

He quickened his steps and came abreast of the house. It stood back from the street, bay-windowed, narrow, and primly austere, wedged between an empty confectionery shop and a shuttered red-brick building. It rose above these like a faded and impoverished spinster jostled by vulgarians. Jeffery ran his eyes over the house and nodded. If Mary Marlowe had sought seclusion, she had certainly achieved her ideal in this desolate backwater. He pushed through the gate, made his way across a broken tiled pavement and mounted three steps to the door. Pressing a finger on the bell-push, he waited.

It was almost a minute before the sound of footsteps was heard inside. The door swung back, to reveal an old woman in a faded dressing-gown. Untidy grey hair escaped from a net dragged hurriedly over her head. Her face was wrinkled and brown, and from this parchment two beady black eyes like boot-buttons scrutinized him. A shrill voice quavered: "What might you be wanting?"

Mr. Blackburn summoned his most charming smile. "Good afternoon, madam. I understand that there is a flat to let in this house?" His eyes twinkled at her. "I am looking for the landlady."

The old woman thrust back a wisp of hair that settled across her eyes. She thrust up a Punch-like chin. "There's been a mighty big run on this flat," she sniffed. "An' that poor girl not yet cold, as you might say!"

"Indeed?" said Jeffery.

The woman nodded with melancholy satisfaction. "I was talking to her in this very spot last night—jus' before she went to that there place. An' the next thing I know is that there's a pleeceman tellin' me she's been taken with her heart." She reached out a claw of a hand and touched his arm. "Them young people can't stand up to it like us old ones. I'm seventy-five next month and—"

"Impossible!" exclaimed Jeffery gallantly. He insinuated himself in the doorway. "I was told by a friend about the young lady's death. Very sad! She was a very quiet young lady, I'm told, the last one you might expect to suffer from a heart attack."

"Quiet—and ladylike!" The crone nodded her grey head. "And kept herself to herself, not that that's anything to be ashamed of." She peered up into his face. "That girl was with me here for three months, an' all that time I've barely as much as 'changed the time o' day with her."

Jeffery nodded. "You said that there had been some demand for this flat?"

"You're the second this morning. The other jus' left about five minutes back. Smart young chap in a moty-car." She wrinkled her face at him. "P'raps you saw him?"

"I believe I passed a motor-car coming out of this street," Jeffery admitted. "And—did he take the flat?"

"I dunno. He jus' gave me back the key and said he'd let me know." She stood aside. "But there'll be no harm done in you looking over it, sir. Come inside."

Jeffery did so. She closed the door. The contrast of the dark hall and the brilliant sunshine outside made him blink. As his eyes became accustomed to the change, he made out a set of stairs descending to a basement. The old woman saw his scrutiny and nodded.

"It's a lovely flat," she crooned. "And you'll have the whole 'ouse to yourself, sir, same as Miss Marlowe did. I've got the basement—an' you'll never see me from one week's end to the other." She fumbled in the pocket of her gown and brought forth a key. "The pleeceman brought this back last night—found it in that pore girl's bag." She pressed it into his hand. "You won't mind looking for yourself, sir. I've got my dinner on the stove downstairs." She nodded and moved to the head of the steps. "Jus' give me a call when you're ready, sir. I'll come up." She leered at him, turned and hobbled slowly down to the basement.

Jeffery waited until her grey head had disappeared below. Then he walked to the door facing the stairs, thrust the key in the lock and passed through. Next moment he halted on the threshold, petrified at the sight that met his eyes. For some seconds he remained thus, then he turned and clicked the door shut behind him. Mentally he thanked his stars that he was alone.

For the room, obviously the living-room of the flat, was in the wildest disorder. The furniture had been dragged from position, the chairs turned upside down, and the cushions of the chesterfield ripped open and tossed aside. An oaken bookcase had been laid on its side and the volumes tumbled in a heap on the floor. Papers from a bureau were scattered over the carpet, which was jerked from its tackings and rucked in careless folds. Even the pictures on the walls were askew and the glass of one had been splintered into glistening spears.

"Good Lord!" exclaimed Jeffery softly.

He made his way delicately through the chaos to the next room. It was a bedroom, once tastefully furnished and fluffily feminine with taffeta and silk. Now it gave the impression of an apartment struck by a tornado. The pink cushions were slit and vomited feathers everywhere. The bed-clothes were tossed in a heap, the bolster dragged from the mattress and gutted cruelly. A small chest of drawers had its polished surface scarred and rutted where the locks had been forced; the drawers were dragged out and their contents dripped over the sides. Jeffery continued his way through the flat, to find that this brutal vandalism extended to the kitchen and the bath-room. The ashes of the chip heater were strewn across the floor and a small cabinet housing toilet soaps, powders, and sponges reeled drunkenly in one corner.

Mr. Blackburn drew a long whistling breath of astonishment. Automatically his fingers moved to his pocket for a cigarette. Lighting it, he moved back to the disordered living-room, up-ended one of the chairs and sat down. He stared around, attempting to reproduce in his mind the arrangement of the room as it had been. It was useless!

The saturnalia was too complete and it confused his brain with a dozen questions.

Who had done this thing? What secret had this flat contained that made such a reckless and destructive search necessary? Had the unknown violator found what he sought? And when had the search taken place? In that moment his thoughts flew to the scene he had witnessed in the street. He shook his head. It seemed impossible that Rodda could have perpetrated this wholesale vandalism while the old lady waited on the floor below. This frenzied search must have taken some considerable time and caused no little commotion. Was it not more likely that Steinie, suspecting the secret, had come to recover it for himself only to find that another had forestalled him, leaving this ruin? That would account for the young man's ill-temper and his vicious negative to Lusinska's question. Also it explained his eagerness to get away before the upheaval was discovered. How, then, did Lusinska fit into this dark riddle? And what was the secret? And what, in the name of all mystery, did it have to do with Mary Marlowe's death?

He puffed absently at his cigarette, thoughts flickering like lightning against a lowering sky.

It seemed obvious that the landlady was in complete ignorance of the havoc in the flat. Therefore it must have been perpetrated without her knowledge. Jeffery recalled that the Chief Inspector had told him that the old woman had accompanied a police officer back to headquarters to make a statement regarding her tenant. Had the unknown violator taken advantage of her absence to search the flat? But the landlady held the only key! Which meant that the searcher must have had a key of his own . . . a key to this flat that was so comfortably furnished for a girl who earned, apparently, only a few chance guineas now and then. Jeffery shook a wise head. It was peculiar, to say the least.

His agile mind swarmed over the known facts. The flat had been in perfect order when the police officer examined it shortly after eleven o'clock last night. On the other hand, had the search been made after the landlady returned from headquarters, it seemed impossible that she could have remained unaware of the commotion.

That narrowed the time-limit to somewhere between eleven o'clock and midnight . . . which was shortly after the actual death in the studio. In that case . . .

Jeffery leapt to his feet.

In that case, the person who had visited and searched this flat must have been somebody who was already aware that Mary Marlowe was dead—somebody who knew this before it became common knowledge through the newspapers! And the only people who had this information were those individuals in the studio at the time of the girl's collapse! Was this another link in the chain? And if so, could it mean that Mary Marlowe had been murdered . . . and that one of the people in that studio was responsible for her death?

But how had she died? By what dark means had the girl been struck down?

Jeffery crushed his cigarette under his heel. It was useless to attempt any reconstruction of theories until that one vital point had been clarified. It would be a saving of time and mental effort to await the Chief Medical Officer's report on the autopsy of the body.

He crossed to the heap of volumes pyramiding on the floor and turned them over thoughtfully with one toe. A title caught his eye—held it. His face tensed and he dropped on one knee beside the pile, glancing closely at each book. Again he felt that queer surging excitement, that sensation of glimpsing something dangerous and unnamable. Piled on the rucked carpet was a small but complete library on obscure toxicology!

There was a bulky volume of Blyth's *Poisons, their Effect and Detection,* another of that comprehensive work of Maschaka's *Handbuch der Gerichtlichen Medicin,* and Robert Christian's *Treatise on Poisons* together with Hemming's *Aids to Forensic Medicine and Toxicology.* Jeffery squatted down, pushed aside bound copies of the Medical and Surgical Report to pick up F. Selmi's *Studi di Tossicologio Chimica* and a small volume by the father of modern toxicology, Matthieu Orfila. It was *Traite de Toxicologie.* Delving among the pile like a terrier in a wood-heap, he pulled out a rare copy of *Traite de Toxicolgie Generale,* published in 1835. There were also accounts of famous poisoning trials, of Henry Seddon, of Palmer, of Dr. Pritchard, and this heap included Andre Soussan's work on *Life and Trial of Marquise de Brinvilliers.*

Every phase of the horrible craft was covered among the pages of that sprawled collection. The volumes covered the history of poisoning from the dawn of mythology when Medea and Circe and pale Hecate mixed love philtres and death potions, on through the sullen glamour of the Venetian courts to the ghastly notoriety of the Borgias when Caesar and Lucrezia prepared death in a hundred unexpected and fearsome ways. With squirming stomach and dilated nostrils, Jeffery read on, fascinated by a curiosity stronger than his repulsion. He glanced through pages crowded with details of poisoned shirts that sent men mad with agony, poisoned gloves causing slow atrophy of the hand, poisoned rings, poisoned wines. And so on down to such recent cases as Mrs. Maybrick and Madame L'Beradi of Paris.

A little sick, a little shaken, Mr. Blackburn tossed aside the last volume and straightened his back. His mind was numbed with the wholesale malevolence of mankind, drugged with the suggestion of hemlock and nightshade and aconite.

Poison!

Why did this dark strain thread its way through the problem like some sinister, half-heard, yet omnipresent *motif* dominating a Satanic symphony? It had recurred again and again, a whispered suggestion that seemed intangible yet always behind his ear. Restlessly he shifted—and gave a sudden surprised gasp. Some object, penetrating the carpet, had pricked him.

The sudden pain acted like a cold douche. Jeffery sprang to his feet, kicked back the carpet and dived inquiring fingers into the weave. He found the object by sense of touch, then his eyes followed. It was some long, thin spike that had, apparently, rolled under the carpet during the upheaval. He disengaged it gently, brought it to eye-level and stared. It was some moments before he recognized the object.

It was a hatpin, and from the blunt end the ornament had been roughly torn off.

4

Mr. Blackburn said plaintively: "I may be lacking in a sense of humour, Chief, but I see no reason for this ribald mirth. There's nothing particularly amusing in being stuck in the nether portion by a hatpin!"

The Chief Inspector held his side and rocked. "Oh, my aunt!" he sniggered. "You've a whole floor surface to park yourself on—yet you must go and squat down on a hatpin! If only I could have seen it!"

"It was not at all spectacular," Jeffery assured him coldly. He walked across the room and seated himself rather gingerly on the chesterfield. "And now that I've brought that momentary ray of sunshine into your life, perhaps we can get down to some serious business."

Eight hours had elapsed since Jeffery's discovery in the wrecked flat at Bayswater. He had spent the afternoon about some mysterious business on which he remained irritatingly vague, and had returned to his rooms just in time for dinner. The meal over, he had put the Chief Inspector in possession of his morning adventure, concluding with the incident of the hatpin. Read found this intensely amusing.

" 'As the crackling of thorns under a pot'," quoted Jeffery bitterly, as Read continued to guffaw. "Come on, Chief! You've had your fun!" And as the Chief Inspector repressed his elephantine ripples, he continued, "What are you going to do about this new development?"

Read lowered himself into a chair, selected a cigar from the box on the small table and cut the end with due reverence. He looked up. "Darn me if I don't round up Steinie and that Russian dame and put the screws on them just for luck," he grunted.

"Indeed?" snapped Jeffery. "On what charge, may I ask? You can't go around throwing people into the Bastille for the sake of innocent amusement!"

"We'd soon find a charge," the other muttered darkly.

"I'd very much like to hear it." Jeffery leaned forward. "Breaking and entry?" He shook his head. "Steinie entered that flat quite lawfully and I'm positive those breakages weren't the work of his lily-white fingers. You might get him on playing tag with the traffic laws, except that I definitely refuse to testify. And you certainly won't get him on the charge that's most important—suspicion of being concerned in a murder—because we don't know yet that it is murder—"

"You seemed dashed positive about it this morning," the big man interrupted.

"I'm convinced beyond all doubt," Blackburn assured him. "Of course Mary Marlowe was murdered! But who am I among so many? You're the policeman, Mr. Read! Yours the task of convincing twelve stout oak-hearted Englishmen. And juries want solid, watertight proofs, backed by the indisputable corroboration of Scotland Yard! And," continued Jeffery maliciously, "that's just what you can't give them! That's where the murderer has been too clever for you!"

The Chief Inspector's foot scuffed the Turkish rug on the floor. "Providing," he said stolidly, "that the case comes in the category of murder."

Jeffery leapt to his feet. "You're being purposely obtuse," he snapped. "If this business is so innocent, what's the reason for that search in the flat? Why did Rodda go there? And why is Newland so positive that some other agency than heart failure brought about the girl's death?"

His companion puffed phlegmatically. "I prefer to save my breath until Conroy arrives," he returned.

"And when will that be?"

Read screwed his eyes at the clock. "Within a few minutes now. He said nine o'clock. It's five minutes to the hour."

"Did he say he had any news?"

The Chief Inspector's tone was sour. "You know that man as well as I do, son! He can make an oyster look like a side-show barker when he likes! All I can tell you at the moment is that he's had that body in his department for twelve hours with three officers working on it. If there's anything to be found, Miles Conroy is the man to discover it!" He waved his cigar at the divan. "Now, for Pete's sake, stop behaving like a kid at the dentist's!"

"Hogwash!" snapped Jeffery.

He began to prowl the sitting-room. Read shrugged, picked up the evening paper and settled himself to scan the pages. Behind him, his companion continued his unquiet perambulation. He moved to the table, straightened the books thereon, brushed a tiny coil of ash from the cover and peered over Read's shoulder at the newspaper. The Chief Inspector signified his disapproval by rapidly turning the page. Whereupon Jeffery wandered aimlessly to the writing-desk, thrust restless fingers among the papers and stood tapping a pencil against his teeth. From here he moved to the window and stared down the empty street. It was very quiet in the room. From somewhere came the scream of a train whistle and the shunt of steam. Jeffery wheeled, glanced at his wrist-watch, compared it with the clock on the mantelpiece and addressed the man in the chair.

"Is that clock right, Chief?"

"Right as Big Ben," said Read imperturbably. He rustled the leaves of his paper. "You've certainly got ants in your pants tonight, son!"

Jeffery did not reply. He returned to his seat on the chesterfield and flung himself down, shoulders hunched, fingers drumming. He stared at the changing green and gold flame of the gas-fire, making hissing progress about the coils. The Chief Inspector read steadily on, his nose buried among the printed lines. Thus, when a sharp rap sounded at the door, Read started as abruptly as his companion. He tossed aside the newspaper and called "Come in." Jeffery was on his feet, eager and trembling as a thoroughbred facing the barrier.

The door opened and Miles Conroy entered.

Miles Aloysius Conroy, "Mac" to his associates, Chief Medical Officer of the Criminal Investigation Department, was a neat precise little man, bearded in the manner of King Edward the Seventh. With his high forehead emphasized by thinning hair, his twinkling black eyes and a bitter, sardonic mouth, he had something of the appearance of a dissolute and very worldly apostle. He nodded to his hosts, strutted across the room and lowered himself into the chair that Read pulled forward. Waving aside Jeffery's offer of cigarettes, he produced a pipe and tobacco-pouch. He was looking from one man to another, that fine forehead seamed.

"Well, this is a hell of a fine welcome," he snapped. "Aren't you two speaking? And where's the famous hospitality? Don't I get a drink?"

"All right—all right!" The Chief Inspector, wise from experience, was already busying himself at the sideboard. He came across and thrust a glass into Conroy's hand. "Here, you monkey! Spill that down your handsome beard!"

"I shouldn't have had to ask for it," their guest reproved. He sipped and made a wry face. "Shocking taste in liquor you have, Read."

"Never mind about that," the other grunted. "Come on, Mac! Spill the beans. What have you discovered?"

Conroy balanced his glass between tapering fingers. "Precisely nothing," he said primly.

Read, in the act of sitting, stared. "What d'you mean—nothing?"

"The tympaneous membrane becoming calloused?" inquired their visitor pleasantly. "I'll elaborate. After twelve hours examination of that girl's body, we found nothing! Nothing except for one small point that you already suspect." He lifted his glass and examined the contents against the light.

"That girl no more died of heart weakness than she did of psittacosis!"

"Ah!" exclaimed Jeffery. He relaxed like a man who has passed through a severe strain.

Read grunted. "Well, at least that's a step!"

"In which direction?" inquired Conroy blandly. He drained his glass and placed it on the table. "From what I can see of the business, we're as much in the dark as ever. Even more so! If that girl's collapse was due to cardiac weakness, then I'm Hippocrates' grandmother! And if it wasn't, how did she die?"

"Don't you know?" barked Read.

Conroy shook his head. "I do not! Personally, I have never known such a remarkable case. It's fascinating, intriguing—and as baffling as hell's inner circle! No wonder your Dr. Townsend took the easiest way out!"

"Easiest way?" echoed Jeffery. He leaned elbows on the arm of the chesterfield. "How did he take the easiest way out?"

"By refusing to admit his ignorance. By covering that ignorance with the diagnosis of cardiac weakness. Not that he could be blamed for that," added the Medical Officer quickly. "To the average G.P., the symptoms of that death have all the appearance of a severe cardiac lesion. Townsend did merely what nine out of every ten doctors would have done under the same circumstances. But I happen to be the tenth." Dr. Conroy leaned back, placed his finger-tips together and exuded complacency. "You see, I'm really a very brilliant fellow!"

"You're a bearded bladder of wind!" snapped the Chief Inspector. "Now, cut out this back-slapping and get down to details! One minute you say that girl's death isn't heart failure and the next breath you announce that it has all the symptoms. Let's stop chasing each other round the mulberry bush and get down to business!"

"Very well!" Miles Conroy straightened and took the pipe from his lips. "Here are the facts, gentlemen. The post-mortem appearance of that body, with its rigidity, convulsions, the clenched hands and slightly cyanosed features, all are symptoms of a sudden abrupt lesion of the cardiac organs. Or what is popularly known as heart failure. Now, there is no need for me to detail the outward symptoms of cardiac disease during life. What does concern us at the moment is that these symptoms leave undeniable traces on the body of the sufferer."

He paused and his eyes wandered past Read to the eager Jeffery. "Now, the outstanding evidence of cardiac weakness during life is usually found in the enlarged veins of the neck while the patient is upright, increased visibility of the pulsation of the caratoid, dropsy of the lower extremities—and dyspnoea."

"And what might—?" began Read, when Conroy interrupted.

"It means difficulty in breathing," he explained. "As you know, I didn't see the patient alive. You did! Therefore, both of you are in a better position than I to say if these symptoms were present."

Jeffery shook his head. "I believe I speak for both of us when I say that there were no such indications noticeable to the layman's eye," he said quietly. "Of course, we saw the girl only for a few minutes. But her closest friend, a person who spent a considerable amount of time with her, denies that the girl ever exhibited symptoms of heart weakness in any shape or form!"

Read nodded. "I told you about that, Mac."

"Certainly you did," Conroy agreed. "We next come to the business of *rigor,* a point which you say was brought up by a young chap in the studio. While it wasn't his place to instruct a professional man, he was certainly right as far as his information went. A body struck down with heart trouble usually retains flaccidity for some time after death, the actual interval varying from time to time. However, here we are faced with a peculiar anomaly. *Rigor* apparently set in almost immediately, and this would appear a definite negation of heart disease!"

Dr. Conroy paused. Read nodded. Jeffery did not speak.

"When the body came into my laboratory," the Medical Officer continued, "a superficial examination bore out these conflicting points. The cadaver was that of a person in the best of health. The lower extremities were certainly not dropsical and there seemed no indication of swelling in the larger veins of the throat.

"Puzzled, I went over every inch of that body first by sight alone and then with the glass." The little medico's tone was weighted. "On no part of the body was the skin so much as broken. There was no trace of puncture or scratch. I examined the hair, the scalp, the fingernails, the soles of the feet and the skin between the toes. The result was the same—a complete and absolute negative.

"Thoroughly interested, I proceeded with the autopsy. I looked for a heart dilated and hypertrophied—and found that organ as sound as a bell! I sought enfeeblement of the walls through excessive blood pressure—and found them stronger than mine could ever hope to be! Also, there was no trace of pulmonary or tricuspid valve diseases, no indication of paroxysmal tachycardia—"

"Just a moment—just a moment," interrupted Read. "Give us a chance, Mac! You're not in the lecture-hall! I get enough vocabulary from Jeffery. Give us plain English!"

Conroy was applying a match to his pipe. "You've had it! In plain English, Read, our autopsy completely failed to bring forth any evidence in support of the diagnosis of heart failure!"

A pause. A wind brushed the walls and rattled the windows with a stealthy hand. For some moments, no one spoke. Then:

"Well?" barked Read. "What *was* the cause of death?"

Conroy surveyed him levelly. Something too vague to be called a smile shadowed his lips. "You tell me," he suggested.

"But you're the Chief Medical Officer—"

"I'm not God Almighty!" Conroy's mouth was hard. "I can't work miracles, Read! I may be clever, but I can't make the dead speak!"

Jeffery was staring at the doctor with thoughtful eyes. He said vaguely. "Saint Stanislaus could! He was the Bishop of Cracow about 1050. He brought to life a Polish farmer to testify regarding some church land he had sold the Bishop and which King Boleslaus wanted to confiscate."

Conroy raised his eyebrows and his tone dripped irony. "You don't say! That was, of course, a little before my time."

"Ease up, Jeff," Read said gruffly. "This is no time for your apocryphal droolings! What has Saint What's-his-name got to do with this discussion?"

"Just another example of the advantages that have passed with an age of miracles," returned Jeffery gently. "You see, if that poor girl were permitted the gift of tongues, she could naturally testify to the cause of her death. And do you know what she would say?"

Conroy twisted his thin lips. "I am waiting to hear you tell me!"

"She would tell you she was poisoned," Jeffery returned.

5

The clock on the mantelpiece chimed the half-hour. Miles Conroy drew a long breath that hissed softly through his parted lips. Two daubs of colour fired his cheeks, widened and spread slowly across the high forehead. Very deliberately he turned and placed his pipe on the table at his side. Then he wheeled on the young man, and his words shot forth with the vindictive precision of machine-gun bullets.

"You're a hell of a clever fellow, aren't you, my cocky! So the young lady was poisoned, was she? And it was introduced through her mouth, I suppose? You've got it all worked out very neatly, haven't you?" His mouth was a thin, bitter line. "Now, let me tell you something, my clever young man! I've had three of the finest men in England working on that body since early this morning! And if you can tell me what poison was used to kill that girl, you—you can take my name off my door and paint your own up in its place! Yes—!" He swung round on the Chief Inspector. "And I'll foot the bill out of my own pocket!"

Mr. Blackburn refused to be ruffled. To show his indifference, he lit a cigarette. "She was poisoned," he insisted, blowing smoke. "Probably by some form of obscure toxicology—"

"Obscure my backside!" Conroy's beard quivered with indignation. "Do you think you're talking to a first-year medical student? Obscure toxicology—Arrrrh!" He made a contemptuous noise deep in his throat.

"Now then, you two!" barked Read. He thrust out a hand and pushed Conroy back in his chair. "What you need is a drink, Mac." He crossed and mixed a whisky-and-soda. "Here—take this."

The doctor hesitated, then he relaxed and took the glass with a grunt. "All right," he growled. "But I've a perfect right to be touchy! If you could only realize the work I put in on that autopsy, simply because I wouldn't admit defeat . . ." His voice was drowned in a gurgle as he up-ended his glass. He wiped his lips with his free hand and sat back. "Well, the witness is yours, Blackburn," he announced with ferocious geniality. "What do you want to know?"

"Did you examine for poison?" asked Jeffery.

"Of course! When I found the skin on the girl's body unbroken and our first autopsy abrogated the theory of heart failure, naturally my mind turned to the subject of poisons." He groped on the table for his pipe. "Now, you ask the questions and I'll answer them." Something of the old twinkle flickered in his eyes. "I rather fancy we'll get along better that way."

Jeffery leaned back and crossed one leg over the other. "Are there any poisons, Mac, that cause death immediately or within a few minutes of ingestion?"

"Certainly," nodded Conroy. "Omitting the strong mineral acids, carbon monoxide, carbon dioxide, and the irrespirable gases—Prussic acid, the cyanides, oxalic acid, and occasionally strychnine are the chief poisons coming under this heading."

"And are the symptoms of that girl's death in any way analogous with poisoning?"

"Yes," the Medical Officer admitted. "It is analogous with strychnine poisoning. Strychnine is a spinal poison—it is believed that the inhibitory power of the grey matter in the spinal cord is paralysed by strychnine. There is, at first, a catching of the respiration, usually followed by a convulsive seizure. The convulsions take the form of a violent general tetanus; the limbs are stretched out involuntarily, the hands are clenched, and at the height of the paroxysm the back may be curved and rigid as a board. The body becomes very stiff after death, and generally the rigidity remains a long time. In the case of one of William Palmer's victims, the body was rigid for two months after death. On the other hand, the *rigor mortis* has been known to disappear within twenty-four hours."

Read's bushy eyebrows raised. "Surely those are almost the identical symptoms—" he began.

"It is," said Conroy testily. "Except that when we used Allerton Cushman's test on the viscera, there wasn't a trace of the alkaloid! To be doubly sure, we tested for other poisons in the tetanus-producing group—nux vomica, brucine, and igasurine. We might as well have saved our time for all the results we achieved!"

Jeffery was frowning. "Isn't it possible for strychnine to work out of a body?" he asked. "Could this have happened in the present instance?"

"Impossible," answered Conroy shortly. "For one thing, the interval between ingestion and death, assuming, that is, that the girl was poisoned at the studio, would be much too short for elimination to take place. Secondly, the poison could not pass through the body without leaving some trace, or being deposited, minutely perhaps but unmistakably nevertheless, in such organs as the brain, the liver, spinal cord, spleen, the duodenum and the kidneys." Conroy paused and flashed his black eyes at them. "Such was not the case here. The organs mentioned were completely free from any traces of irritant poison!"

"Arsenic?" suggested the Chief Inspector.

Again the doctor shook his head. "Arsenic is not an instantaneous poison," he explained. "Even in its most acute form, the symptoms take from twenty minutes to half an hour to develop, although in isolated cases it has been known to mature within eight minutes. But we have a much stronger proof than this that arsenic was not used. With this poison, the indications preceding the death are unmistakable. The victim vomits freely, then collapses into a coma. It is true that certain convulsive movements of the limbs have been observed, but always on the approach of death the face is pale, the eyes hollow, first the mucous membrane then the skin takes on a bluish tint. In this particular case, there was no vomiting and certainly no collapse into a coma, although it is true that the face was cyanosed."

"You tested for arsenic?"

"Most decidedly! We did one test with the Marsh-Berzelius apparatus and another with Reinsch's method. But it was an unnecessary precaution. One look at those healthy organs might have told us it was labour in vain! Because arsenic leaves a decided effect upon the body. The most marked change occurs in the mucous membrane of the stomach and the intestines where there is a very pronounced inflammatory action. In most cases, the coating of the stomach is covered with a pasty skin. Sometimes, the membrane is dotted with minute ulcers." Conroy paused and a reminiscent gleam came into his eyes. "For instance, in the museum at the University College, I remember examining a most interesting example of the effect of arsenic on the stomach. There were spots of aborescent extravasation and a slight congestion of the summits of the rugae—"

"Hold it—hold it!" Read barked. "You're running off the rails again, Mac! And making us feel slightly ill, although we don't understand half your gibberish! Come down to earth!"

"Well," announced Conroy with some asperity. "I'm waiting for your questions!"

"If you were so certain from the healthy appearance of the organs that arsenic was not present," demanded Read, "why trouble to test?"

The little doctor spread himself in his chair. "It's our job to do things thoroughly," he pointed out. "Again, arsenic is a particularly tricky poison. It's what we call a wanderer."

Jeffery nodded. "You mean it moves about in the body?"

"A proper nomad," Conroy assured him with a wag of his beard. "It gets everywhere! Remember the notorious Maybrick case in 1889, when Mrs. Maybrick was accused of poisoning her husband with arsenical fly-papers? It looked like an open-and-shut case, yet in the autopsy no trace of arsenic was found either in the stomach or its contents, or in the spleen. The poison had worked into the liver, the intestines, and the kidneys." He reached over and dipped his fingers into Read's cigar cabinet, talking all the while.

"That is why, in a poison autopsy, it is always a mistake to examine the stomach only. Such findings are most inconclusive, since the rapid absorption of the poison may leave no traces in that organ. When poisons are taken through the mouth, they are certainly absorbed by the stomach in the first place. But they afterwards pass into the blood which circulates them through the body and deposits the toxins in the tissues of the liver, kidneys, and other organs mentioned. Naturally, the stomach is free from traces."

"And an examination of the other organs excluding the stomach revealed nothing?" queried Blackburn.

"Nothing," repeated Conroy. He clipped the end of his cigar with a pocket-knife, returned the instrument to his pocket and lit up. The fragrant smoke rose about his head. Jeffery shifted restlessly.

"Did you test for other poisons?" he persisted, after a pause.

"We tested for those producing effects concomitant with the symptoms of the collapse," replied Conroy. He withdrew the cigar and blew a neat smoke-ring. "Any of the alkaloids would produce similar representations. Aconitine paralyses the heart. It is what we call a protoplasmic poison, affecting the central nervous system and the muscles. Dyspnoea and convulsions are likewise prevalent. Atropine works rapidly while potassic or hydric cyanide brings about symptoms analogous with epilepsy. I could name a dozen others but it would merely be a waste of time. I am willing to stake my professional reputation and the reputation of my department that there is no trace of poison in that girl's body—nor has there been poison administered to her at any time!"

Doctor Conroy's eyes rested on both men for a fraction as he spoke. Then with a brief nod he sat back in enjoyment of his cigar. The Chief Inspector said slowly, his tone groping like a hand in the dark.

"She wasn't poisoned. She didn't die of heart failure. There is no mark nor is the skin broken on the body!" His voice rose. "Then how the devil did that girl die?" He swung round on Jeffery. "I thought we'd cleaned up witchcraft when we finished with the Mannikin Murders, son. This looks like a recrudescence of the business!" [1]

Jeffery jumped to his feet. Hands thrust deep in his pockets, he was pacing the floor, his face frowning, his eyes

[1] Read was referring to the fantastic affair of the Rochester family and the Dolls of Death, which case formed the subject of the adventure retailed in *Death's Mannikins.*

anxious. "Nonsense," he said curtly. "That girl met her end by some thoroughly tangible means! We must keep that fact in our minds and not go wandering off in some murky Cloud-Cuckoo land of horrors!" He halted his perambulating opposite the doctor. There was a note almost of pleading in his voice.

"Mac—haven't you any idea?"

Conroy shook his head slowly. "Frankly, I haven't!" he admitted. "I told you that this was the most baffling and intriguing case it's ever been my misfortune to stumble on! If it is a homicide, it comes pretty near the Perfect Murder so beloved of the mystery scribblers!"

Blackburn moved to the mantel. He leaned on it, looking down at Conroy. "There's one question, Mac," he began.

The little doctor raised his head. "What is it?"

"I take it," said Jeffery quietly, "that the absence of any determinable poison in the body does not necessarily clinch the fact that poison was not used?" And as Conroy continued to stare at him: "To make my meaning clearer—is there a known poison that could cause death and remain in the organs of the body, yet resist detection even under the most stringent chemical test?"

Doctor Conroy dropped his eyes to the cigar, turned it in his fingers, examining it idly. He seemed making up his mind about answering. He spoke quietly, his gaze still on the smoking weed.

"Yes. There are several poisons which may remain in the body and yet elude the closest search. When mixed with certain chemicals contained in the various organs of the body, these toxins are converted into harmless substances. Substances that the investigating specialist ordinarily expects to find in a normally healthy body."

Jeffery did not move. He stood, tall and lean, his shadow, distorted by the table-lamp, clawing blackly on the wall above him. Only his tone trembled with some hidden emotion as he asked. "In other words, Mac, a person possessing knowledge of the right poison to use might take a life without leaving any traces in the body to reveal the action?"

"Well, now—" the dapper Medical Officer pursed his lips. He moved the cigar to and fro under his nostrils, as though sampling the fragrance. Suddenly, Jeffery dropped into his seat on the chesterfield.

"Yes or no, Mac! Is there such a poison—a poison that can kill and leave no trace?"

Conroy faced him. He nodded his head slowly. "I must admit that there are such poisons," he said quietly, "Naturally, we don't make such information common knowledge! But every modern scientist and toxicologist knows them quite well. It is a fact that there are certain organic poisons which, as I say, can be converted into constituents commonly present in the human body. And I could name several vegetable poisons not chemically identifiable nor which betray their existence by causing any actual lesion. Then there are the volatile poisons, some of which may be dissipated entirely before the suspected organs reach the specialist for examination."

Jeffery nodded. "Briefly, we're as far from the solution of that girl's death as we were last night," he said helplessly. "Whichever way we turn, we seem faced with a blank wall! There are so many theories that *might* be true, but every time we attempt to reduce these suggestions to mathematical certainty, we're blocked by our inability to prove a conclusion!"

"So that's what's been playing on your young mind?" said Conroy grimly. "You're off your balance because this case refuses to reduce into the terms of a mathematical problem!" He shook a wise head and the prim lines about his mouth relaxed. "Give it up, Blackburn! You'll never do it! The fundamentals are against you from the start. Good heavens, man, algebra and physiology are poles apart!"

The young man sighed. "I'm beginning to realize how right you are, Mac. Certainly we are fearfully and wonderfully made, but far, far from mathematically planned. Now I understand what Chesterton meant when he said that the most fallible machine of the machine age was man himself!"

The Chief Medical Officer sat up so abruptly that an inch of ash scattered his coat. As he brushed it away: "Both of *you* seem to have overlooked the paramount fact that we're trying to build bricks without straw," he snapped. He levelled his cigar at Read. "Have you any proof that this girl was murdered?"

The Chief Inspector waved a hand at Jeffery, a gesture of negation. "It's the lad's idea," he grunted. "Argue it out with him!"

"There's no question of argument," stated Jeffery. "The further we probe, the less we discover! And it is that very fact that assures me that Mary Marlowe was murdered—murdered by some brilliant piece of planning that closely approaches genius in crime." He took up his position of elbows on the arm of the chesterfield and his voice was very earnest. "You haven't heard half of the business, Mac. Listen."

Clearly and concisely, he outlined the affair from the time of their entrance to the studio, touching on the details of the death, the incident of the locked door, and concluding with an account of his visit to the wrecked flat in Bayswater. Jeffery omitted nothing. Even the incident of the hatpin came in for its share of description. Conroy listened without interrupting, nodding from time to time. Barely had the young man finished his recital when the telephone rang sharply. Read was about to cross the room when the doctor rose and stopped him with a gesture. A curious half-smile shadowed his bearded lips.

"Just a moment!" He spoke above the insistent shrilling of the instrument. "This is my big surprise!" As his hosts stared at him, the smile broadened to a grin. "At last I believe I have something of interest for you both. I hesitated to mention it before, because I wasn't sure. You see, I set some investigators to work off my own bat—and this sounds like the result!"

The Chief Inspector leaned across the table. "Anything to do with the autopsy?" he asked quickly.

"Oh no." Conroy walked to the telephone and spoke over his shoulder. "Nothing whatever to do with that body after death. This concerns the body before death!"

He stilled the agitation of the instrument by lifting the receiver. The hush was so pronounced that the two listeners some distance from the telephone could hear the tinny chirruping syllables of the speaker at the other end of the line. Of words, however, they could distinguish nothing. Conroy was nodding, an expression of satisfaction on his face. Presently, he uttered a few curt monosyllables and replaced the receiver. Turning, he glanced at both men slyly, running his fingers through his beard like some diminutive and particularly artful Shylock about to play a trump card.

"Well?" barked the Chief Inspector impatiently.

Conroy smiled at him. "They talk about the long arm of coincidence," he murmured conversationally. "But the arm of the law is much longer and certainly more reliable." He walked across to the small table and picked up his glass. "During the autopsy this afternoon, one of my assistants happened to notice that girl's fingers. They were extraordinarily rough and calloused—not at all like the fingers of the modern miss, who strives for the skin you love to touch. Rather," said Conroy blandly, "were they the hands of a person who had been, for some years at least, working at hard manual labour. The kind of manual labour that young women are forced to do in prisons. . . ."

Glass in hand, he crossed to the sideboard and mixed himself a drink with dainty precision. Read and Blackburn continued to stare at him, as if afraid to break the trembling, swollen silence that followed his words. Miles Conroy turned, faced them. He spoke crisply.

"Out of sheer curiosity, I had a check-up made on that girl. Your Criminal Record Office is reliable as ever, Read! It identified that woman as Isabelle Simms, released from prison a little over twelve months ago. She had been sentenced for incendiarism, but was originally arrested on suspicion of being concerned in the mysterious death of Adolph Gallasch, an analytical chemist. Simms was his assistant at the time when Gallasch died of arsenical poisoning!"

The Chief Inspector straightened and expelled a long breath. "Well, I'll be the monkey's uncle!" His voice sharpened. "You're not making a mistake, Mac?"

Conroy shrugged. "The plastic surgeons have done a neat little job in altering her nose and mouth," he said primly. "But the evidence of the fingerprints is unmistakable. There's only one chance in sixty-four thousand million of a slip-up, I understand. Well, unless that has happened, the fingerprints of the girl you knew as Mary Marlowe and the prints of Isabelle Simms are identical in every detail!"

CHAPTER V

VIA THE EAR!

Of this I feel assured: there is no such thing as ultimate forgetting. Traces once impressed upon the memory are indestructible!

DE QUINCEY.

I

WILLIAM ALLAN PINKERTON, that bulldog force behind the famous private detective agency, once remarked that the capital crimes were solved not so much by brilliant feats of deduction, not by reconstruction or esoteric scientific machines, as by solid spadework, the individual and often maddeningly dull routine work of a number of officers, each working on his special detail in the pattern of the crime, finally weaving each isolated thread into the rope that would inevitably fit about the murderer's neck. In just the same manner, Scotland Yard maintains law and order throughout Britain not so much by extravagant nights of imagination as by system allied in some measure to science.

The Criminal Record Office at Scotland Yard is a miracle of condensed efficiency. Its range is encyclopaedic, its existence the most dangerous threat that shadows the law-breaker. Every police force in the country can draw on the C.R.O. for information. The finger-print bureau each year identifies about 300,000 criminals by their prints and guarantees to supply any police-station with information within twenty-four hours. It has over half a million records, each tabulated and filed. It contains more than 200,000 photographs of criminals which are always kept up-to-date, dead men being eliminated as the information conies to hand. The Criminal Record Office costs £15,000 a year to maintain and Scotland Yard does not begrudge one penny of the amount.

It was to the Criminal Record Office that Jeffery Blackburn made his way on the morning following Dr. Conroy's dramatic statement in the flat regarding the dead woman's past. Jeffery, reversing the order of things and without a word of explanation regarding such eccentric behaviour, had left the Chief Inspector snoring among the blankets. After a thoughtful breakfast of tea, toast, and half a dozen cigarettes at a café, he had sauntered through St. James's Park and on to Whitehall. The Cenotaph, clean and pallid as stripped willow, glowed coldly in the morning sunlight. He tarried here and there. Clocks were striking the hour of nine when he entered the Yard.

Jeffery spent almost an hour in the C.R.O. transferring information from the files to a scribbling-pad. At length he rose from the table, slipped the pad into his pocket and turned to the hovering officer. "May I borrow these photographs for a while?" he asked. "I'm taking them along to the Chief Inspector's office."

The officer nodded. "That's all right, Mr. Blackburn." He smiled. "We can trust you, sir. Anything else?"

Jeffery shook his head. "No, thank you." He glanced rather ruefully at the littered table. "I'm afraid I've left things in something of a mess," he began.

The officer said cheerfully: "Don't worry about that, sir. We'll soon have that straight."

And Mr. Blackburn, reflecting that the world was quite a sound place after all, picked up the photographs and, with a nod to the officer, made his way to Read's sanctum.

He knocked, and without waiting for an answer pushed open the door and entered. The Chief Inspector was standing by the window, frowning over the Embankment. He turned as Jeffery came in, eyeing the young man with sour surprise. It was evident that William Read was not in the sweetest of tempers.

"What the devil brought you here so early?" he grunted.

" 'The business that we love, we rise betimes and go to with delight'," said Jeffery brightly. He crossed the room and pulled a chair up to Read's desk. "I gather that the world has rather a dull-brown taste to you this morning, Chief?" And as Read growled something, the young man wagged an admonishing finger at him. "You're just annoyed because you've got a job on hand!" He pulled the scribbling-pad from his pocket and slapped it on the desk. "And let me warn you that this is the biggest thing that's ever happened within the square mile since the Sidney

Street siege! It's going to keep your mind off radio for the next three months!"

The big man wheeled from the window like a goaded bull. "I wish you'd kept your interfering nose out of radio altogether," he snarled. "You're never satisfied unless you're pulling the roof down on someone's head! This is a lovely mess you've gotten me into!"

"Well, I like that!" retorted Jeffery warmly. "How am I responsible? Who dragged me into this business in the first place? Who was the inquisitive one on that night? You know perfectly well that you were breaking your neck to get to that opening! And just because you poke your fatuous head into a murder case, you put the blame on to me!" He shook a reproving head. "Chief, I'm ashamed of you!"

Read snorted. "We're a damn' long time proving that it is murder, even with Mac's departmental aid," he grunted.

Jeffery tipped his chair back.

"Exactly," he cried. "That's just what makes this case so remarkable! Chief, I'm satisfied that we're getting to grips with the crime of the century! This is no business of a dark lane, a purse, and two blockheads to kill and be killed, to paraphrase De Quincey. This is a crime that has probably been months in preparation, a crime intelligently planned, delicately balanced, brilliantly executed." His eyes wandered past Read and fixed themselves dreamily on a large framed photograph of a former Chief Inspector staring down from the wall. "You know," mused Jeffery, "were I not so scrupulously honest and raised to respect the well-known Chaucerian phrase, this is just the kind of crime that I would plan and achieve!"

"Rot!" growled Read. He walked across to his desk and, sitting in his swivel-chair, began to shuffle restlessly through some papers before him. "Come on, son! I haven't got all day to waste listening to you shoot hot air! Get to the point. What have you got there?"

"This?" Jeffery pulled up his chair and tapped the pad. "This is a condensed *dossier* of Mary Marlowe, *nee* Isabelle Simms. And a very interesting *dossier* it is, too! I put the past hour into its compilation."

Read grunted. "So that's what's routed you out so early?" He glanced at the pad. "Well, did you light on anything that makes for progress in the case?"

" 'I have toiled hard nor vainly'," retorted Jeffery. "But as for the progress you demand, I'm afraid disappointment is your lot. What I've unearthed merely moves us back a step." His eyes lighted and he glanced up into Read's troubled face. "Y'know, that's not a bad title for this whole business—'The Crime that Moved Backwards!' "

The Chief Inspector's forefinger beat a slow, measured pulse on the desk.

"I'm waiting," he said icily, "for you to get down to facts, young man."

Jeffery was lighting a cigarette. He tossed the matches on the desk and picked up his pad, ruffling through the leaves.

"Here we go," he announced.

"It seems that early in May, 1933, the Kinofilm Company in Berlin sent a unit to London for the production of short educational pictures. They were silent films and they were primarily meant for universities and colleges. Several of these films concerned toxicology, and to this end they brought with them a chemist by the name of Adolph Gallasch. He was employed mainly to authenticate the technical data about which the films were made. The unit took a studio near Shepherd's Bush. While in London, they took on the services of a young woman as assistant to Gallasch. This was a girl named Isabelle Simms. Miss Simms had studied chemistry and emerged with the usual qualifications. Everything seems to have gone quite well for about three months. Several films were shot, cut, edited and stored.

"One night, a close, hot night in August, a fire broke out in the studios. Film studios being what they are, it gained a rapid hold and spread to the room containing the highly combustible chemicals. By the time the brigade arrived, the studio was what our daily newspapers so picturesquely term 'a raging inferno'. The brigade did its best, but they might as well have poured petrol on the flames. Within three hours, the studio was burnt out.

"No one appears to have known, at the time, how the conflagration started," continued Jeffery, with a quick glance at his notes. "But for one tragic event, the whole business was not at all serious. The studios were covered by insurance, and though some of the films were destroyed, together with the negatives, the loss could not have been great. And so the whole business might have been just another ephemeral half-column in the newspapers, but for one nasty detail that thrust the fire into high prominence among the news of the day."

The young man paused and puffed at his cigarette. "This was a rather shocking discovery made on the morning after the fire, when the officers were poking around the still smoking ruins. Amongst what was left of the chemical room they found the charred body of a man. He was dead, of course, but due to the fact that some heat-neutralizing chemical had drenched him, the body was not badly burned, and the unfortunate individual was easily identified. It was Adolph Gallasch.

"The room in which the chemicals were stored was steel insulated. While the walls were naturally twisted and buckled by the great heat, they were not destroyed. The investigating officers made the discovery that the lock on the door of the chemical room was sprung. It was then decided that the unhappy Gallasch had accidentally locked himself in the chemical room and, being overcome by the heat and fumes, had collapsed before he could free himself and dash for safety. It was all very sad, but apparently a perfectly normal accident, if I may use the term. The unit disbanded. Some of the employees returned to their native Germany. Some stayed in London. A month passed, and the whole incident had faded from the public mind when it was recalled in a most startling manner."

Blackburn tipped back on his chair and stared past the Chief Inspector out of the window.

"A month later, as I say, the great newspaper-reading public were given the thrill of their lives. It appeared that the Home Secretary had received a letter, a letter stating that the fire at the Shepherd's Bush studio was not the result of an accident. It had been started deliberately. With the intention of covering a murder! For the writer announced that Adolph Gallasch had been dead before the fire began—that he had been poisoned, the dead body locked in the chemical room, and the conflagration started with the express purpose of destroying the corpse!"

Read jerked upright. "Holy mackerel! But surely no notice was taken of a letter like that?"

Jeffery smiled grimly. "Notice certainly *was* taken of it! An investigation started immediately."

"But who wrote the letter?"

"That,", said Jeffery, "is a little job of work for you, my Chief! The press reports remain irritatingly vague about that missive. You must get hold of a copy of the letter. The writer was obviously someone of importance, otherwise the business would have been shelved along with the dozens of other cranky notes that follow any public incident."

The Chief Inspector was frowning. "That does strike a chord in the memory," he admitted. "Weren't we out of England at the time—?"

"September, 1933," interrupted Jeffery, "we were on the high seas bound for Australia.[2] Weaver Patterson occupied your chair. We read accounts of the case in the newspapers at that time."

Read nodded. "Of course! Go on, Jeff."

"As I said," Blackburn continued, "an investigation began almost immediately. Not only did the Commissioner reopen the case of the Shepherd's Bush studio, as it came to be known, but also he ordered an autopsy on the body of the dead chemist. Within a week, sensational news rocked England! Not only was it proved that the fire at the studio was the deliberate work of an incendiary, but an examination of Gallasch's body revealed undoubted traces of arsenic! Something like 1.0 grain was taken from the viscera!"

The young man paused.

"I haven't had time to get down the finer details," he admitted. "The investigations continued for three weeks, and at the end of that period Isabelle Simms was arrested on a charge of incendiarism and murder. The evidence of her guilt regarding the first charge is unmistakable, but the second—for this, the evidence was purely circumstantial. Briefly, Simms had quarrelled with Gallasch over the disappearance of some expensive chemicals. The man had accused the girl of stealing them, and had given her twenty-four hours to return the chemicals before he re-

---

[2] It was during their stay in Australia that Read and Blackburn became embroiled in the nightmare business of the Melbourne Centenary murders, one of the strangest and most remarkable cases this couple have worked upon. How they brought it to a successful conclusion is told in an earlier novel, *Blood on His Hands.*

ported the matter to the authorities. This incident occurred on the morning preceding the fire. Later, when the unit stopped work for afternoon tea, Gallasch complained that his brew tasted bitter, but as the tea was rather strong, this passed without comment. Simms had brought the tea into the laboratory and left it on a shelf because Gallasch was absent at the time. No other person save Simms and Gallasch had access to the laboratory and the chemical room.

"This was at four o'clock on the afternoon preceding the fire," continued Jeffery. "Gallasch was not seen again until his body was discovered the following morning among the burnt-out remains of the studio.

"When she was arrested, Simms made a statement that she was, all unwittingly, responsible for the studio fire. Her story was that she had attempted to destroy some waste film and the inflammable material got beyond control. She had not given the alarm because of the fear that she would be held responsible for the conflagration. Regarding the murder charge, she declared herself innocent. She stated that the incident of the chemicals was a misunderstanding; Gallasch had discovered them hidden behind other material in the laboratory. However, as the fire had destroyed all trace of chemicals, her story had no corroboration."

Blackburn gestured to Read to push across the ashtray. The other obeyed. Jeffery squashed his cigarette end among the ashes before he continued.

"The trial of Isabelle Simms aroused tremendous interest throughout the country. Public opinion was divided into two factions governed by the sexes. As a whole, the menfolk were inclined to believe the girl more sinned against than sinning. The women, on the other hand, considered her guilty as Satan. Call it feminine intuition if you will, but the ladies were definitely set against the girl. Strange," mused Mr. Blackburn, "how *les femmes* are always willing to believe the worst of their sisters in misfortune when—"

"Spare the sermon!" Read snapped. "Stick to your story!"

Jeffery grunted something uncomplimentary and referred to his notes again.

"At the trial, Simms was defended by Sir Evan Rosslyn, who was then without his title. Graham Lambert appeared for the Crown. As the majority of the evidence was purely of a circumstantial nature, Lambert played heavily on the finding of the arsenic in the body. But on the third day of the trial, when everything seemed dead against Simms, Sir Evan brought forth a remarkable attestation. He produced evidence to show that Gallasch was one of those extraordinary individuals—*an arsenic eater!"*

"Good Lord!" grunted the Chief Inspector.

"Gallasch," continued Blackburn, "was a fine-figured, handsome man approaching his fiftieth year. He was married and had five children, but was living apart from his wife. There were vague rumours of a love-affair with another woman, but nothing could be proved. Sir Evan put forth the suggestion that Gallasch had cultivated this habit in the belief that the arsenic had certain revitalizing effects. Counsel went on to point out that it is a well-known fact that mountain climbers in the Tyrol take microscopic doses of arsenic for the increasing of stamina, while horses are frequently given arsenic in their food to bolster up their staying powers.

"Also, a habitual arsenic eater, starting with the smallest part of a grain, could eventually ingest an extraordinary amount of the poison with no ill effects.

"And thus Rosslyn toppled over the Crown case like a house of cards. Whether or no his evidence on this point was conclusive, none can say. But it gave him the foundation for a brilliant speech that germinated the seeds of doubt already sown in the minds of the jury. Sir Evan's address brought the trial to a close. The jury were empanelled for three hours. At the end of that time, they returned with their verdict. They found Isabelle Simms innocent of the poisoning charge, but guilty of the incendiary accusation."

Jeffery paused. The Chief Inspector nodded to him to continue.

"The court-room was packed with women who had come to hear the verdict. When the judge passed the sentence of eighteen months' imprisonment, there was quite a demonstration in the court. Some of the women hooted and one wildly emotional lady screamed that the girl was a murderess of the most cowardly type. This female was promptly ejected, of course, but it showed pretty plainly the feeling against Simms. Small wonder that she changed her name and her appearance when she emerged from prison."

"Have we got anything on her after she came out?" asked the Chief Inspector.

Jeffery nodded. "I regret to say that we have," he confessed. "She was released in March of last year, when she seems to have gone thoroughly to the bad! Simms alive," added the young man thoughtfully, "is almost as intriguing a problem as Simms defunct. Was she a vicious murderess, guilty of a poisoning crime, or was she an innocent victim of circumstantial evidence? Did she go to the bad because of her inherently evil nature or was she contaminated and embittered by her sojourn among hardened criminals? And if our existing prison system makes for such unfortunate happenings—"

"Skip it," grunted Read laconically. "I can get all that from Havelock Ellis! What have we got on her after she came out of prison?"

"Specifically, nothing," said Jeffery, with a glance at his notes. "Theoretically, quite a lot. There are three nasty cases of blackmail in which she figures vaguely. It's also suspected that she soiled those calloused hands in the confidence game frequently. Then there's the business of the Duke of Torrington's tapestries that were stolen. That takes us to September of last year, when she fled to the Continent because the temperature over here was getting a trifle warm for her. And then," he concluded, "hey presto! She vanishes!" He waved his hands widely. "To reappear as Mary Marlowe!"

The Chief Inspector rocked back in his chair. "With a new face, eh?" He tugged at his short moustache. "It looks mighty queer to me, son! There's much more in Simms' reappearance than meets the eye!"

"Meaning—?" queried Jeffery.

"It shouts, doesn't it?" demanded Read. "Here's this girl, as crooked as they come if her record counts for anything. She disappears to the Continent, to turn up in London some months later with a new face, a new name, and a new personality. Good-bye, Isabella Simms, the tough little tart! Here is Miss Mary Marlowe, the modest shrinking violet, so shy of meeting people, a lone girl struggling with life on a few shillings a week, so pure, such a brave, virtuous little figure—perhaps!" And Read's chair jerked forward to emphasize his derision.

Jeffery grinned, then sobered. "And she cultivates socialite Andrew Newland as an admirable smoke-screen of respectability," he mused. "Yes, it must be so! It explains a lot of details. No wonder Simms preferred lonely rides and deserted tea-shops to mixing with crowds who might recognize her in spite of the change in her appearance! It also explains why she'd never talk about her past, why she apparently had no relatives and seemed so alone. Also why she'd never come to the point about their attachment. Noble Mary Marlowe marrying Andrew Newland for his money! Perish the thought!" The young man shook his head sombrely. "The rotten part of it is that Newland seems to have fallen hard for this girl. I'm afraid that young man is in for a very rude awakening!"

"And that flat!" Read's florid face was alight. "Now we know why she could afford to furnish the place the way it was! Of course, she had another source of income—a pretty fat income, too, judging by the look of things! Who was putting up that money? And why?" The Chief Inspector thumped the desk. "I'll tell you why, son! Isabelle Simms was in London this time for a special purpose. She had some kind of a job to do. And if it wasn't something crooked, I'm—I'm Diana of the Ephesians!"

Jeffery stood up, thrust his hands into his pockets, and crossed to the window. He stood looking out for a few moments, then he turned. He spoke quietly.

"Theories are the easiest things in the world to build, Chief! You've summed up a pretty feasible case based on the presumption that Isabelle Simms is a callous little vixen, without conscience or morals. Now, I can give you a perfectly logical explanation, covering all the facts even to her death, founded on the premise that she is an extremely wronged woman!"

"Bilge!" snorted Read. "Look at the records!"

Jeffery ignored the interruption. "Chief," he said quietly, "I want to ask you just one question. Has it ever occurred to you that Simms may have committed suicide?"

"Suicide?"

"That's what I said." Jeffery walked back to his chair, sat down and rested his elbows on the desk. "You've been assuming that Simms was guilty. I'm going to assume that she was innocent. Here we have a sensitive, intelligent girl who has passed through the unnerving ordeal of a murder trial, topped by eighteen months' imprisonment. She contacts with criminals that warp her judgment and her nature, already embittered by her persecution, isn't strong enough to stand up against these eroding influences.

"She comes out of prison to find every door closed against her. What might have been a lucrative career has been ruined by this tragedy! Inevitably, she takes to crime. But after some months, either her fear of the law or her better self warns her of the inevitable end to such a life. She decides to go straight! First, however, she must rid herself of the smear that Isabelle Simms has cast on her career, so she travels to the Continent, has her appearance altered, changes her name and reappears in London as Mary Marlowe."

Read did not speak as Jeffery paused, but his sniff was eloquence itself.

"In London, she finds the going hard," the young man continued. "She earns a few guineas here and there until at length, driven to it by sheer desperation, she takes to the world's oldest profession. Hence her well-furnished flat and her intermittent periods of prosperity. Then she meets Andrew Newland. Here is a clean-living, unsophisticated young man, not particularly intelligent, perhaps, but something of an idealist where women are concerned. Certainly a lad with decided ideas on right and wrong! This young man falls deeply in love with her and she with him. What is she to do? Always she lives in hourly dread of his discovering, not only her murky past but also her illicit present. Sooner or later, he must find out the truth! Sooner or later, she must be betrayed.

"This constant anxiety plays heavily upon her mind. She sees only one way out—suicide! And one night, after a particularly depressing day, she decides to take her life!"

"So she decides to take poison during a radio play!" Read's sneer was mingled with contemptuous amusement. "For the love of Pete, Jeff—you ought to be writing serials for Aunt Agatha's magazine!"

Jeffery frowned. "Wasn't it Flaubert who advised de Maupassant never to be afraid of portraying life as melodrama, because melodrama was life?" he murmured. "Why shouldn't she take poison? She has the means at her fingertips, since her knowledge gives her a quick-acting, untraceable poison such as Conroy mentioned last night. And she determines to do this thing during the darkened interval of the play.

"In a frenzy of self-reproach, she wrecks the flat that her sordid earnings have acquired. She leaves the place in ruin and goes to the studio. Once inside the smaller studio, she locks the door and keeps the key so that the barrier of the locked door will delay a doctor until the poison has done its work. Then, waiting for that darkened sequence, she swallows the poison," Jeffery concluded with a vague gesture.

"*Vale,* Mary Marlowe!"

There was a lame, flat silence. The Chief Inspector did not speak. He stared at the young man, amusement and scorn in the expression that twisted his mouth. Then a voice spoke from the doorway:

"You've left out something, young man," it announced. "Why didn't you have a white-haired mother setting a light in the window of the little cottage in the valley?"

They pivoted simultaneously. Miles Conroy stood there, smoothing his beard with long fingers. There was wicked mockery in those twinkling black eyes, and his mouth was an ugly sneer. He came forward.

"Seems a shame to have to ruin that pretty idyll by pointing out that it's as untrue to facts as it is to life itself," he chuckled. "Because it's got a flaw in it as big as Marble Arch!" He halted opposite the desk.

"Isabelle Simms certainly didn't commit suicide!"

Read was on his feet, leaning over the desk. His big fists clenched. "You've discovered what killed that girl?"

Conroy smiled provokingly. "Oh yes," he purred, "I've discovered what killed her."

"What was it?"

The little Medical Officer clasped his hands behind his back and raised his eyes to the ceiling. "Something so amazing and so remarkable, yet so essentially simple, that it's almost staggering!" He sniggered. "And you'll never guess it in a thousand years!"

Jeffery said sharply: "Don't clown, Mac! Tell us the truth! Did that girl die naturally—or was she murdered?"

Conroy lowered his eyes to Blackburn's eager face. "She was murdered, of course!" he snapped. "Murdered in a manner so devilishly ingenious that if it hadn't been for the merest chance, I'd still be groping in the dark!"

The Chief Inspector's face was scarlet. He drew a deep breath that swelled his massive chest. A tiny vein in his forehead twitched like an impaled moth. "I'm asking you for the last time, Mac"—he spoke through his teeth, slowly, dangerously: *"What killed that girl?"*

There was a silence in which a pin could have been heard to drop. Jeffery, listening, had the queer impression that the whole world had stopped to listen. When he spoke, Conroy's voice had the sharp brittleness of a bird pecking at a window.

"What killed her? It was a hatpin. A ten-inch hatpin!"

Read said slowly: "What do you mean?"

"I mean," said Dr. Conroy clearly, "that some gentle soul ran it through her left ear into the brain!"

2

"Good God in heaven!" whispered Read.

He dropped back slowly into his chair, his big frame sagging, his eyes never leaving Conroy's face. Then he released that pent-up breath in a long, soundless whistle. Jeffery was staring as though hypnotized at the little doctor. All the sickening horror that crowded in on the realization of Conroy's words trembled his voice as he spoke.

"That's the most terrible thing I've heard in all my experience of crime." He sat down almost abruptly, as though his legs had weakened under him.

Dr. Conroy was staring from face to face, his high forehead puckered. "Why the sensation?" he demanded. "If you're brooding on that method, let me assure you that it sounds much worse than it actually is! As a matter of fact, except for the first momentary numbing shock, there'd be no pain at all! Infinitely much less than would be caused by a knife stab or a bullet wound!"

He glanced at both men in turn. Jeffery said quietly: "I'm glad of that, Mac. All the same, it seems particularly horrible—"

"Particularly brilliant, you mean," retorted Conroy. "Why, it's positive genius in murder! Imagine it! Death without sound, wound, or blood! Death, leaving post-mortem symptoms that might well baffle any doctor! From a technical point of view, it's the cleverest thing I've met with in my career!"

Jeffery turned to the Chief Inspector. "We're fighting a very worthy opponent this time," he said grimly. "If and when we get this murderer, I'd like to shake his hands before you clip the manacles on them, Chief. My admiration for him grows with each discovery!"

"Him?" It was Conroy who spoke. He pulled up a chair and sat down. "Perhaps it's merely association of ideas, but I had a woman in mind. Hatpins and stabbing seem an accepted feminine prerogative!"

Read gave a little jerk to his head, like a man waking from a dream. "A hatpin through the ear, eh?" he muttered. "Say—Jeff! Think that pin you found in Simms' flat has anything to do with this?" He gnawed his moustache. "It's a vast pity you didn't think to bring it away with you."

Blackburn shrugged. "How was I to know that it was going to be of such importance? I suggest, Chief, that you get a man on that right away. He'd better bring that pin back before anyone else finds it. Providing, of course, that it was the pin used!" He turned to Conroy. "You'd know, wouldn't you, Mac?"

"After an examination—certainly," replied the doctor.

Read's finger was already on the key of his desk telephone. He barked a few sharp orders at the instrument and sat back.

"It won't be long now," he announced.

"And we mustn't forget," said Jeffery, "that there was a hatpin in that studio on the night of the murder. Remember it?—used with the oiled silk for the water-dropping business." His eyes wandered past Read to the window. "It would be interesting to discover if it was the one I found in the flat."

"Surely you would have known it again—" began the Chief Inspector, when Jeffery shook his head.

"The only means of identification, the ornament, had been torn away," the young man explained. "But there's no need to sit here guessing," he added. "Put a call through to that effects man—what's his name—?"

"Martin."

"Yes—Martin. Ask him if he still has the hatpin used in the effects for that play. That should clinch the business at once."

Again Read manipulated the telephone. Then he nodded. "The call's going through right away."

"A hatpin," repeated Jeffery thoughtfully. "Y'know, there's something very significant about that. Remember the Sheldon murder when the killing was done with a paper-file, and how the very nature of the weapon helped us to narrow down the list of suspects?" And as both men nodded, he went on: "It seems to me that this might be a similar business. The very individuality of the weapon should be an advantage to us. Because hatpins aren't the ubiquitous objects now that they were in mother's day. I doubt whether one woman in five hundred uses hatpins these times."

Read nodded. "That makes sense," he admitted. "And here's another point! The murderer was so sure that we wouldn't discover the method of killing that he could take the risk of using an uncommon weapon—"

"He had to use a hatpin," Conroy interrupted. "No other object would have been suitable!"

"What do you mean?"

"Only a thin strong length of steel could do that job," the little doctor repeated. "Of course, the murderer had to have some rudimentary idea of anatomy since he must know the direction that the pin would take." Conroy pursed his lips. "Your murderer can also congratulate himself on being well in with Lady Luck!"

"What do you mean?" Jeffery was frowning.

The Chief Medical Officer placed his knuckles on the desk-edge and leaned over it. "Do you realize," he said slowly, "that to bring about a death in this manner is the most difficult of all murders? There is only one course that pin could take without being blocked by the cranial wall. Yet, with one chance in a hundred of finding the vital channel, our murderer brought it off! Although I haven't examined the body closely, I can say that the only possible entrance was through the tympaneous membrane of the ear, penetrating the acoustic canal and—" He broke off as Read made a gesture of repulsion. The big man hunched his shoulders uncomfortably.

"Break it down, Mac," he muttered. "You're giving me the willies!"

Jeffery asked: "How did you stumble on this method?"

Conroy thrust his thumbs in the armholes of his waistcoat. His eyes twinkled. "I've been waiting for you to ask me that," he said. "I could spin you a tale about a second long and brain-fagging search, but as a matter of fact, Blackburn, you put me on to the thing yourself!"

"I did?"

Conroy nodded. "You—and the blind chance that ruins even the most carefully planned schemes." His eyes raked the young man's face. "Do you remember last night—when you mentioned about getting that hatpin stuck in your beam ends while you were at the flat? Well, as you spoke about it, something clicked in my mind. I had one of those queer sensations of having heard it all before—you know how it is? It didn't mean much to me at the time, except that it kept nagging at me, an elusive memory that I couldn't place. Somewhere or other, I had heard of a case in which a hatpin and a death went together. I fell asleep last night thinking over it."

He paused. "This morning, when I woke, I remembered the whole thing quite clearly!"

"You mean," demanded Read, "that this method of murder has been used before?"

"Of course," Conroy assured him. "There's nothing new under the sun. The first case happened during the war—it was in Paris during the end of 1916. I was in charge of a crowd of R.A.M.C. chaps who were on leave in that naughty city. While we were there, a murder was committed on the Left Bank—an American artist killed his mistress, who was making trouble over his model. I forget the exact details, but jealousy was at the bottom of the business. Anyhow, he caught her listening at his door one night and ran a hatpin through the keyhole. By sheer chance, the pin took the right track and, although the artist didn't realize it at the time, he had evolved the perfect murder! The cause of the death would still be a mystery if the man hadn't soaked himself in absinthe on the following day and blabbed about the whole business. It was a nine days' wonder, even in wartime! So there's your answer. Whoever did this thing apparently heard of the Parisian murder and decided to duplicate it. And by a miracle, he succeeded!"

"Then let's hope this person likewise decides to duplicate the absinthe incident," growled Read. "It seems to me that it's the only way we'll ever get to the bottom of this crazy affair. The farther we probe, the more complex the case becomes!"

Jeffery moved restlessly. "That doesn't make it any easier," he murmured. "You say that this first murder caused a sensation? Then every paper in the world probably had a reference to it. Which means that the knowledge became common property. Of course, not every person would remember, but if this thing has been as carefully planned as I imagine, it goes well back into—"

The buzz of the desk telephone stilled the words on his lips. Read's hand flew to it, depressed the key and he barked, "What is it?"

"It's Connolly here, Chief," replied the instrument metalliferously. "It's about that hatpin—"

"Well, Dennis?"

"I spoke t' the bird in charge of the effects at th' studio, the bird with the adenoids, and he tells me he ain't seen th' hatpin that was used with those effects since th' night of th' play. It's gone, vamoosed, no-findy!"

Read's eyebrows came down. "O.K., Dennis," he said after a pause.

"Anything else, Chief?"

"Hang around," said his superior briefly. The key shot up and Read turned. Conroy was regarding him with quizzical eyes. "Inside job, eh?"

"I'm not surprised," returned Jeffery. "There was that peculiar business of the locked door. I have a rather interesting idea in the back of my mind over that!" He looked at Conroy. "Mac, provided the murder was committed as we believe, how long would the actual operation take?"

The other pursed his lips. "Five seconds would be ample. It needed nothing except a straight thrust. Might be rather difficult to accomplish in pitch darkness, however."

"And the symptoms would be those of a heart attack?"

"Undoubtedly! Violent convulsions would rack the body. The respiratory organs would stop immediately, although the heart might go on beating for some little time until it slowed down of its own accord. Confronted with such symptoms, added to the absence of a haemorrhage and no visible sign of wound, not one doctor in a hundred could tell the right cause of death!" Conroy pushed back his chair and rose. "Well, I'll be getting along, Read. If you want me, I'll be in the charnel house." He waved a hand airily.

Jeffery rose likewise. "I'm going, too. You'll find me at home if anything fresh turns up, Chief. I'm going to soliloquize in solitude."

The Chief Inspector grunted. "To what end?" Jeffery paused half-way across the room. "I'm going to transport myself into the fifth dimension," he returned.

"Y'see, I'm burning to discover by what means a person can walk through a locked studio door—and yet click it shut after them!"

3

Mr. Blackburn was extremely fortunate in that, being unofficially connected with Scotland Yard, he was likewise absolved of all the responsibilities. Thus he was free to spend the remainder of the day unharassed and fettered by nothing more worrying than his own personal affairs. Not so the Chief Inspector. Now that the business of the broadcasting station had passed from the category of a curious though quite impersonal problem to the status of a particularly callous and carefully planned murder case, the liabilities entailed by his position fell about him with extraordinary rapidity. There were a hundred and one details for his consideration. With the Chief Medical Officer's discovery, the smooth and efficient mechanism of Scotland Yard was set in motion and Read's was the hand that must guide and control.

The remainder of his day was a frenzied programme of orders, interviews, discussions, explanations, and signatures on documents. Detective Armstrong returned shortly before lunch with the hatpin from the Bayswater flat. It was examined and pronounced to be the weapon that had taken the life of Isabelle Simms in such an unconventional manner. An officer was dispatched to procure a copy of the letter which had reached the Home Secretary and reopened the Shepherd's Bush Studio case. A third was assigned the task of acquainting George Nickerson with the latest development. Thus it was that the afternoon had begun to wane before Read escaped to the privacy of. his office. He sank down in his swivel chair, one hand hovering over the cigar-box on his desk. Then the telephone at his elbow screamed at him.

William Read ejaculated a particularly vulgar word and laid violent hands on the instrument. His manner was extremely curt as he answered, then as Jeffery's voice floated over the wire—"Oh, it's you! Had a good afternoon's sleep?"

"Let's cut out the cross-talk, Chief!" The eagerness in the young man's voice was apparent. "This is serious! Listen, I think I've stumbled on something rather important. It may be all wrong, but it's at least worth trying out. So I want you to do something for me."

Read's tone was surly. "I guessed as much!"

The other ignored the interpolation. "Chief—I want you to get every person who was in that studio on the night of the murder back in there this evening! And I want the place fitted up exactly as it was on that night! Can you do that for me?"

Read sneered. "What's this? Another of your brilliant reconstructions?"

"Don't be difficult!" Jeffery snapped. "You know I've never yet made a request of you without there being something definite behind it. And this is vitally important. Can you do it?"

"I suppose I must," grunted Read. "I'll get no peace until I do. But what's the idea of it all?"

"I'm going to try an experiment in acoustics," chuckled the receiver, and it clicked rudely in the Chief Inspector's ear.

VI

ASTONISHING ILLUSION OF SOUND WITHOUT SIGHT

"Believe only half of what you see, Davey, my boy, and even less of what you hear!"

David Copperfield.

JEFFERY BLACKBURN ran his eyes over the people assembled in Studio Number Two of the subsidiary broadcast studio in Wigmore Street. He nodded to the Chief Inspector. Read shut the door, turned the key in the lock, and set his broad back against it.

The studio had the queer appearance of having shrunk, the walls of having moved closer like the inquisitorial chamber in the Poe story. And this feeling of claustration appeared to be sensed by each group which stood, apprehensive and silent, about the room.

Von Bethke was there, his bullet-head thrust forward, those hard black eyes darting here and there. There were tiny beads of perspiration forming on the rolls of fat that overhung his collar. He stood, plucking at his lips, between a sullen, defiant Lusinska and a patently disturbed Martha Rockwell. The middle-aged actress seemed to have become a different personality; tragedy or fear had damped the mischievous sparkle in her eyes and wiped the humour from her face. Now she looked nothing more than a dumpy, plain, and badly frightened woman.

In one corner the sleek dark head of Gordon Finniss formed the apex of a triangle of which the fair hair of Garnett and the red curls of Bob Hammond constituted the basic points. Under the light, pallor, overlying the swarthiness of his skin, gave to Finniss' face a peculiar dirty-white appearance, and his hands were like restless leaves in a breeze. The two younger actors were plainly nervous. Their eyes wandered between the Chief Inspector's uncompromising visage and Jeffery's tight, pale features.

The clown face of Ted Martin hung like some lugubrious Benda mask over the effects table. Near him, George Nickerson shuffled uneasy feet, a harassed, sombre-eyed

Nickerson from whose bowed shoulders that cloak of snapping efficiency had long fallen. He was muttering in an undertone to Anthony Stewart, the announcer. They paused as Jeffery moved, and there fell on that studio something of the electric hush of a packed theatre as the curtain gives a preliminary twitch before rising.

Every eye was focused on Blackburn as he crossed the room and took up his position near the effects table. When he spoke his voice had a low penetrating quality that quivered the close atmosphere as a wind ripples water.

"Ladies and gentlemen," he said quietly, "you are probably wondering why you have been summoned here tonight. Without elaborate preamble, you are asked here to aid the cause of justice. This morning, following an autopsy on the body of the woman you knew as Mary Marlowe, it was revealed beyond all doubt that the cause of her death was not heart failure, as we were led to believe. This woman was murdered—murdered in a manner particularly clever and unbelievably cruel! She met her death by a hatpin that was thrust through her left ear into her brain!"

He paused for the anticipated consternation. Amazingly, none came. Somewhere a tight, choked breath was released, a gasp that may have been horror or fear. He saw Olga Lusinska's fingers close slowly. Gordon Finniss paused in the act of lighting a cigarette, his cupped hands hiding his face, only his eyes revealing the sickening shock. Vance Garnett and young Hammond stared, their faces reflecting something of the awed incredulity of a child listening to an impossible fairy-story. Martha Rockwell's hand climbed to her throat and she breathed heavily.

"This is neither the time nor the place to go into anatomical details. Sufficient is it to explain that the symptoms of death by such horrible means have all the appearance of a heart seizure. Other and more important matters concern us at the moment. The first of these is that among the sound effects used in this studio on the night of the murder was a long hatpin. That hatpin is now missing. Martin tells me that it was not among the effects when they were packed away that night. Therefore, it must have been removed from this studio by some person who was in the room at the time. We will return to this point in a moment.

"Secondly, we must remember that although no person at present in this studio knew it until after the murder, the victim had locked the door of this room and retained the key in her hand during the presentation of the play!"

Again he paused. And as before there was silence. No sound came from the groups. Either they did not realize the grim conclusion to which Blackburn was leading or else they realized it only too well and were stunned by the horror of the thing.

"Now, consider the facts as we know them." Jeffery's voice was quiet. "That girl was killed during the darkened sequence of the play. She was killed with a hatpin, an instrument similar to the one that lay at hand within a few feet of every person in this studio. And all the time the studio door was locked on the inside, thus *making entry from outside impossible!*

It was as though, at that moment, the people in the studio realized their position. From chained numbness, the pendulum swung to gesticulating babel, a bursting spate of fulmination that flooded to the very walls of the studio. The guttural protestations of Von Bethke, the vicious expletives of Lusinska, and the excited titubulation of Ted Martin clashed and merged with the deep resonance of Finniss and the clipped exclamations of George Nickerson. Jeffery held up his hand and the clamour died. There were panting indrawn breaths and half-formed words, then silence. George Nickerson spoke and in that sound-proof room his voice sounded flat, colourless, a voice not quite human. He turned a prematurely lined face to the young man.

"How can you say that, Blackburn! We know that someone came out of this studio while the lights were lowered!"

Jeffery said quietly: "Through a locked door, Mr. Nickerson?"

The manager raised his hand and dropped it again. "But we *heard* them," he insisted. "You admit it yourself! We heard the click of a door and the sound of footsteps! Then there was that noise of a motor-car driven away! Why—even the men in the control room heard those sounds!"

"Exactly!" Blackburn pounced on his words. "Yes—we all heard those sounds! But did they come from outside—from the corridor? Or did they come from inside this studio?"

Nickerson said contemptuously: "Hear those noises through sound-proof walls? That's an absurd suggestion!"

"We didn't have to hear them through sound-proof walls, Mr. Nickerson. The microphone in this studio was open all the time. Every sound made in this studio would be transmitted by the microphone to our ears—and to the ears of the men listening in the control room—*through the speakers!"*

In the same thin tone Nickerson whispered: "What do you mean?"

"I'll demonstrate," said Jeffery curtly. He turned to the effects table. "Early in the evening on that last occasion we were here, your studio director was good enough to explain this bewildering collection to us. His exact words were, as far as I can recall, *'We can get every noise from a crying baby to an elephant stampede or an avalanche with these things.'* He also demonstrated this model door. But there were two other sound effects on this table that were to be used during the action of the play that he did not mention." Jeffery paused and his hand flew to the table. "Martin has since volunteered the information. The first is this little box which, when a button is pressed on the side, gives a perfect representation of stealthy footsteps. The other is this gadget that reproduces the noise of a motor-car starting and driving away!" He glanced up quickly. "Mr. Martin?"

The effects man licked his lips. "Yeah?"

"You are more accustomed to handling these articles than I. Imagining that a script called for a character to leave a room, click a door shut after him, walk down the corridor, get into a motor-car, start and drive it away—how long would that sequence of effects take to manipulate?"

Martin swallowed something in his throat. "About—'bout fifteen seconds, sir."

"Very good," Blackburn nodded. "Now, would you manipulate those effects in the order named to get that specific result?" And as the effects man reached out to the table, Jeffery said quickly: "Wait—let's have those lights out!"

Without a word, the Chief Inspector lifted a hand to the switch by the door and the studio was plunged into darkness. Out of the gloom came excited little murmurs: "Quiet, please!" Jeffery cried sharply. The muttering died. "Ready, Martin? Now listen carefully, everyone!"

Silence. In the darkness something blacker shifted about the effects table. Out of the shadows came a ghostly echo of the sounds heard on that unforgettable night. And such dark recollections did it inspire that Jeffery felt the short hair on his neck prickle uncomfortably. First came the unmistakable click of a door shutting, then the gentle, furtive slither of footsteps, and finally, the throb of an electric starter that was swallowed in the surge of the engine, to fade in a humming diminuendo to silence once more.

"Lights!" called Jeffery. They blazed up, to reveal pale faces, twitching lips, unsteady hands. "Thanks, Martin." He turned. "Satisfied, Mr. Nickerson?" The studio manager said huskily: "I admit it's possible, Blackburn. But after all, it's merely theory! You will never convince me that the murder wasn't the work of an outsider!"

For the first time, the Chief Inspector gave tongue and his voice held a menacing undertone that rumbled like distant thunder. "We don't have to convince you, Mr. Nickerson. You have to convince us! You can't get away from the fact that this door was locked!"

"That doesn't mean anything!" the manager retorted. "What about the master-keys? They were hanging in the commissionaire's office within the reach of any person who cared to take them!"

Jeffery shook his head. "Impossible! Remember, that murder had to be committed under the cover of the darkened sequence of the play! I'm told that because a new technique was being used, the details of this production were kept a close secret. Therefore, how could any outsider have known of the black-out at all?"

Nickerson made a vague gesture. "These things get around," he said lamely.

"No," said Jeffery. "It won't do! Even if we assume that this theoretical outsider *did* know of the darkened sequence, we face a much more formidable barrier in that locked door. So your outsider must push his way through the crowd, come to the door of this studio with the intention of murder, find the door locked, move again through the crowd, obtain the keys from the commissionaire's office, make his way through the crowd for the third time, return to this door, unlock it, slip in and commit the crime. Not only must he accomplish all this within thirty seconds, but he must push his way through the crowd for the last time and return the keys to the office so that your studio director finds them there almost immediately the lights are turned up and the murder revealed." Again he shook his head. "I'm sorry, Mr. Nickerson, but it isn't at all logical."

The manager's expression was ugly. "It's certainly as logical as accusing any of these people here of the murder!"

Jeffery glanced at Nickerson for a moment, then stepped forward. He stared about the studio, allowing his eyes to rest on every face.

"I think there is some misunderstanding about this business," he said pleasantly. "We are accusing no person of murder! And please get it out of your heads, all of you, that this is some kind of psychological third degree. It's nothing of the kind! It is merely an experiment—a process of elimination. When we discover the various ways in which the murder could have been committed and, with the help of you all, eliminated the methods that are logically unsound, we must inevitably arrive at the correct solution. That is all we are attempting at the moment."

He paused, noticing a relaxing of their attitudes. "One of the most intriguing details of this affair is the location," he went on. "Why was the murder committed in a radio studio? And why, in heaven's name, in the middle of a play?" He smiled. "We have, of course, all heard, seen, or read of the murder in the radio studio in which the character in a play, killed in masquerade, is actually murdered. Now, if we follow this line of thought, Miss Lusinska, who was playing the part of the victim in the play, should naturally be the person who was attacked. Then why Mary Marlowe? There appears to me only one reasonable answer. The murderer chose this most unorthodox location *because the environment assisted his crime* in some manner. These experiments are merely to isolate and reveal that manner. When we have accomplished that, we shall be a definite step forward!"

Warm colour had crept into George Nickerson's face. "Sorry," he muttered. His shoulders moved awkwardly. A little stir ran through the studio, an uneasy movement that was like the shifting of a heavy load. Only the Chief Inspector, stern as Draco by that perplexing door, remained motionless as some figure rough-hewn from granite.

Jeffery cleared his throat. "Those remarks were necessary in view of the crime reconstruction that I am about to give you," he explained quietly. "This reconstruction may be wrong. I hope that it is! Again, you people are more familiar with the mysteries of broadcasting than I, and you maybe able to fault my theory on technical grounds. That is why I ask you to listen carefully, bearing in mind that fundamentally it is only a theory!"

Automatically they nodded. Jeffery indicated the chairs. "If the ladies care to sit . . .?" he suggested, and Lusinska and Miss Rockwell shook their heads almost simultaneously. The young man shrugged. He leant against the table.

"Regarding this theory," he began. "It appears to me that the person who committed this crime must have been in possession of three important facts. Assuming for the sake of clarity that the murderer is a man, he must have been aware of that darkened interval during the play. He must have known that among the sound effects to be used in connection with the play was a hatpin—and he must have known that the last-minute re-arrangement of the studios would bring those sound effects into this room. In other words, that they would be close at hand during the black-out. This person may have even tampered with the line that made such rearrangement necessary! Obviously, only one group of people are possessed of those qualifications and they are the people who were in this studio at the time of the murder!"

He paused. The groups in the room seemed to have moved closer and eyes that had been furtive and lowered were now bright with defiance and some other quality not so easily named.

"Now, follow the reasoning of this criminal," invited Blackburn. "He has some definite motive for wishing the girl dead. I understand that there was a rehearsal with full effects on the afternoon preceding the actual production. As a person concerned in this play, the murderer thus has opportunity to time his routine to perfection. He knows that the hatpin will be among the effects, remember, also that these effects are close to hand. He has evolved the really brilliant plan of producing death with all the symptoms of heart attack. This can be accomplished within ten seconds, leaving him ample time to manipulate the sound effects which give the illusion of a person leaving the studio and driving away in a motor-car."

Gordon Finniss interrupted, his mouth contemptuous, "I don't follow your reasoning there," he objected. "If your murderer went to such pains to evolve this enigmatic method of killing, why trouble about the sound effects since the death might never be suspected as murder at all?"

"A good point," Blackburn replied. "The answer lies in the fact that we are dealing with a person whose cunning and forethought approaches genius! The average criminal would consider that he had covered his tracks sufficiently by this unconventional method of murder, but our man is well above the average! He covers even the unlikely possibilities, realizing that, should the death by any chance be proved a homicide and investigations begun, we would naturally focus our attentions on the studio. Sooner or later, during the cross-examination, someone is bound to remember those betraying noises.

"Consequently, our criminal reasons, the investigators will dismiss from their minds the possibility of the crime being the work of someone *inside* the studio. He believes that we will deduce that the murder was the work of some outsider who escaped into the darkness." Jeffery paused. "And we certainly would have reasoned that way but for a most remarkable contingency that the murderer could not have known. *His victim has locked the door of the studio!* By that simple action, she has ruined the entire success of that brilliant piece of planning, since obviously it is impossible to fake the escape of a person through a locked door!"

Silence, thick, heavy, brooding. In that moment he was aware of a subtle change in their attitude. It was as though something hot and dangerous had crept into that room, something primitive, newly sensed but old as the day Cain struck Abel to the earth. When he continued, Jeffery's voice had the cold gravity of a judge pronouncing sentence.

"Imagine the feelings of this criminal when he discovered that his clever manipulation of the sound effects had been in vain. But he kept his head. Nothing was suspected at the time. It wasn't until this morning that we discovered murder had been committed, and by that time the criminal could cover the tracks to the best of his ability." He faced them levelly. "That, ladies and gentlemen, is my theory. Now I am waiting to hear from you. What is your opinion?"

Someone gave a chuckle, a harsh cackling that held no suggestion of mirth. Eyes flew here and there, to rest on

Carl von Bethke. The producer shook with some inward amusement so that the loose skin about his throat trembled like the dewlap of a panting hound.

"You ask us what we think of that story?" he smirked. "I think it is the biggest piece of nonsense ever I have heard!" He waved a fat white hand about the studio. "That these people do not laugh in your face is indeed a wonder!"

"Really?" Jeffery said coldly. "And just why do you find it so amusing?"

"Why?" The producer took a half-step forward. His mouth curled in a grin of derision beneath eyes that were jet-black stones. "Surely you can nothing of wireless know to make such silly statements!"

Read thrust his head forward. "Come to the point, Mr. von Bethke!" he snapped. "What do you mean?"

The producer's small head turned on his shoulders. "I mean three things, Mr. Read," he said slowly. "If any such person was to have gone near that table when the lights were out, we in here should have seen him surely! Even as we could see Martin moving there when the lights were out a few minutes ago! And recall—Martin was standing by the effects table during the darkness. If any person had touched the effects, he would know at once!"

Martin said heavily. "I'm willing to wager my month's salary no guy laid a finger on these noises!"

Von Bethke rubbed plump hands and glanced at Jeffery. "You know your Goethe—yes? '*Warum wahlst Du den schuierigen Bergeswieg, wenn der leichte Pfad Dir offensteht?*' You are trying to make something very hard from something very simple! Also this you forget. If those noises were made in here as you say, we must have heard them ourselves. Yet no one in here heard a single sound as you describe!"

Read grunted. "We've only your word—"

"But no," the producer interrupted. "You have the word of every person listening to the play." His smirk broadened. "The control men say the microphone was not switched off until the lights came on. You heard those sounds before that. And if you heard them, those sounds you say came from this studio, then every other person listening in must have heard them also!" He paused and shook his head. "That is the best proof that can be offered. Make your inquiries about it!"

Jeffery did not speak. He stood motionless, his eyes never leaving von Bethke's face. The Chief Inspector turned to Nickerson. "Any way of checking up on that?"

"Certainly," returned the manager promptly. "I'll put a call through to our engineers at Droitwich. They check up on everything that goes over the air from here." He strode across to the wall-telephone and spoke to the switch-girl. As he turned—

"There was a third objection, I believe?" said Jeffery quietly.

"Oh yes—there is a third objection," chuckled von Bethke. "You say that Marlowe was stabbed through the left ear? Then, unless they are miracle workers, the people in this studio are innocent. I can prove that!"

"How?" snapped Read.

"Because,"—and the producer's hands caressed each other—"because all the time the lights were out, Marlowe had her left ear pressed against the keyhole of this door!"

"What's that?" Jeffery's hand, resting on the effects table, clenched. "What did you say?"

The amusement had faded from von Bethke's face. He spoke quietly, his tone almost earnest in its conviction.

"It was because of the new technique. We were, as you saw, acting the play physically as well as orally. So that when Marlowe's lines called for her to listen at a keyhole, I insisted that she carry them out actually. I insisted that she rise from the table, go across to this door and put her ear to this keyhole! Not only did it give added realism to the part, but at that afternoon rehearsal in this studio, it gave just the correct voice-distance from the microphone!"

Jeffery cried, "But how can you be sure—?"

The Chief Inspector cut in on his words. "We'll soon prove it, son! If that girl put her ear to this keyhole, she'd leave a print on the metal! I'll get the boys on that right away!"

George Nickerson gave a sudden ejaculation. His face was glowing, lit as by some inward exciting fire. "Then, if she stood in that position, it can mean only one thing! The hatpin that killed her was thrust through the keyhole—thrust through by somebody standing outside the door!" His voice rose. "And those sounds we heard were actually the noises made by the murderer as he escaped!

That click was probably one of the outer doors of the studio shutting behind him!"

No one had noticed the winking eye of the wall-telephone until that moment. Jeffery was nearest. He stepped forward, unhooked the receiver and spoke for almost a minute. Then he turned. His voice was as brooding as the heavy, frustrated expression that blanked his face.

"That was your engineers," he said levelly. "They are emphatic that no sounds such as I described went over the air on the night of the murder!"

Jeffery swung the wheel of the Bentley and the car turned into Grosvenor Place. In the subdued reflection from the dashboard his face was ineffably weary.

"I thought it was too easy," he muttered bitterly to a silent Chief Inspector beside him. "The whole thing was too damn' pat!" He shrugged. "Well, after all, it was only an experiment. At least it's advanced us one step. We've proved that the trail leads somewhere beyond that studio door."

The Chief Inspector shifted restlessly. "And beyond that studio door is a corridor," he grunted. "Beyond the corridor is a street—and that street leads out into the heart of London! Which means that instead of having to pick out a murderer from six suspects, we now have to pick him out of six million!" He craned his neck over the side of the car and spat disgustedly. "And that, Mr. Blackburn, is what you call advancing!"

Book Two

PLOT FOR A DETECTIVE NOVEL

Man, not satisfied with the mental confusion and unhappiness to be derived from contemplating the cruelties of life and the riddle of the Universe, delights to occupy his leisure moments with puzzles and bugaboos. It may be that in them he finds a sort of catharsis or purging of his fears and self-questionings. Or it may be that his animal faculties of fear and inquisitiveness demand more exercise than his daily round affords. Or it may be sheer perversity.

DOROTHY SAYERS.

I

JOURNEY TO NOWHERE

"Now, here, you see, it takes all the running you can do to keep in the same place. If you want to get somewhere else, you must run at least twice as fast as that!"

Alice Through a Looking Glass.

IT WAS ON the following morning that the documents made their inexplicable appearance. Their arrival brought an evening of tragic surprises to a day that had been grey with disappointment and negation.

Jeffery's ingenious theory regarding the sound effects was torn to shreds by the investigations set in motion by the indefatigable Read on the morning following the young man's discussion at the studio. The Chief Inspector's finger-print experts visited the sound-proof room, photographed the door and placed upon their superior's desk a perfect print of the outlines of a human ear enclosing a keyhole. An additional check-up of a dozen unbiased listeners proved beyond all doubt that the sounds heard by the trio on the night of the murder could not have emanated from the dramatic studio. The hatpin found in the Bayswater flat was passed on to Ted Martin, who completely failed to identify it as the pin missing from the effects. He had gestured to the blunt end and muttered—"Without them fancy jiggers, pins look as alike as a coupla dollar bills. This might be the pin and it might not. I can't say!"

A squad of men were detailed to search the dramatic studio and they obeyed with the thoroughness for which the Criminal Investigation Department is famous—and found nothing. A similar operation was performed at Isabella Simms' flat—with similar results! Read, who flung himself against this wall of frustration with the angry resentment of a small child kicking a post, even attempted an auditing of the guests on the night of the opening. The result was not only failure, but a rather inglorious and painful experience, since the Chief Inspector leaned more toward brute force than tact. And every person who was either in or about the small studio on the night of the murder walked through London with what is known in criminological vernacular as "a tail".

In this manner the Chief Inspector spent the morning at his flat, a morning that was a nightmare whirl of insistently ringing telephones, interviews, callers, snapped orders and snarled vituperation as each avenue of exploration came to a blank end.

Mr. Blackburn remembers it as one of the most unpleasant experiences of his life. He spent the hours lolling about in a dressing-gown, striving to close his ears and disassociate his mind from his companion's concentrated but fruitless energy. "For the first time," he said later, "I could sympathize with old Attaxerxes when he commanded 3000 slaves to thrash an ocean because storms delayed him. I had the same sensation of pent-up irritation against the power of this riddle which remained so inscrutable despite our fervent attempts to probe its secret!"

Over a tasty but unappreciated lunch they discussed the case for the hundredth time, and their unproductive groping touched on the business of the locked studio door. "I still maintain," said Jeffery, toying with his tasteless cigarette, "that the girl was in some way afraid of an attack on her life. It seems to me the only logical reason."

Read looked up from a barely disturbed plate. "Listen, son. Something's just occurred to me! One of the people in that studio must have blabbed about that darkened sequence. Otherwise, how could the murderer have known when Simms was actually listening at that door?"

"Not necessarily," Jeffery returned. He pushed aside his plate and traced idle patterns on the cloth with his finger. "Don't forget that the crowd in the large studio could see the lights from the smaller room reflected through the window of the control room."

Read nibbled a piece of bread. "Then there's that business of the pin! How did it get from the effects table to Simms' flat?"

Jeffery flicked ash from his cigarette. "That, I grant you, is a poser! Again, if the murderer stood outside the door, how could he have obtained that pin from inside? And if the pin among the effects wasn't the weapon used, where the devil is it now? Why should it be missing?"

Read considered. "If the ornament at the top was broken off, the steel portion could have been slipped through the keyhole by someone inside to a confederate on the outside," he pointed out.

"If we consider that," Jeffery said wryly, "we're back where we started! It means that the murder was an inside job after all!"

The Chief Inspector ran a serviette across his lips. "Here's how I see it," he announced. "Bound up somewhere in Simms' past is an enemy who has threatened her. Perhaps she was blackmailing somebody. She learns that he is to attack her on the night of the broadcast during the play, so she locks herself in the studio.

"However, the murder is accomplished. The criminal goes to her flat, waits until the landlady is absent, and makes that search. During this, he loses the pin." He paused and his companion cut in quickly:

"Won't do, Chief!" Jeffery shook his head. "The most illogical part of your theory is the fact that's been sneering at me ever since we began this investigation: *Why was that girl murdered during a radio play?*" He thrust a forefinger at Read. "Consider it! Simms lived alone in her flat! She walked alone through London! There must have been a hundred better opportunities for the murderer to strike!"

He crushed out his cigarette and faced the elder man. "You know, Chief," he said quietly, "there's something very extraordinary about this case—about its very lack of any conceivable form! There's too much bewilderment for the natural flow of events—a feeling of premeditated anticlimax to each fresh discovery. Throughout the whole business there is deliberate contradiction in every move, the sort of thing that recalls the carefully planned and intentional mystification of a brilliant detective story!"

Read frowned. " 'Fraid I haven't got your imagination, son," he grunted. "All I can visualize is a curt note from the A.C. if we don't deliver something in the way of goods very shortly." He glanced up. "And I think you've put your finger on the main point of the case when you ask—why a radio station and why in the middle of a radio play?"

"In other words, the most incongruous and unlikely location," retorted Jeffery. "You see what I mean about deliberate mystification?"

Read said grimly: "I'll keep my two feet on the ground, thank you! I'd prefer to believe that the murder was committed in the studio because, as you said, the location aided the murderer in some way!"

"That theory would have been excellent had my experiments with the sound effects proved successful," replied Jeffery dryly. "Now we must look about for an alternate reason. Frankly, Chief, I'm completely stymied. I can think of no conceivable motive why the murderer should expose himself to the enormous risk of killing this girl in a room filled with people, while half a million strangers listen in to his crime—" His lips clicked shut on the last word. Up came his head. His eyes, narrowed and gleaming, caught and held those of the Chief Inspector. "By Jove!" he whispered.

"What's wrong?" Read demanded.

"The crime with half a million witnesses," murmured Jeffery. "Now, I wonder—" His tone sharpened.

"Listen, Chief, I have an idea—a crazy, outlandish notion that might contain a germ of something really worthwhile! I'm going to take the Bentley and drive out of the city—somewhere—anywhere!"

"But what's the idea, son?"

"It occurred to me that we're tackling this thing from the wrong end!" Jeffery was stuffing cigarettes and matches into his pockets. "I'm going to get away from these surroundings—attempt to blank my mind of everything except the actual crime and start all over again! No, Chief,"—as Read started to speak—"don't ask me anything further. I'll see you back here tonight at dinner!"

The Chief Inspector was late at his office that morning. When he arrived, the parcel was already on his desk.

Read was surprised. He rang for his officer and, on appearance, that gentleman vouchsafed the information that the parcel had arrived with the morning mail. The Chief Inspector dismissed him and, crossing to the desk, sat down and eyed that package somewhat in the manner of a bull terrier regarding a sleeping kitten.

It was a suspiciously unimpressive parcel. Roughly the size of a small cigar-box, it was wrapped in coarse brown paper and the folded ends pasted instead of being tied into place with string. The Chief Inspector's name, together with the address, was printed in capitals with black ink. Read, whom experience had made wise, brought the parcel closer and peered at the postmark. He was rewarded with nothing save the information that the parcel had been posted at the G.P.O, E.C.I. on the previous afternoon.

Frowning, the big man took up a paper-knife and slit the brown wrapper carefully. The paper fell away, to reveal a plain white cardboard box. Pasted on the lid was the typewritten message—"Documents found in the flat occupied by the late Mary Marlowe."

The Chief Inspector almost dropped the paper-knife in astonishment. For some seconds he remained staring at this unexpected manifestation, black brows drawn down over slitted eyes. His hand moved to the bell-push beneath his desk, then hesitated. He shook his head. Instead, he pulled open a drawer and took out a pair of wash-leather gloves, slipping them on his hands. Slowly, cautiously, he reached for the box and his fingers prized open the tight cover. Inside, neatly packed and bound with tape, was a number of folded documents. Read lifted them out, pulled the looped tape free and spread the folded papers before him on the desk. . . .

The Bentley roared up Blackheath Hill as Jeffery's foot depressed the accelerator. Sitting deep in his seat, the young man was only half-conscious of the road before him, a road bisected by the spokes of the driving-wheel. He sucked at an unlighted cigarette between his lips. At the intersection of Charlton Way and Shooters Hill, he swung the car just in time to avoid a collision with a coasting truck, and this move caused him to turn abruptly into the Way. Again he trod the accelerator; the Bentley trembled and leapt forward like a stone from a catapult. . . .

Read picked up the first envelope, drew forth the folded note inside and ran his eyes over the wording. The clipped grey moustache bristled as his florid face tightened. Putting the letter on one side, he took up the next document. This proved to be larger than the letter—smoothed out it resolved into a map of certain portions of Calais. Various localities were enclosed in red circles numbered from one to ten. The Chief Inspector placed this aside for further consideration and selected a fat parchment-like envelope. On the outside, in a similar spidery handwriting to that which marked all the envelopes, were the words—"Instructions for 65". Read opened the missive and screwed his eyes at the spindling calligraphy. Feeling in his pocket, he produced a pair of spectacles, hooked them on his ears and began to scan the handwriting afresh. For some seconds he read, then looked up with a face blank with astonishment. He expelled a long whistling breath of amazement, then his expression gave place to another, a look of grim satisfaction. The swivel-chair creaked as he sat back, eyes glued to that neat, old-maidish handwriting. . . .

On the Plumstead road, the Bentley gave a reproachful choking cough and its speed slackened appreciably. A few moments later, it was seized by a slight paroxysm culminating in a despairing wheeze. Jeffery, transferred to his present surroundings by this phenomena, trod the accelerator furiously. The engine responded by stopping with a curt backfire. Jeffery muttered something uncomplimentary and his eyes moved to the petrol gauge, to find the indicator at zero. He cursed his carelessness and drew the car to a halt opposite the Royal Arsenal.

Climbing out, he stared around for the familiar colours of a petrol-station and picked one out at least half a mile down the road. Shrugging, he tossed aside his sadly chewed cigarette, lit another, and thrusting his hands into his pockets, proceeded to trudge. . . .

The Chief Inspector laid down the last of the documents and raised his eyes, staring thoughtfully into space. Almost unconsciously, he removed his spectacles and slipped them back into his pocket. He rose and crossed to the window, looking out. From time to time he nodded his head heavily, as though in silent approval of secret thoughts. He glanced at his wrist-watch, then with a swift movement crossed to the desk telephone and depressed the key. Carter, his official secretary, answered. "Get Mr. Andrew Newland at the Winchester Hotel," ordered Read. "Tell him to see me at my flat tonight. If he happens to be out—leave a message. It's urgent!" And as Carter murmured obedience, the Chief Inspector added—"And get Bankston for me. I want to see him in here."

Five minutes later, Thomas Bankston, head of the fingerprint bureau, entered. Read was peeling off his gloves. He returned the other's greeting curtly and gestured to the parcel.

"See that, Thomas? I want you to take it, wrapping-paper, box, and contents—and dust them all for prints. Take your time, but do it well! And treat these documents as you would a Shakespeare first folio! They're just about as precious!"

Bankston, man of few words, grunted. Gathering up the parcel, he nodded and disappeared. Read waited until the door closed behind him, then pressed the bell under his desk. The young officer, notebook and pencil in hand, entered. The Chief Inspector nodded to a chair.

"Sit down, Carter!" And as the young officer obeyed—"Did you put through that call to Mr. Newland?"

Carter nodded. "Yes, sir. He took the message himself. Said he would be around about eight o'clock."

"Good!" Read began to pace the floor, hands behind his back, face screwed in an agony of composition. Then he turned. "Ready?" And as Carter raised pencil and notebook, the Chief Inspector said crisply: "I want you to take an urgent wire to M. Faubourg, of the Police Judicaire, Surete . . ."

". . . and you'll have to lend me something to carry it in," Mr. Blackburn was explaining to a mechanic in greasy overalls. "Y'see, my car stalled about half a mile down the road!"

2

Two men sat quietly in the flat at Victoria that night listening to a third man speaking.

The Chief Inspector, standing before the fire-place, paused for a moment and allowed his eyes to rest upon his audience. Jeffery was curled in the arm-chair, his face shadowed, his head nodding from time to time. Opposite him, Andrew Newland sagged limply in his seat like a pricked balloon, a man sucked of all fibre and stiffening, his heavy face the wide-eyed, open-mouthed mask of a buffoon. And like a clown's face it was bloodless, drawn, and deep in those staring eyes was something of the pain and bitterness of the clown's heartache.

Read's voice, gruffly gentle, went on: "And so it is only right, son, that you should know the truth about this girl who called herself Mary Marlowe. Because of the discoveries of this afternoon, it is inevitable that the truth must reach the newspapers in the morning. That's why I've taken this unpleasant task on my shoulders tonight." He paused. "So there you are!"

Andrew Newland shifted, slowly, heavily, as though his extremities were dead weights. He blinked once or twice like a man who comes out of darkness into blinding light. He raised his head.

"It's not—not quite such a surprise as you might think, Mr. Read," he said quietly. An expression too bitter to be called a smile shadowed his lips. "I'm not as clever as most chaps, but I'd have to be the complete fool not to have realized that there was something very wrong with—" he hesitated—"with that girl."

Read said quietly. "I hoped that you'd take it that way, lad." He rambled on, clumsily kind: "Anyhow, perhaps it was best to turn out this way. If it had happened after you were married . . ." the suggestion hung limply.

Newland had been staring at his clasped fingers. He looked up, and for an instant hope lingered in that pale face. "I—I suppose there's no chance of all this being a ghastly mistake—?"

" 'Fraid not, son." The Chief Inspector's tone was weighted. "What I discovered today makes it certain that Simms was up to her neck in crooked business, apart from her past record. *'De mortuis . . .'* " Read hesitated and waved a hand—"Jeffery's much better at this quotation business than I am. But without wishing to libel the dead, it looks as though Simms was a pretty bad lot. She was playing with fire for years and ended by getting herself badly burned."

Newland's jaw set grimly. He ran his fingers through his curling black hair. "You've hit on something else?" he said miserably.

"Yes. That's one of the reasons I asked you around here, son. I've run across some documents which throw a light on certain aspects of the crime. I want you to be in this. But first, there are a few questions I'd like to ask you."

"Anything I can do . . ." muttered the young man.

The Chief Inspector shifted his bulk from one leg to the other. "There is, son. Listen. You told us a few days ago that Simms urged you to get her a part in a radio play. What reason did she give?"

Newland's lip curled. "That she needed the money—to pay her way."

"Before Simms actually had a part in the play," Read went on, "did you give her any indication that she might broadcast over the air?"

The other hesitated. "I—well—I suppose I did," he admitted. "She was terribly keen to get into radio—she was always urging me, in a quiet way, to use my influence with Nickerson to give her parts. Always, of course, on the pretext that she needed the money."

"Of course—of course!" Read rubbed his hands briskly. "It all fits in perfectly!"

Their visitor said wearily: "How does it fit in? To me, the whole thing is upside-down! Every single detail! If this girl is the bad lot that you say she is—why did she take up with me, of all people?"

"Because," said the other quietly, "you were a most effective screen to her background, son. But there was a much more important reason. It was because you were one of the few people who could get her into radio!"

Newland shook a bewildered head. "But why *should* she want to get into radio?" he demanded hoarsely. "Especially if she didn't need the money! Why trouble about it at all if, as you say, she was doing some crooked job for which she was being well paid?"

The Chief Inspector folded his arms, a slow deliberate movement.

"Because," he said, "that *was* Simms' job! She had to get into radio, because the air was the only method left to her of transferring a particularly vital message . . . a message which Isabella Simms had been specially sent to London to get!"

Jeffery started up in his chair as though the seat had suddenly become white-hot. "Good Lord!" he exclaimed.

The elder man was smiling grimly. "That's the answer to the question that's been worrying us all along," he nodded. "Why was the murder committed in a radio studio? Simply because that message had to be stopped from going over the air at all costs! And the murderer took the most efficient means of preventing the transmission!"

"That's it!" Blackburn clicked his fingers. "And it also explains why Simms locked the door of the studio—obviously to prevent outside interference with this important message!" He sat back. "Thank heaven something's falling into place at last!"

"Is it?" Read grunted. "I wonder?"

Newland was staring, his head jerking from one face' to the other during this rapid interplay of words. His eyes fastened on the Chief Inspector and he half-raised himself from the chair. "What is all this about?" he demanded.

Read moved from the fire-place and pulled up a chair. It creaked under his weight as he sat.

"It probably doesn't make much sense to you, son," he commented. "I'd better start at the beginning." He leaned back and crossed his legs.

"What I'm going to tell you is pieced together, not only from actual documents—documents found in Simms' flat—but also from confirmatory evidence given by my old friend Pierre Faubourg, of the Police Judicaire. Together, this information weaves itself into an amazing story.

"Now, recall that we traced Simms' movements as far as September of last year, when she disappeared to the Continent, to turn up again in London last December. This girl fled to Paris because we were getting a little too familiar with her work over here. And in the French capital, she soon found her own level. A week after she arrived, she teemed up with an organization that was building up a flourishing business in the wholesale distribution of dope—cocaine, heroin, opium and all the trimmings. They had a clearing-house in an underground cafe on the Calais waterfront, and from this central point they distributed the drugs throughout France."

He paused and nodded to Jeffery to push over the cigars. Selecting a weed, he brought out a pocket-knife and began to cut the end.

"This organization were keen to build up a similar ring in London," he continued. "To this end, they took Isabelle Simms, had a plastic surgeon work on her face, gave her a new name and sent her back here. She arrived about the beginning of December. Simms had orders to hook up with another shady customer already here. The girl did so and everything appears to have gone swimmingly for some months. Simms and her partner organized the business well. Among the documents is a plan of the city divided into various zones. An agent was to control each of these. A central clearing-house was to be established at Wapping. Simms, because of her chemical knowledge, was to dispense the drugs and her partner's job was to distribute them to the minor agents. In short, toward the end of January, everything was ready for a widespread flooding of London."

The Chief Inspector scratched a match on the tall smoke-stand and applied the light to his cigar. Jeffery was leaning back, eyes half closed, following every word. Newland sat hunched forward, his head bowed.

"In the meantime, however," Read went on, "something happened which threw a monkey-wrench into the whole plan. The Police Nationale in France became aware of the activities of the organization and offered a reward of five thousand francs for information. They got it within two days, a comprehensive account of the entire business. Acting on this, they raided the waterfront cafe and caught the gang red-handed. With one exception. The ringleader, the brains behind the organization, was missing.

"The police were fairly certain of this man's identity. He was a Parisian stockbroker named Paul Viardin and was reputed to have had his finger in a number of unsavoury pies. He was wealthy and rather a power in the city. Therefore, they could do nothing without proof. And they set about obtaining that evidence by means peculiar to the French police. M. Viardin was shadowed day and night. His home was watched. Every piece of correspondence that reached him was first opened and read. His outgoing mail was likewise examined. This vigilance continued for three weeks, and in that time not a single trace of evidence against the man could be found."

Read paused to blow fragrant smoke. He cleared his throat.

"Now, M. Viardin knew exactly what was happening. And with the breaking-up of the organization he recalled Simms to Paris. Eluding the police by a clever trick, he met her and she confided to him her suspicions. Simms said that she was sure her partner in London had betrayed the gang for the reward. Whereupon Viardin gave her instructions to return to London and investigate her partner's private affairs. As soon as she was sure of his treachery, she was to report the fact to him.

"But some method of transmitting this information had to be achieved. Simms could not write nor telegraph, since everything received by Viardin in that manner was closely examined. She must not visit him personally, since the police dogged his every step and, although he had managed to elude them on this occasion, the risk was too great to attempt a repetition. Moreover, in case this meeting had been watched, Simms was ordered never to set foot on the Continent again. Yet Viardin was determined to have the evidence of the traitor's guilt. And this is the manner in which he set about overcoming the difficulty.

"He instructed Simms to return to London and get the proofs of her partner's treachery. Then she must, by fair means or foul, get a part in a radio production! They agreed on two code-words—two words in French. One was to be used in the case of the partner's innocence, the other if he were guilty of the betrayal. Simms was to interpolate this word somewhere in her dialogue during the play! She could even repeat it again and again if necessary. And Viardin, listening in on the Continent, could thus be informed of the partner's innocence or guilt without Simms moving from London." Read nodded grimly. "And that's exactly how it came about!"

From his chair, Jeffery spoke. "Just a minute, Chief! You don't mean to tell me that Viardin was prepared to sit by his wireless set day and night for weeks on end—listening for one particular word out of the millions that poured through his speaker?"

"Not at all," the Chief Inspector returned. "Remember that the casts of all big productions are printed in a hundred wireless journals and magazines. It was only necessary for Viardin to follow the programmes and wait until he saw the name of Mary Marlowe mentioned. In this particular case, he couldn't possibly miss it! Because of the fact that Marlowe took over the part from another actress, there were paragraphs to this effect printed in all the wireless journals, thus giving the business additional publicity!"

Jeffery nodded slowly. "Of course, it's so simple as to be really brilliant! No wonder we never thought of a scheme like this behind the murder."

The Chief Inspector shifted and looked at Newland. "Simms returned to London and got to work. All the time she was filling your mind, son, with the suggestion of putting her in a radio play. About a fortnight ago, she obtained the proofs she sought—evidence showing beyond all doubt that her partner was guilty of betraying the organization for the reward. She redoubled her efforts to get on the air. Then you gave her the greatest opportunity of her life when you requested that she replace the other actress."

Newland groaned. "But how was I to know—"

"That's all right, son," Read grunted. "We don't blame you—you haven't got second sight!" He knocked ash from his cigar into the glass bowl of the stand.

"Now," he continued, "we come to the point where theory must replace facts. Just how the partner became suspicious of Simms, how he discovered that she was to betray him over the air, and by what means he found out about the darkened sequence and Simms' business at the door during the play are matters that we can only guess at until we hear the truth from this man's own lips! On the other hand, Simms undoubtedly knew of his suspicions. Her act in locking the studio door and retaining the key proves that she feared an attempt would be made to stop her giving the code-word. She was, as you remember, playing the part of a Frenchwoman—therefore it would have been the easiest thing in the world to slip that all-important word into the dialogue any number of times. The players were not working from scripts and if the producer did notice that word, which is extremely unlikely, she could have put forward the excuse that she slipped on her dialogue, substituting the first word that came into her head to save a break in the continuity."

Jeffery was gazing into space. "And so her partner waited until she was listening at the door and thrust the hatpin through the keyhole," he murmured. "Yes—it's quite feasible." He looked up. "It wasn't necessary for him to know the script, Chief. If he followed the play, he would have known those lights were out! Especially, as I pointed out before, if he was in the main studio!"

Read's lips tightened. "He was in the studio all right! You saw him there yourself!"

"But there were over two hundred people there—"

"I'll read you a description of the man who claimed that reward for information against the gang," the big man said grimly. He extracted a folded piece of paper from his pocket. "This," he explained, "came from M. Faubourg late this afternoon in answer to my urgent wire." He unfolded the paper, slanted it to the light, and ran his eyes over it.

"Ummm—yes—here we are! Aged between twenty-five and thirty . . . average height . . . slim build . . . very dark eyes set in pale-complexioned face—"

"Steinie Rodda!" cried Blackburn, and jumped from his seat.

The Chief Inspector nodded heavily and slipped the message back into his pocket.

"You've got it, son! Steinie Rodda was Simms' partner in this drug business—the man who betrayed the French gang—and the little cherub who murdered Isabelle Simms at the radio studio!"

A heavy lorry rumbled past the flat, setting the windows quivering in their frames and causing the glasses on the sideboard to ring gently. This died away and no sound was heard in that room of indrawn breaths save the cheerful pulsation of the mantel-clock. Jeffery stood motionless before his chair, fingers fumbling automatically for his cigarette-case. Andrew Newland sat looking undecidedly from one man to the other. Suddenly Blackburn wheeled on the elder man.

"But, Chief, if you received that information this afternoon, where is Rodda now? Surely you didn't wait—"

The Chief Inspector pushed him back into his seat. "Sit down, son—sit down," he growled. "Are you trying to teach me my business? Take it from me that Rodda's being taken care of!"

"But where *is* he?"

"Connolly and Donlin are waiting outside his hotel," Read said gruffly. "They called there at five o'clock this afternoon. Our slippery friend had gone out—the desk-clerk didn't know where. He's taken no baggage. I told the boys to wait at the hotel until he came back and then to bring him around here."

Jeffrey glanced at the clock. "But that's four hours ago! He can't have been away all this time. They must have missed him."

Read showed his teeth. "Yeah? Then they'll both go back to pounding the pavements before they can say knife!"

Jeffery's restless fingers toyed with his cigarette-case. "They must find him, Chief! Can't you understand that Rodda is the key to the whole riddle?"

"There's no riddle now, son." The Chief Inspector chewed his cigar. "The whole thing's open-and-shut! Steinie murdered Simms to prevent her squealing on him. He was in the studio that night, remember? He escaped through the back corridor, slipped out of the side door and drove away in his car. We heard him!"

"Yes, but—"

"Never mind your buts!" The cigar protruded truculently. "The whole thing's as plain as a Belisha beacon! On the following morning, Steinie remembered that the documents in Simms' flat would give him away, so he drives over to get them and—" his words splintered and the cigar dropped as Read's lips fell apart.

Jeffery was watching him grimly. "Go on," he said heavily. "Continue, Oedipus. Steinie drives over to get those documents—only to find that someone has forestalled him, wrecked the flat and found the papers." He snapped suddenly. "The case is open-and-shut, all right—except for the two most important details!"

Read did not speak. Outside the open window, something that may have been the shadow of a prowling cat passed quickly. Jeffery rose and stabbed a finger at the elder man. "Before you can call this case open-and-shut," he rapped, "I want you to answer two questions: *Who took the documents from Simms' flat and sent them to you? And why were they sent?"*

The young man began to pace the room. "And do you know why those documents were sent to you? Because they constitute an almost water-tight case against Steinie Rodda! And that brings us to the question of *who* sent them!"

Read grunted. "Perhaps the person who found them was prompted by a desire to aid justice—"

"Rats! A barrel of rats! If this person wanted to aid justice, why weren't the documents delivered in person? Why were they sent anonymously? And with such blatant anonymity! Complete lack of fingerprints and every possible trace of the sender obliterated!" Jeffery shook his head. "No, Chief! That person wasn't aiding the cause of justice. He sent those documents to incriminate Rodda—and he wants to remain anonymous because he's up to his ears in this dirty business himself!"

"But how could he incriminate Rodda," Read argued, "when there's no mention of Rodda made in those documents? I had to send away to the Police Judicaire to find out the description of the man who claimed the reward before I recognized the likeness to Steinie!"

"Because this person knows all about it," Jeffery retorted. "I said he was deep in this business and so he is! He knows about the Simms-Marlowe masquerade—every detail of it. That's why, when he sent the documents, he knew that you'd make a full investigation and that investigation would eventually build a perfect case about Rodda!"

The Chief Inspector shook a stubborn head. "No, Jeff. It's too far-fetched! I'm satisfied that Rodda's our man!"

Jeffery walked round the chair occupied by Newland, who sat with faintly bewildered expression, listening to this rapid duologue in silence. He looked down at the elder man.

"Chief," he said quietly. "Do you remember my reconstruction of the time element in connection with that wrecked flat? I figured that the search must have taken place during the absence of the landlady, somewhere between eleven and twelve on the night of the murder. Consequently, that searcher, the person who found the documents, must have known of Simms' death, must have been aware of it hours before it was published in the newspapers! Therefore, it must have been someone who was in that studio at the time of the murder!" His words slowed. "And is it too fantastic to suggest that it was the murderer himself who searched that flat?"

"Now, now—son," began Read when Jeffery cut in.

"Look to the motive—the motive that animated the dispatch of those documents to you! We can brush aside as absurd the idea of some innocent bystander who wishes to aid the cause of justice. Innocent bystanders don't wreck a stranger's flat at midnight in search of material to aid the cause of justice! Therefore, we are forced back on the more logical premise—that the documents were sent to you with the intention of incriminating Rodda. And who could possibly wish to do this but the actual murderer?"

Read said slowly: "You don't believe Steinie Rodda murdered Simms?"

"Of course I don't," snapped Jeffery. "And that's the very reason I'm worried sick over his non-appearance here!"

"Cut out the riddles," grunted the other. "What do you mean by that?"

"Can't you see?"—the young man made an impatient gesture. "The murderer has gone to endless risk to build up a clever case against Rodda—a case that would convince any jury of his guilt! Granted it's circumstantial—but then ninety per cent of murderers are convicted on circumstantial evidence. And Rodda would be convicted without the jury leaving the box! His record would be against him, for one thing! For another, he had ample opportunity, being actually on the scene of the crime at the time of the murder. Thirdly, he had the strongest motives in the world for killing Simms at that particular time! I tell you—once this case came into court, Rodda would be as good as dead!"

"Well—?"

"The murderer knows that there can be only one possible flaw in his brilliant scheme. Rodda may have an alibi for the time that Simms was murdered! And if this is so, he can destroy that carefully woven net about him simply by opening his lips. Consequently, the murderer means to prevent that at all costs! The entire success of his plan rests on the fact that Rodda must die before he can prove his innocence!"

The Chief Inspector was on his feet. "Rodda . . . dead!" he exclaimed incredulously. "Jeff! You don't mean that this unknown would murder . . .?"

"Why not?" snapped Jeffery. "The real murderer is out to save his own skin, at all costs!"

The big man's florid face had gone pale. "But if Rodda was murdered . . . why, it would only prove his innocence . . . prove that the murderer of Simms was still at large!"

Jeffery folded his arms. "Not necessarily," he said gravely. "You forget one important point, Chief: *We can't be sure if Simms had a chance to put over the code-word during the play!'* If she did put it over before she was killed, *there's another party out after Rodda's life—a* life that must be taken in return for his betrayal of the drug organization!"

The young man measured his superior with shadowed eyes.

"And the murderer realizes this! He believes that if we find Rodda murdered, *we can never be sure whether or not that killing is the work of the drug organization!* The murderer believes that we would tell ourselves that Rodda, the murderer of Simms, met a just end. The hue and cry for his killer would automatically move to France and we, he believes, would consider the Simms case closed—"

He broke off as the door-bell hummed into his words. Both men congealed, only their eyes meeting in mute interrogation. Andrew Newland rose from his chair and stood awkwardly, his eyes searching the faces of his hosts. Read and Jeffery were oblivious of his presence. Five dragging seconds passed and then the Chief Inspector called:

"Come in."

The door opened. Dennis Connolly, a lumbering, moon-faced Irishman, moved into the room. He was obviously ill at ease and stood inside the door fumbling with his hat. The Chief Inspector strode forward, his cold eyes lacing the detective from head to foot. And as Connolly did not speak—

"Where the devil have you been?" Something curiously hollow robbed Read's snarl of its bite. "I told you to wait and bring Rodda along! Didn't you find him?"

"Yes, Chief—we found him all right!" Connolly dropped his head and surveyed the other from the corners of his eyes. "Yeah—we found him. Lyin' on the floor of his room with a hole blown in his chest!"

"What's that?" Read's tone was dry.

The big detective said woodenly. "It happened about twenty minutes ago, Chief. Someone got into Steinie Rodda's room before us and blew the livin' daylights outa him!"

3

The proprietors of the Hotel Splendide, that ten-storied edifice overlooking Hyde Park, will tell you that their vast marble mausoleum is built within sight of the infamous "Tyburn trees" of gruesome memory. In this, their proud association with violence and horror is, of course, definitely in the abstract; it is deliberately fostered to give a background of romantic tradition to something that is the epitome of modernity. These sentiments, however, took an abrupt *volte-face* when the murder of Mr. Steinie Rodda in room number 231 brought their association with crime to an alarmingly concrete basis.

Twenty minutes later, Chief Inspector William Read, with Jeffery and Detective Connolly, pushed their way through the revolving doors that led into the softly lighted lobby. Read had waited only long enough to dispatch Andrew Newland to his own hotel and ring through to Miles Conroy's home. Then Jeffery had packed Read and the elephantine Connolly into the Bentley and careered to the Hotel Splendide as fast as spinning tyres could take them.

The three men were met in the foyer by a sallow-faced, frock-coated manager, who rippled excited explanations in broken English and wrung his hands in extravagant Gallic gestures. Read brushed him aside like a pestiferous fly and began to ascend the broad staircase. From pillared alcoves, bellboys watched their progress with wide eyes, and the obsequious faces of black-coated clerks peered at them from corners. At the top of the stairs, the Chief Inspector wheeled on the manager, who was trotting at his heels. "Push off," he snapped. "We'll call you when we need you!" He halted and looked along the carpeted corridor.

Some distance away, Detective Donlin, a lean dry stick of a man, paced restlessly before a door. He turned at the sound of voices and came forward. "Doc. Conroy's inside," was his greeting as Read advanced to meet him.

The Chief Inspector nodded. "Now that you're both here," he barked, "let's get down to facts! What happened?"

Donlin glanced at Connolly and the latter took it on himself to explain. "There's not much to tell, Chief," he mumbled. "We hung about like you told us, waiting in the foyer. About half an hour ago, a bellboy comes downstairs and says something to the clerk on the desk. He beckons us over and tells us that Rodda musta come in the side entrance, because the bellboy's just seen him go into his room.

"Ted and I starts upstairs and as soon as we gets to the top, there's the sound of a shot. An' a crash. We rushed down to this room—the door's open and it's black as pitch inside. Ted goes to the light switch and presses it down, but nothing happens—"

"We found out afterwards that the electric globe had been removed," supplemented Donlin.

Connolly nodded. "So we rings for the manager and he brings up a torch. We flashes it around and there by the open window is Rodda, sprawled in a heap with a hole in his chest. The revolver, an automatic, was on the floor beside him. Outside the open window is a fire escape leading to the ground. Rodda looked like he'd just come in. He still had on overcoat, gloves, and a scarf and he was facing the open window when he was shot." The big detective frowned. "If you ask me, Chief, someone was waiting for him outside that window—"

"I didn't ask you," Read snapped. "You're the biggest pair of bone-headed gorillas that ever cluttered up the Department! I might have known that you'd bungle the whole thing!"

Donlin flushed. "But, sir, how could we foresee that Rodda would come in through the side entrance?"

"You couldn't foresee a good dinner!" stormed the Chief Inspector. "I suppose you were doing crossword puzzles down there while the murderer made his getaway!" He turned on his heel. "Ach—! You make me sick!"

He strode into the room, a silent Jeffery at his heels. The two detectives followed sheepishly at some little distance.

Miles Conroy was already at work on the body, which had fallen by the window of the room. A small table by the wall had been overturned in the crash. The Medical Officer, his slim dapper figure looking very svelte in a dinner-suit, was in a bad temper. He was kneeling beside the body and raised a flushed face as the others entered.

"So here you are!" he snapped. "What's the idea of calling me out at this hour? Don't I get any private life? I was in the middle of a bridge game!"

Read strode over to him. "Cut out the cackle, Mac," he said tersely. "This is trouble with a capital T." He nodded to the body. "What happened to him?"

Conroy rose and wiped his hands delicately on a handkerchief. "Got an automatic bullet smack in the chest," he said sourly. He touched one outflung hand with a fastidious, patent-leather toe and Jeffery, looking down, saw that the gloved fingers were pulped and bloody. "Made a grab for that gun with his left hand, it appears," Conroy grunted. "There's black powder all over those mangled fingers."

"Anything else?"

Conroy considered. "Weapon fired at fairly close quarters—eighteen inches to two feet away, I should say. It was an automatic. I believe they found it on the floor beside the body." He stared down. "That seems to be all. Fairly straight-out shooting."

The Chief Inspector teased his moustache. "How do you think it happened, Mac?"

Conroy shrugged. "That's your job, Read! I'm no flatfoot. However, from what I can see, I should say that this fellow went to the window—or perhaps he was called—and someone popped him from outside. He dropped and brought the table down with him. That's the best I can do."

"And the wounds are in keeping with that idea?"

"Decidedly!" The Medical Officer crossed to the round table in the centre of the room and began to repack his bag. "If that's all you want, I'll get along," he suggested. "And I'll ring a couple of the boys to collect your friend on my way home."

"All right!" Read nodded and the little doctor moved off with a grunt. Jeffery walked around the body, his eyes taking in every detail. He looked up. "Dennis—you say that the automatic was found under the window?"

Connolly advanced into the room. "That's so, Mr. Blackburn." He crossed to the table and picked up an object wrapped in a handkerchief. Unfolding it, he exhibited a small black automatic. "One shot fired from it," he said laconically. "And there's blood on the barrel where that chap grabbed at it."

Read had turned and was listening. "Seems funny to me that the gun should be found in the room when the murderer was outside," he observed.

Jeffery shook his head. "I don't think we can make much mystery out of that," he said moodily. "Rodda grabbed at that gun on the point of explosion. This would probably knock it out of the other's hand. As that hand was protruding through the window, naturally the gun would fall inside!"

"Then why didn't the murderer pick it up?"

"He hadn't time," Jeffery pointed out. "Remember, Connolly and Donlin were racing along that corridor outside. The murderer scarcely had time to get away—let alone think about retrieving his gun." He shook his head. "I'm not worrying about the actual method of killing. That seems straight-out and plain. Our headache lies now in the problem of who did this murder—whether it was the work of Simms' killer or a thrust from the organization that Rodda betrayed!"

The Chief Inspector made a helpless movement of his hands. "P'raps the prints on the gun might help us."

"If any," returned Blackburn bitterly. His face was etched with some expression very close to despair. "Don't you see, Chief, that even if we can determine that point, it doesn't help us at all! We're no nearer the solution of the murder or the identity of the criminal." He flung out his arms. "Look at us now! For all our brain-fagging theories, for all your spade-work, we've merely been spinning a squirrel's cage round and round. Here we are—three days after that girl's murder—three days of ceaseless effort—and we've advanced not a single step! We're in exactly the same place as we started!"

There was a pause. Then the Chief Inspector squared his shoulders and thrust out a jaw like a ploughshare.

"All right," he rapped. "We're through with theories—finished with this deduction business! This looks like one case where it won't work. Instead, we'll see where some good old-fashioned strong-arm methods can get us!" He rubbed his big hands together. "I'm going to put the fear of God through this entire hotel!" He wheeled on Connolly. "Let's have that manager up here. We'll start the works on him!"

A shuddering yawn racked Jeffery's body as the big detective shambled away. The young man crossed the room and flung himself down in a chair, rubbing weary eyes. He spoke without looking at Read.

"Chief—before you begin your inquisition, there's one thing I'd like to know. Was Steinie Rodda left-handed?"

Read's lips were tight. "Not that I know of, son. Why?"

"He was ambidextrous?"

"I don't think so. What's the idea, anyhow?"

Jeffery leaned back in his chair and closed his eyes. "I'm curious to know why, if Rodda was normally right-handed, he grabbed at his assailant's gun with his left hand!"

II

DARKNESS IS DANGER!

Thy hand, great Anarch, lets the curtain fall;
And universal darkness buries all.

POPE, *The Dunciad.*

THE dragnet was out for Olga Lusinska.

From the harassed hours of research following the murder of Steinie Rodda, one important fact was gleaned. The person who had waited outside the window of Rodda's apartment was the Russian actress.

The desk-clerk testified that, at half past three that afternoon, a telephone-call had come through for Rodda. About four o'clock the man had gone out of the hotel. A few minutes after nine o'clock that night, a woman had come in, approached the desk-clerk, and requested that he put a call through to Rodda's apartments. The clerk had done so, but, receiving no answer, concluded that the occupant was still away. The woman, who had given no name, seemed upset at this information. She had lingered for some time in the foyer, and at length she went away.

Half an hour later, the caretaker and his wife, who occupied a back flat in the hotel, noticed a woman climb the fire escape to the first-floor landing and stand peering through the window into a room. Assuming that it was a guest locked out of her apartments by some mischance, he had called to the woman. She had not answered—instead, she covered her face and almost ran down the fire escape and out across the back garden into the street. She passed quite close to the caretaker. This was some ten minutes before the actual shooting occurred. The caretaker had then gone back to his own rooms. He could not say if the woman returned.

Both witnesses were closely interrogated as to a description of the woman. Both agreed on an identification that could fit only one person.

Olga Lusinska!

The bellboy who had seen Rodda going to his room reported that the man was dressed just as he was found and he had entered the hotel either very ill or very drunk. He had swayed along the corridor muttering to himself, his fumbling, uncertain movements those of a man in the last stages of intoxication. It had taken him some little time to unlock the door of his room.

There were no fingerprints found on the automatic revolver. Neither Read nor Jeffery was particularly disappointed in this.

With the confirmation of Lusinska's presence in the hotel that night, the organization of Scotland Yard was once more set in motion. Two detectives visited the actress's flat in St. John's Wood, only to find it empty. Then, indeed, did the Chief Inspector exercise those methods which he termed "good and old-fashioned". He sent a squad to comb Lusinska's rooms; they discovered nothing more than the evidence of a hasty and unpremeditated flight. Read, despite the lateness of the hour, dragged Carl von Bethke from his bed and subjected him to a merciless interrogation. That gentleman would not—or could not—help them in the slightest way. He stated that he had not seen Lusinska for the past two days and stuck to his point with the tenacity of a limpet.

Then it was that Read threw out his dragnet and the entire country became one wide Cyclopean eye searching for the elusive actress. And at three o'clock in the morning, the weary investigator moved back to the flat and fell upon his bed.

Despite this, Read was in his office at nine o'clock on the following morning, spectacles hooked on his ears, scanning the reports that had already begun to filter in. Not so Jeffery! Mr. Blackburn slept through half the morning, a restless nightmare tossing that mocked at the term "repose". He was awakened by the shrilling of the telephone. Hobbling in flapping slippers to the instrument, he heard the voice of Andrew Newland on the wire. Newland informed him that he had received an urgent message to return to the Towers. His aunt's illness had taken a decided turn for the worse. If Blackburn or Read wished to get in touch with him, he expected to be there for the next few days. Jeffery thanked him, muttered polite condolences regarding his relative's condition, and hung up. It was then almost noon. Mr. Blackburn decided to combine breakfast and lunch and set about the ordering of it.

Thus it was almost two o'clock before he made his way to the Chief Inspector's office, eager to know what progress Read's efforts had made. Read's chair, however, was vacant, his room untenanted. Jeffery passed through to the outer office where he encountered Dennis Connolly brushing his hat on his sleeve. The detective nodded as the young man entered.

"Anything fresh?" queried Jeffery, sitting on the edge of the table and lighting a cigarette.

"Very little," Connolly assured him. "Th' Chief's gone down to that studio to see if they've heard anything of that Russian dame." He pulled on his hat and jerked at the lapels of his coat.

"And where might you be going?" asked Blackburn.

The detective thrust a ham-like hand into his pocket. "Th' Chief and I went through Rodda's personal belongings this morning," he explained, "and among the things we found this." He produced a small key and held it up.

Jeffery nodded. "And just what does it unlock?"

"It's branded 'United Safe Deposit'," he returned, twisting the key in his fingers. "I'm going down to see what it is that Steinie keeps hidden away so securely. I'm on my way now."

"And so am I!" Jeffery got on his feet. "We are as Pylades and Orestes in this thing, Dennis! And if you can pack your gargantuan frame into the Bentley, I'll drive you down!"

A slow grin spread across Connolly's face. "O.K., Mr. Blackburn. Let's go!"

The offices of the United Safe Deposit Company occupied the ground floor of a building in Chancery Lane. Jeffery drew the car to a halt on the opposite side of the road and the two men climbed out, crossed the street, and entered the building. They were directed to the basement, one end of which was partitioned off with a steel grille. Behind this barricade, half a dozen clerks worked' industriously, and from somewhere near came the squashy thud of a "silent" typewriter.

There was a rather irritating delay while Connolly explained to a clerk and the clerk to an accountant and the accountant to his direct superior. Eventually, however, a stoop-shouldered man in a shabby black silk office-coat very shiny about the cuffs came forward. "Our Mr. Robinson will take care of you," the chief accountant promised, and the shabby little man tugged at his drooping moustache and gave them a watery smile of acknowledgment.

Mr. Robinson pressed a button under the desk and the electric grille slid back noiselessly. Connolly, followed by Blackburn, passed through. The clerk led them through a gigantic Catherine-wheel of a door and they passed into a long, brilliantly lit corridor flanked by walls of steel. Their footsteps rang and echoed back on the steel insulated flooring. On either side were more of these monstrous doors, guardians of strongrooms holding heaven alone knew what secrets. Then the steel walls moved closer and became reticulated with squares studded with a thousand keyholes. In this portion, their guide paused and turned back to the big detective.

"What is the number of your key?" he asked.

Connolly screwed his eyes at the tiny object and read the number aloud. Mr. Robinson nodded, ran his eyes over the array of boxes, and paused at one set low near the floor. He bent and slipped his master-key in the lock, clicked it back and gestured to the detective to do likewise. Connolly crouched and inserted his key. He gave the shallow drawer a tug and it slid open in his hands.

The drawer contained only one object. This was a circular tin canister, a few inches deep and roughly eighteen inches wide. It glittered in the strong light. Connolly lifted it out and weighed it in both hands.

"Reasonably heavy," he grunted, passing the canister to Jeffery. "What do you make of it?"

Head on one side, Blackburn shook the can gently. Something moved within. He lowered the canister and measured it with thoughtful eyes. "If it didn't sound perfectly ridiculous," he murmured, "I'd wager that this was a reel of cinema film."

Connolly's expression was incredulous. "Movie stuff? Why should anyone go to this trouble over a tin of that?"

Mr. Robinson, who had been a silent spectator of this polemic interlude, coughed. "It isn't quite as absurd as it may seem, gentlemen," he said. "We have all manner of queer things stored away in these vaults, although we don't know one quarter of the contents. But I can personally vouch for a pair of false teeth on a dental plate, a set of child's marbles, and a bunch of imitation flowers that—"

Connolly interrupted what promised to be a lengthy predication. "Never mind about that," he said curtly. "Let's get this thing open!" A pocket-knife appeared in his fingers and he pulled open the strongest blade, "Just hold that can on the floor, would you, Mr. Blackburn?"

Jeffery obeyed. The detective knelt beside the container and inserted the blade under the lid. He probed for some seconds, then gave a mighty wrench and the steel snapped like a dry stick. The edge of the tin gaped. Connolly muttered something, tossed the broken knife on the floor and laid muscular hands on the canister. The lid flew off with a spiteful *zing* and rolled across the room.

Inside lay a wide black roll of cinematograph film, the loose end secured by a rubber band.

Without a word, Jeffery stooped and lifted out the reel, slipping off the constricting fastener. Disengaging, the loose end, he unwound twenty feet of the perforated celluloid and held the strip up to the light. Connolly, sucking a bleeding thumb, watched him meditatively. The stoop-shouldered clerk eyed the film-littered floor rather anxiously.

Blackburn was staring at the tiny thumbnail partitions of the film, his face frowning. Running the length of the strip, the neatly lettered title of the picture repeated itself.

Kinofilm Company
Presents

DEATH IN THE FIELD

A KINOFILM SILENT SHORT SUBJECT

"Kinofilms, eh?" murmured Jeffery. "Now, what have we stumbled upon here?"

He began to rewind the film on the spool. Clipping the rubber band in position, he replaced the reel in the canister and, with Connolly's aid, jammed the lid into position. Then he thrust the whole into his companion's hands. "Take charge of this," he said crisply. "The sooner we get it safe inside the Yard, the better!"

The big detective was eyeing him curiously. "What do you make of it?" he asked, tucking the canister beneath his arm. "Why should Rodda go to such trouble over a reel of movie film?"

"Ours not to reason why—as yet," retorted Blackburn evasively. He bent and picked up the broken penknife, slipping it into the detective's coat pocket. Then he turned and nodded to the clerk. "Thank you, Mr. Robinson."

The other inclined his head. He led the couple through the plated corridor to the grille. A few minutes later Blackburn and his companion were standing on the pavement, waiting an opportunity to slip through the stream of traffic to their car on the opposite side of the street. Connolly spied a break in the procession, a gap of twenty yards between a heavy lorry and a big blue sedan car, crawling at snail's pace along the road.

"Come along," he said, and the two men began to cross. Connolly was in the lead, some few feet in front of Jeffery, that precious canister hugged closely to his body.

What happened then occurred with such speed that the eye could scarcely follow it.

Connolly was almost to the centre of the road and the big blue car was roughly ten feet away from him. Suddenly it roared like some angry behemoth and leapt forward with an abrupt pouncing movement. That heavy wedge-shaped radiator flashed like a guillotine knife straight for the astonished detective, who stood petrified in its path. . . .

"Look out!" screamed Jeffery.

And in that split second, Connolly jumped forward. One mudguard brushed his side, sending him spinning across the street. The can of film went bowling into the gutter. The blue car twisted violently, danced madly on two wheels and roared down a side street.

Blackburn rushed over. Already a crowd had gathered, and amid this swelling tide of perturbation Dennis Connolly was picking himself up. Jeffery waited only to see that he was uninjured, then retrieved the canister from the culvert. When he returned, his companion was grunting something at an anxious policeman. Connolly turned as Jeffery approached.

"Let's get going," he scowled, brushing the mud from his clothes. His big hands were trembling. An angry red graze, pricked with blood, covered one side of his face from forehead to chin. "Yes—I'm all right!" he replied to Jeffery's unspoken inquiry. "Did you get the film?"

"I did!" returned Blackburn grimly. They pushed their way through the crowd and climbed into the Bentley. Neither spoke until they were clear of the street. Then Connolly spat on his handkerchief and wiped the blood from his face. "You didn't get that swine's number, I suppose?"

Jeffery's tone was abysmal with regret. "I didn't! It all happened so quickly. I was too busy watching you and looking after the film. Because that's what he wanted—that canister!"

And Connolly repeated. "What do you make of it all?"

"Only that someone is very anxious to prevent us seeing that film," Jeffery retorted. "Apparently, they mean to stop at nothing to hinder the screening." He glanced at his companion. "I'm going to drop you at the nearest pub for a stiff brandy, Dennis, then I'm driving back to the Yard as fast as the car will take me. If the Chief's there, we'll probe the secret of 'Death in the Field' before anything else unforeseen occurs!"

Mr. Blackburn was given a further illustration of Robbie Burns' contention regarding the best-laid schemes when he pushed his way into the Chief Inspector's office ten minutes later, to find the room untenanted and Read's chair vacant. With that precious tin of film under his arm, he crossed the floor, opened the door of Carter's office and addressed the uniformed secretary, who was dancing his fingers over the keys of a typewriter.

"Where's the Chief?"

Carter's fingers poised in mid air as he looked up. "Mr. Read came in and went away again only a few minutes ago, Mr. Blackburn," he said. "I told him you had called—and he left this note for you." The secretary pulled open a drawer and produced a folded slip of paper. He held it out. "I was to give you this as soon as you came in."

Jeffery nodded. He unfolded the message, a sheet from a scribbling-pad scrawled with Read's large, angular calligraphy. The wording was brief and to the point: *On something that may turn out important. May be very late. Don't wait up for me.* Jeffery read. He crumpled the note in his fingers and tapped a toe, perpending. Eager as he was to screen this film, he felt it would be unfair to do so without the company of the Chief Inspector. *Don't wait up for me.*

That appeared to indicate Read's absence all night. In which case, the showing of the film must be postponed until tomorrow. It was disappointing but unavoidable. Jeffery balanced the container in his hands.

"Oh, Carter?"

"Yes, Mr. Blackburn?"

"You see this container? I want you to lock it in the Chief Inspector's strongroom."

That important ceremony completed, Jeffery left Scotland Yard, deliberated for a few moments between driving or walking, and decided to walk. He strolled in the direction of the Embankment. It was, he felt sure, going to be a singularly lengthy afternoon. He considered the possibility of a picture show, then discarded the idea. There was only one film he wanted to see and that was for private exhibition only. He was in much the same mood as the afternoon he had visited the Bayswater flat, conscious of the same urge, inspired by this latest development, to grapple afresh with the amazing problem.

Two outstanding questions ticked and vibrated in his mind. What important connection was there between the Kinofilm reel and the murder of Isabelle Simms and her treacherous partner? Or were the two murders separate cases, the latter killing the work of the drug organization? That was the point that blocked every theory, the barrier to each fresh line of investigation.

Despair settled about Jeffery's heart. He realized that he was already threshing helplessly in that sticky web which the criminal had spun so widely. Had Rodda been killed by the drug ring? If so, the Hotel Splendide case was a complete and self-contained business, entirely outside of the murder at the broadcasting studio. In which case they could dismiss it from their minds and leave the responsibility to the Police Judicaire. *But could they?* Was not this just the conclusion that the murderer of Simms wanted—provided that he was also the murderer of Rodda? But how could he be sure? Desperately he fumbled, groping in a shadowy maze of conjecture, dragging shackled feet on the quicksands of doubt.

"The whole case is absolutely without parallel," Jeffery. muttered. "With every other investigation, there have been loose ends somewhere to grasp. In this business, the whole is rounded into a perfectly logical case that simply defies analysis!"

Yet, somewhere, something was wrong. The whole thing was too compact, the ends dovetailed too neatly. Steinie Rodda had murdered Isabelle Simms to prevent her betraying him to the drug organization. By some ironic mischance, he had struck too late! She had passed on the information *before* her death. And just retribution, in the form of an avenging member of the gang, had shot Steinie.

All loose ends tied. The perfect plot.

The perfect plot! Too perfect for real life! It had everything—excitement, suspense, a piquant dash of irony and a surprising though perfectly logical ending! The perfect plot! That was what was wrong! The whole thing was too artificial, too mechanical, too mathematically balanced for real life. It was like some ordered fiction plot in which the characters moved, step by step, along the tortuous path planned for them. And yet this was no puppet-show enclosed between cardboard covers. It was not printer's ink that had gushed from the bullet-wound in Rodda's chest.

Then somebody clapped him on the shoulder and Jeffery dropped out of the clouds of conjecture with a bump. He blinked at the grin that split the cheerful face before him.

"Rollo!" he cried.

"Hello, you broody old owl," said Rollo Morgan, and pumped the outstretched hand delightedly.

Jeffery's smile chased the shadows from his eyes. "Gosh, Rollo—you're positively obese! Is that what married life does for you?"

Blackburn had not seen Rollo Morgan for close on twelve months. Their slender acquaintanceship which had begun at Oxford did not ripen into actual friendship until the sinister business of the Mannikin Murders. It was Rollo who had begged Blackburn to step in and investigate the dark cloud of witchcraft and murder which threatened the very existence of the unhappy Rochester family. The successful conclusion of this case brought fresh laurels to Jeffery and one of the prettiest wives in England to his friend, for it was only a few months later that Miss Jan Rochester became Mrs. Rollo Morgan. Marriage appeared to have agreed with the cheerful, uncomplaining Rollo, for there was a suggestion of a double chin and an undeniable bulge about his waistline that bespoke satisfactory home comforts.

"And how is Jan?" Jeffery was saying.

"Right as a bank," Rollo assured him. "Although she's in a bit of a stew at the moment," he added. "Our maid walked out on us last week and we've had the fun o' Cork getting another."

Jeffery eyed his companion's corpulence and grinned. "Wouldn't do you any harm to scrub a few area steps, my lad."

Rollo grimaced. "I dashed well look like doing it, too! Good domestics are rare as hen's teeth, old boy! We thought we had one, Annie Peters, but she wanted two half-days off every week, besides Saturday and Wednesday nights!"

Jeffery smiled. The same old Rollo, garrulous as ever, settling down more or less easily into the groove of domesticity. One of those fortunate souls whom Time seems to ignore, perhaps because they themselves ignore Time.

". . . Jan asked her why she left her last place," Morgan was rambling on. "She told the wife that it was no place for a young girl, because she couldn't get away to picture shows and dances and there wasn't a phonograph or a radio set anywhere in the house—"

Mr. Blackburn flinched. "Don't mention wireless, please!"

Rollo paused, his mouth open, then he nodded comprehendingly. "Of course! You're working on this crime at the B.B.C. The newspapers are full of it."

"Are you following it at all?"

Morgan shook his head. "No, thank you," he said promptly. "Neither is Jan. We've had our fill of crime and detection. It's all terribly interesting until it strikes home, as we know!"

"You're very wise to ignore it," Jeffery assured him. "I only wish I could do the same!" He shrugged. "I suppose I could if I made up my mind about it. Officially, I've been sacked!"

"Sacked?"

Jeffery nodded. "Tried out one or two theories that turned around and bit me," he explained. "Consequently, the Chief Inspector is a trifle terse about my co-operation. He's tipped deduction into the dust-bin and dusted off the rack and the thumbscrews. At the moment, the Chief is spiritually in tune with Caligula, who maintained that a few moments' force was much more effective than an hour of eloquence."

Rollo chuckled, his twinkling eyes sinking into chubby cheeks. "How is the old war-horse? Still breathing fire and pawing the steel-shod hoof?"

"More or less. But there's a pretty valid excuse for his fireworks at the moment. This business has us both worried!" Blackburn's expression was wry. "Frankly, Rollo, for the time being, I'm completely at a loose end—haven't the faintest idea what to do."

"I have!" Rollo grasped his arm. "Now is your chance to come along and say hello to Jan and have a bite of dinner with us. Now, don't hedge. . .!" as Jeffery began to murmur. "You've admitted to being at a loose end!"

Jeffery hesitated a moment. Then he grinned and shook his companion's hand. "Rollo," he said, "you're a very substantial spirit of good! You have saved me from a fate worse than death! Lead on, my trusty Virgil!"

2

It was fortunate that Mr. Blackburn decided to walk from the Morgans' house in Chelsea Bridge Road to his own flat. Certainly he had left the Bentley at Scotland Yard and would have had to travel an appreciable distance out of his way to reclaim it; on the other hand, had he driven home in the car, he could not have made so silent an approach and it is almost certain that he would not have noticed that queer phenomenon on the window of his flat.

Big Ben was chiming eleven when Rollo and Jan Morgan wished him *au revoir* and Jeffery began his trek along Pimlico Road. It was a beautiful night, unusually warm for the time of the year, and there was that velvety softness in the air that makes walking so delightful. Hands in pockets and cigarette between his lips, Mr. Blackburn strode along, humming to himself. The evening with the Morgans had refreshed his mind and relaxed his nerves. The dark menace of the murder problem no longer loomed omnipresent in his consciousness. The young man was thinking of other things as he walked, memories invoked by the softness of the night and the gay insouciance of a new moon swinging low in a spangled sky. There was that hilarious occasion (how long ago it seemed now) when Rollo had brought an odorous chemical into the class-room and tipped it into Professor Wilkinson's inkwell while that venerable old gentleman was demonstrating the essential binomials at the blackboard. And that occasion when Morgan, breaking bounds, had slipped in traversing the dangerous barbed-wire maze over a spear-pointed wall and had hung for some hours from the spikes by the seat of his trousers, unable to release himself. The world was a very good place in those undergraduate days—they had planned their lives with all the reckless grandiloquence of youth. What was it that Thoreau had said?—something about youth getting together his materials to build a bridge to the moon, a palace or a temple on earth . . . and the middle-aged man building a woodshed with the same materials. Heigh-ho. It was a wise providence which ordained that the future should be veiled and the morrow—

Quite by chance, Jeffery glanced up and his train of thought snapped like a severed tape.

So engrossing had been these whimsical cogitations that he had approached almost to his flat without actually being aware of its proximity. Happening to raise his eyes to the window of the sitting-room, he was surprised to note that the glass was illuminated for a brief space. His first thought was that it had reflected the gleam of motorcar headlights, but the street was barren of any vehicle. Jeffery drew back into the shadows of a doorway, his eyes focused on that window. After a few minutes, it was repeated . . . a circular arc of light splashed the glass, moved across the surface and vanished. As identification came to him, Jeffery's body tensed. That circle of light emanated from an electric torch. Someone was searching the flat and it did not take lengthy deduction to realize the object of this night prowl.

The can of film!

Moving soundlessly as a bat, Jeffery slipped from alcove to alcove until he commanded a better view. One of the windows looked on to Vauxhall Bridge Road, the other into a *cul-de-sac* which was used as the tradesmen's entrance to the flats. It was this window that was open. The young man thought swiftly.

A few moments later, he walked up to his door, whistling shrilly. He made an astonishing amount of noise inserting his key, pushed a head inside and called, "Are you home, Chief?" Then he slammed the door with unnecessary violence. But he had shut himself outside and was speeding for that *cul-de-sac* as fast as his long legs would carry him. If his ruse had been successful, if he had scared the intruder from his rooms, there was only one way of escape open to the prowler and that was through the mouth of the blind alley. And Mr. Blackburn meant to be there! He swung round a corner and collided with a dim-seen figure. Jeffery grappled with him and the two rolled on the pavement in a swirling tangle of arms and legs.

It was impossible to distinguish anything save a bundle that fought and twisted and panted. His assailant was no weakling and Jeffery thanked his stars that Read had given him a thorough grounding in rough-house methods. Then the man's fist crashed into his mouth and the blood began to trickle down his chin. Blackburn decided that this business had gone far enough; he grabbed at the flailing arm and twisted it cruelly. The man gave a sudden scream of pain and his taut body relaxed. Still gripping his arm, Jeffery jerked the man to his feet.

"Come up, my beauty," he panted. "Let's see who you are."

"Blackburn!"

Jeffery's reply was to drag the man into the lighted street. He stared at that lean bitter face plain under the street lamp. In spite of the dirt, bruises, and scratches, he recognized it instantly.

It was Gordon Finniss!

"And now," snapped Blackburn, still twisting the other's arm behind him, "perhaps you'll explain!"

Finniss struggled. "Let go my arm, damn you! You've some explaining to do yourself! What do you mean by going for me like a street hooligan? Have you gone mad?"

Jeffery wiped the blood from his mouth with his free hand. "What were you doing in my flat?" he rapped.

In the light of the street lamp, Finniss' eyes widened to black pools. "In your flat? Look here, are you quite crazy, Blackburn? I haven't been near your flat!" He writhed again. "And for God's sake, let me go! You're breaking my arm!"

Jeffery dragged the actor closer and ran his other hand over his clothes. From his hip-pocket he drew forth a small black automatic pistol. "So . . .?" he said with a twist of his lips. He transferred the automatic to his own pocket and continued the search. His fingers halted again at the inside coat pocket and fastened on a thin steel object. He brought it out. It was a hatpin.

Blackburn measured Finniss with cold eyes. "What's the meaning of this?"

The actor said sullenly: "It's the hatpin from among the effects."

"And," said Blackburn, "the weapon that killed Isabelle Simms."

Finniss reached out a hand and clutched Jeffery's coat. "No—you're wrong!" His voice was husky. "Don't think that! That's the reason I came round here tonight—to bring that pin back!" He paused and glanced around quickly. "Listen. Can we go into your flat and talk? I've a lot to explain—"

"You certainly have," Jeffery said grimly. "And what did you do with your torch?"

"My torch?"

Blackburn released the man, who stepped back a pace. "Let's not fool about," Jeffery said sharply. "I mean the torch you had searching my flat!"

Finniss moved his hands helplessly. "I tell you I didn't—"

"We'll talk about it inside," the other snapped. "You go first!"

They marched. At the door of the sitting-room, Jeffery clicked on the light and motioned the actor forward. Finniss, blinking, made his way inside and flopped into a chair, brushing the dust from his clothes. "Confound you, Blackburn," he grumbled. "Look what you've done to my coat!"

"You probably won't need it much longer," the other assured him. "They'll give you a broad arrow suit in its place." And as the other started up, he waved him back fiercely. "Sit down! And if you try any monkey-tricks while my back is turned, I'll put every policeman in the city on your tail!"

He looked around the room, frowning. All about was evidence of a hurried search. The furniture was dragged aside. Jeffery's Japanese prints had been torn down from the wall. The bookcase was emptied of its volumes. A bronze head of Leonardo da Vinci was rolled carelessly under the arm-chair. Even the wireless set had the back removed. Fortunately, the investigator had refrained from the vandalism which he had wrought in the Bayswater flat, but Jeffery suspected that this was merely because of the interruption. He crossed and pushed open the door of the bedroom. Nothing appeared to have been disturbed there. Apparently, the searcher had not reached the other rooms. Jeffery, his face dark with anger, turned and stood over the sullen Finniss.

"You dashed sneak-thief," he snapped. "So you were after that can of film, eh?"

The actor gripped the arms of his chair and looked up into the other's face. "Listen, Blackburn," he said. "For the last time, I've never been in your flat before. I know nothing of any film. I was walking down here to see you when you leapt on me like a madman!"

Jeffery's narrowed eyes searched the actor's swollen face. Was that sincerity in his voice and manner the result of careful training in his profession? Or was it genuine? He walked across and took a cigarette from the box on the mantel, hesitated a second, then pushed the box roughly in Finniss' direction. The actor shook his head.

"I want nothing save that you listen to me—and believe me," he said coldly.

Blackburn was lighting his cigarette. He stood by the fire-place and folded his arms. "All right," he said curtly. "What have you got to say?"

"It's about that hatpin." Finniss gestured to the object on the table. "I took it from the studio that night of the murder."

"Well?"

"It was like this." The actor settled in his chair. "On that evening, Ted Martin mislaid his script. He came to me and asked if he could use mine. I consented. So it was my script that he took into the studio with him on the night of the play."

He raised his eyes to Blackburn, who nodded curtly.

"When that black-out occurred," Finniss continued, "Martin put the hatpin in the script to mark the place. During the commotion that followed, the script was closed with the hatpin inside it. When we left the studio, I picked up my script from the effects table and took it home with me. There I tossed it into a drawer. The pin was inside the script all the time."

He paused. Blackburn said levelly. "If this was so, why didn't you return the pin when you knew it played such an important part in our investigations?"

"That's just the point." Finniss licked his lips. "I was afraid. You see, I didn't find the hatpin until after you told us how the girl had been murdered." He swallowed something in his throat. "I thought that if I confessed that I had taken it from the studio accidentally, I wouldn't be believed."

"Why should you think that if you weren't involved?" snapped Jeffery.

"I was involved—in a perfectly innocent way!"

"What do you mean?"

Finniss raised his eyes and regarded the other steadily. "I was in Paris when the former hatpin murder was committed."

Jeffery's eyes glinted. He did not speak.

"On the night of the murder," Finniss continued slowly, "when the doctor was examining that girl's body, I admitted to having been in the R.A.M.C. At the reconstruction, a few days later, you explained how the murder had been committed and that the absence of the hatpin pointed to somebody in the studio being mixed up with the crime. I went home that night puzzling over the murder. Quite by chance, I took out the script of *Darkness is Danger*—and out fell the hatpin!

"Imagine my feelings, Blackburn! I was the only person in that room with knowledge of the previous crime—and now I had the missing hatpin, a replica of the weapon that had killed Simms, actually in my possession! You see my position? I dare not admit the ownership, since you could have easily traced my movements with the R.A.M.C. and discovered my knowledge of the first crime. It would have been too damning! You would never have believed that I had come into possession of the hatpin accidentally!"

"Then why expose yourself to the risk by returning it now?"

Finniss looked surprised. "Surely there's no question of suspicion now?" he said. "I understood that you had proved beyond all doubt that the murder was the work of an outsider and that the people in the studio were exonerated. And, according to the newspaper reports, the hatpin found at the flat in Bayswater was certified as having been the weapon used!"

He paused and as Jeffery did not comment:

"Therefore, I thought it would be perfectly safe to make my explanation." He shrugged. "But I feel that I've cleared myself of one suspicion only to be burdened with another—that of robbing your flat!"

Jeffery said steadily: "Isn't it remarkable that you should have been coming along just at that exact moment—?"

"Coincidence!" Finniss cried. "Nothing more than coincidence!" He half raised himself from the chair and waved a grubby hand at the other. "I swear to you, Blackburn, that I had absolutely nothing to do with the searching of this flat! Why should I? I'm not mixed up in this business in any way! And as far as the murder of that unfortunate girl is concerned, I am one man who has proved himself innocent. You *saw* my movements in that studio! I was standing in that patch of light from the control room—yards away from that girl!"

There was a silence. Blackburn stared at him. "Your story sounds feasible, Finniss," he said shortly. "I'm only wondering if it isn't a trifle too feasible!"

"Martin will bear out my story," the actor returned sullenly. "Get in touch with him! He'll corroborate what I've told you regarding the hatpin in the script."

Jeffery smiled bleakly. "I don't under-estimate your intelligence, Finniss, to the point of believing you would be so foolish as to volunteer a story like this without preparing ample corroboration, should it be needed!" He considered, his eyes thoughtful. "Tell me this," he said abruptly. "Was there any other person in that studio beside yourself with knowledge of the Parisian crime?"

"I don't think so," the actor replied. "Of course, the other members of the cast may have read or heard about it. But I can't—" he broke off suddenly, a new expression creeping into his face. "Now—wait a minute," he said slowly. "Yes. Someone else *did* know of it!"

Jeffery thrust his head forward. "You're sure of that?"

"Positive!" returned Finniss emphatically. "I remember it quite well! It was some weeks ago, when the script of *Darkness is Danger* was being prepared. Katie Knowles asked a friend and myself around to see the rough draught of the plot. She wasn't too sure of the technique of radio writing and asked us to check up on it for her. We stayed to supper and the talk turned naturally to criminology. Then Miss Knowles turned up her scrap-books and snowed us this twenty-year-old clipping from *Le Matin* about the hatpin murder in Paris."

"Well?"

"My friend happened to be rather interested in criminology herself and she asked Miss Knowles to translate it for her. I remember she remarked that it constituted the perfect murder."

A faint colour had flowed in Blackburn's face. "And who was this inquisitive friend of yours?"

"It was Martha Rockwell," Finniss said quietly.

III

DISAPPOINTING MANIFESTO OF SIGHT WITHOUT SOUND

. . . a moving row
Of visionary Shapes that come and go . . .
Rubáiyát of Omar Khayyám.

JEFFERY found it necessary to acquaint the Chief Inspector with an explanation of the disordered flat when the latter returned shortly after midnight. He did not, however, mention the visit of Gordon Finniss. For one thing, Blackburn was still uncertain in his own mind about the man and his story. That the whole business appeared sincere enough on the surface he could not deny, yet the actor's peculiar manifestation coinciding so neatly with the escape of the burglarious prowler seemed highly suspicious. Secondly, Jeffery knew enough of his official companion's temperament to realize that, given even a single hint, Read would have had the actor arrested without a moment's hesitation, so sorely pressed was the big man in his endeavour to find some opening on the blank walls that hemmed him round. Because the Chief Inspector's day had yielded nothing save another series of humiliating discouragements.

Jeffery, changed into pyjamas and dressing-gown, his sore body bathed and iodine smarting on his split lip, had begun on his own account of the day's activities, but Read, morose as the proverbial sore-headed bear, curtly disclaimed all further interest in the matter. He retired to his room, closing the door emphatically behind him.

Blackburn, realizing his companion's position, was keenly sympathetic toward his mood. Despite the almost perpetual logomachy that permeated the flat, each had a deep and sincere affection for the other and Read's grey parade of failure had a correspondingly depressing effect on the younger man. He realized only too well that his friend would be tossing, fretful and worried, on his bed, visualizing stormy interviews with the Assistant Commissioner, letters to newspapers complaining about the "apparent inefficiency of Scotland Yard", recalling that on the morrow, the fifth day of the murder investigation dawned to find practically no appreciable progress made.

Blackburn paced the floor in his slippers, one thoughtful eye on that closed door, deliberating on the wisdom of forcing an entrance and shaking the Chief Inspector from his melancholy brooding with a spirited recital of the day's events. Then he shook his head. Not only was the hour late, but also rather inopportune. Mr. Blackburn sighed, touched his stinging lip gingerly and, gathering up a novel, flapped his way rather despondently to bed.

A great army of poets, from the tragic Aeschylus to the modern Hollywood lyric-writer, have extolled the fact that happiness invariably follows the sunshine and that peace of mind dawns with the morning. Like all trite and popular conceptions, their theorem contains a germ of truth. Certain it is that William Jamieson Read rose to brave a fresh day, if not actually with a smiling morning face, at least a countenance more pleasant than the grim and sullen visage with which he had retired.

Over breakfast, Jeffery put his companion in full possession of facts regarding the can of film and the efforts to retrieve it. Read was aghast. The young man skimmed lightly over his injured mouth, advancing the explanation that he had blundered against the disordered furniture in the darkness. With the exception of Finniss' visit, he outlined each point with such thoroughness that the recital lasted until the couple entered the Chief Inspector's office at Scotland Yard. Jeffery concluded by mentioning that it had come to his knowledge that Martha Rockwell had known for some weeks of the previous hatpin murder.

"Well, I'll be a blue-nosed Buddha!" grunted Read, tipping back in his swivel-chair. "I thought that monkey-faced-dame was a little too interested in things that shouldn't concern her! She ought to be bringing up a family at her age instead of poring over murder trials!"

Jeffery, seated opposite Read, shook his head. "You can't pin anything on that woman merely because she happens to be interested in criminology," he said. "And as far as the knowledge of that Parisian crime goes—well, there might be hundreds of people in London who remember it!" He leaned his elbows on the desk. "What interests me at the moment is the apparent importance of that can of film!"

"They're rigging up a projection machine in the basement," the Chief Inspector told him. "As soon as it's right, we'll run the film through down there."

Jeffery screwed his head and looked at the strongroom. "I suppose it's still intact," he said wryly. "Rather an anti-climax if the unknown had found some means of removing it from the Holy of Holies."

The Chief Inspector's cold blue eyes met his for a moment. Without a word, he rose and walked across the room, pulling a bunch of keys from his pocket. Selecting one, he fitted it into the lock and dragged at the heavy door. Jeffery saw him nod his head, reach forward and reappear with the canister in his hands. "This it?" he queried.

Jeffery nodded. Read returned to the desk, holding the canister as though loath to let it out of his possession. He was staring down at the metal container, black brows drawn. "Got any ideas about this, Jeff?" he said.

Jeffery sat back and folded his arms. "There's one strong connection, Chief. That film is a short from the Kinofilm studios in London—"

"The studio where Simms was employed—the place that was burnt down?"

"Yes." The young man's voice slowed. "The actual subject of the film is a matter of conjecture. But the title, *Death in the Field,* together with the fact that the unit was making films on toxicology, seems to indicate that it has something to do with a vegetable poison."

The Chief Inspector dumped the film on his desk. Turning, he began to pace the floor, hands clasped behind his back. "Why this repeated suggestion of poison?" he said. "With the exception of the Gallasch business, the question of poison has never entered into this case at all. Simms was stabbed with a hatpin and Rodda was shot!"

"I'm not anticipating that the film has anything to do with these recent murders," Jeffery remarked. "That's quite impossible! Remember, that film was made three years ago."

"Then if it has nothing to do with the present murders, why is somebody so keen to prevent us screening the film?"

Jeffery shrugged and his tone had the faint inflection of irritation. "I suggest that we let the screening of the film answer our questions." He paused, then added, "Any news from Paris regarding Viardin?"

The Chief Inspector nodded moodily. "Checkmate again. When they went to arrest Viardin, the cage was empty and the bird flown. They're watching all the outlets, of course, but they have a strong suspicion that he skipped some days previous."

"On the morning following the murder of Simms," nodded Jeffery.

"How do you know?"

Jeffery screwed round in his chair. "Surely it's obvious? Viardin was listening in on that night. One of two things is consequently responsible for his absence. Either he heard Simms put over that code-word and came straight to London to pay a little debt—or else—"

Jeffery slowed his words. "Or else Simms was murdered before she could give the warning. In which case, he heard the whole killing through his speaker. And realizing that something had gone wrong with his scheme—realizing that investigations would be set in motion at once, he fled before those investigations would bring the whole business home to him!"

Read had halted before Jeffery's chair. "So you think that Viardin killed Rodda?" he barked.

Jeffery said wearily. "Either Viardin, or a member of his organization, or the murderer of Simms. Take your choice, Chief!"

The Chief Inspector worried his clipped moustache. "Then who sent those documents to me? That certainly wasn't the work of Viardin! He wouldn't deliberately engineer his own betrayal!"

"Of course not!"

"But," said Read slowly, "it may be Viardin who is so keen to prevent the showing of this film! That might be another reason for his flight."

Blackburn sprang to his feet. "Chief!" he cried. "I believe you've hit on something!" He thrust his hands into his pockets and began to pace the floor, eyes on the carpet. "Let us see how it might work out. . . .

"Rodda, as we know, was Simms' partner in that drug organization. He has this film, a valuable film since he keeps it locked away in a safe deposit. Therefore, is it too much to assume that this film is in some way connected with that organization? It might even contain important knowledge regarding the workings of the gang! Now, Viardin, learning of Rodda's treachery by Simms' code-word over the air, comes to London with the intention of killing the traitorous partner, also of obtaining the film which may hold information which Viardin considers dangerous to his safety. He goes to Rodda's hotel and shoots him as he enters the room."

"Just a minute," Read interrupted. "What about Lusinska? Where does she fit into this? Remember, she was seen about the place, too."

"At the moment, we don't know," returned Blackburn. "She may have been mixed up with the organization herself. She was certainly friendly with Steinie—remember, I saw them together that morning outside Simms' flat in Bayswater? On the other hand, she may have seen Viardin murder Rodda and been spirited away to prevent her talking. That would account for her disappearance, because Viardin may be holding her a prisoner."

Read nodded. "Go on, son."

"Now, Viardin knows that Rodda keeps this film in a safe deposit. He probably ordered him to place it somewhere like that—perhaps Rodda had actually told him the name of the safe deposit. After he has killed Rodda, he plans to get the key from the body, reclaim the film and destroy it. But the entry of our detectives a few seconds after the shot is fired prevents him searching the body.

"Viardin realizes that the key will be found and that the film must inevitably fall into our hands. And that is the last possible thing he wants to occur. Consequently, he dogs our steps until we recover the film and then makes two attempts to retrieve it himself. What secret the film actually holds—"

He broke off as a knock sounded at the door. Carter thrust his head inside.

"Excuse me, sir," he said, addressing the Chief Inspector. "They are waiting for you in the basement when you are ready."

2

The basement was as cheerless as a tomb. The harsh glare of the unshaded electric lights, dangling from hastily rigged flex, flooded stone wall and groined roof, revealing the whitewash peeling from brownish-green splashes of damp and ropes of cobwebs swinging lazily in the musty air. There was a scurry of something in a far corner as Jeffery and Read entered, and a large rat streaked across the stone floor and vanished into the shadows.

In one corner of this crypt, the angular outline of a projection machine was raised some thirty feet away from an improvised screen mounted on a frame against the wall.. The operator was fumbling with connections from a thick rubber cable snaking over the floor. Three uniformed constables, murmuring in a group near the machine, sprang to attention and saluted as Read, the can of film in his hands, approached. The Chief Inspector returned their salute perfunctorily and tossed the metal cylinder to the nearest man.

"Everything ready?" he grunted.

The operator turned. "Yes, sir. I'll thread the film through and we'll make a start."

He probed here and there. From the rear of the machine came a sudden burst of incandescence that flashed, flickered, and burned steadily, shaming the electric lights by its brilliance. The operator nodded. On the screen an illuminated square of white radiance appeared. Next moment the light died to a fierce scarlet glow. Meantime, the constables had removed the reel of film from the canister. They passed the roll to the operator who flicked one end free and held it up to the light. He spoke over his shoulder.

"You won't get any sound with this screening, sir. This is a silent projector."

Jeffery looked surprised. "I understood it was a silent film."

The operator shook his head. "It's a silent so far as dialogue is concerned," he explained. "But there's a musical sound-track. Kinofilm made most of their shorts like that so they could produce in Germany and substitute English sub-titles." He turned and began to slip the reel of film into the upper spool of the machine, deftly threading the celluloid strip through toothed sprocket-wheels. "You'll see a blurred mark down one side of the screen when the film starts," he added. "That's the soundtrack."

He connected the loose end of the film with the lower spool, squinted here and there, and moved to the rear of the machine. At his touch, that steady incandescence burned again. "Lights out," he called, and the basement became dark. The projection machine whirred and the white screen before them danced and flickered with the opening title:

Kinofilm Company
presents

DEATH IN THE FIELD

A KINOFILM SILENT SHORT SUBJECT

Jeffery and Read glued their eyes to those trembling letters. They were followed by the usual list of credits to the director, the scenario writer, the photographer, the film editor, and the gentleman who conducted the orchestra. This in turn faded to a third title:

WARNING
This film is not for public exhibition. It is produced for educational purposes only.

Another change of title:

Under our very feet as we walk, the earth puts forth death in a hundred shapes in the form of vegetable growths. Some are well known, like the hemlock, the deadly nightshade, and the common monk's-head or wolf's-bane, all of which yield alkaloid poisons. There are others not so easily identified. The object of this film is to reveal alkaloid poisons that lurk in the seemingly innocent growths of the earth.

Then came the pictorial interlude. The various plants were shown growing in their natural state and the camera moved closer to reveal certain characteristics by which the plants could be identified. Then the scene dissolved into a whirling phantasmagoria of boiling retorts, test-tubes, masked faces, and glass prisms indicating the stages by which the poison was extracted. Then there came a flash of a professor addressing a class of students and there were many feet of film devoted to his lecture. The film was produced in typical Continental style, photographed from queer angles, heavy with symbolism wrought in shadows and statuary, interpolated with staring eyes and mouthing faces and groping hands. Then another title blackened the screen:

It is not always realized that the familiar potato plant, Solanum Tuberioun, contains in all its tissues, including that of the edible tuber, varying amounts of a poisonous gluco-alkaloid Solanine. It is well known that under certain conditions, this alkaloid may accumulate in the tubers themselves, particularly when sprouting, in amounts which are definitely poisonous.

When the film again flashed into action, it had moved to Cyprus. Beautiful pictorial views of the island were shown, cross-fading into the extreme poverty of the peasant homes. An officer was shown warning the peasants against eating potato shoots, as the quantity of Solanine contained in the peelings and the shoots was greater than in the tuber itself. This was followed by a sub-title explaining that more than fifty cases of Solanine poisoning occurred on the island through the ingestion of tuber shoots and peelings, two cases of which were fatal.

There was a swift shot of a hungry rat approaching a pile of withered potato peelings, sniffing and turning away. On its heels came another merry-go-round of dissolving flashes, demonstrating the extraction of the alkaloid Solanine from the tuber, then, with a click, the last foot of film shot through the projector and a square of illumination dancing on the white screen announced the end.

The brilliant incandescence flickered and died. The electric bulbs put forth their hard glare. The operator turned to the Chief Inspector and his companion. "That's it, sir," he announced.

Read looked at Jeffery, disappointment written large on his face. "Well, son," he muttered, "it looks like just so much wasted time! If you can discover anything pertaining to our case in that fantastic rigmarole, you're cleverer than I think you are!"

Blackburn was staring at the screen. He gave a slight start as the other addressed him. "Er—what's that?" he muttered.

The Chief Inspector was eyeing him curiously. "Well?" he demanded. "Do you want it run through again? Or have you seen enough?"

Jeffery said quietly: "I've seen enough."

Read turned to the operator. "That's all right. Thank you," he said curtly. He began to stride out of the basement, followed by Jeffery. The couple climbed the stairs in silence. They passed through half a dozen corridors and were almost to Read's office before Jeffery spoke again.

"Chief. Did you notice that list of credits on the film?"

"Credits?" grunted the other, "What are they?"

"The list of titles at the beginning telling who had done what to the production."

The big man snorted. "Never read 'em! Waste of time!"

"Not in this case," returned Jeffery slowly. "If you had watched them, you might have noticed something rather interesting."

"Indeed?"

"Yes. According to those credits, Katharine Knowles, the woman who wrote the script of *Darkness is Danger,* also did the scenario for that film."

The Chief Inspector turned a corner. "Well—does that prove anything, except that she's darn' versatile?"

"I think it does," returned Blackburn. "It's started a rather significant train of thought in my mind. It never occurred to me before that Miss Knowles could possibly have been connected with that film unit. But as she obviously was . . ." his voice trailed. He pulled his case from his pocket, lit a cigarette and puffed absently. The couple had reached the Chief Inspector's office. Read was about to push open the door when Jeffery halted in his tracks and thumped one fist into his open hand.

"By Jove!"

Read wheeled and stared at him. Jeffery was standing still, his eyes alight, his cheeks flushed. He looked at the big man as though seeing him for the first time. "What's wrong with you?" Read growled.

A queer expression, almost a slyness, crossed the young man's face. He opened his lips, then closed them and shook his head. "It's nothing," he said, and the evasion in his tone was plain. He pushed past Read. "Let's go inside."

They entered the office. Jeffery strolled across to the window and stood looking out over the Embankment. The Chief Inspector glanced at him, plainly bewildered by his attitude, then with a shrug he crossed to his desk and jerked his chair into position. But in the act of sitting, a long official envelope propped up against the inkwell on his desk caught his attention. He picked it up, slit the gummed flap, and drew out a folded letter. Smoothing it, he ran his eyes over the typewritten lines. It was his turn to ejaculate.

"Great Scott!" he exclaimed. He pursed his lips in a soft whistle of astonishment.

Jeffery turned from the window. "Why the surprise?" he inquired.

Read replaced the letter on the desk. "It's a communication from the Home Secretary," he said. "I asked him to give me the name of the person who wrote that letter asking that the studio fire business should be reopened." A stocky forefinger tapped the paper. "He's just sent the name along. And who do you think it was?"

Jeffery blew a thin feather of smoke. "I don't have to guess," he said calmly. "I know!"

The Chief Inspector glared. "Oh, you do—do you? Then perhaps you can tell me that name?"

"Certainly," assented Mr. Blackburn. "It was Miss Katharine Knowles."

IV

MR. BLACKBURN OUTLINES THE PERFECT PLOT

"It must be admitted that the workings of this unhappy woman's mind were deep and subtle, Watson, so that it was no very simple matter to unravel her plot."

ARTHUR CONAN DOYLE, *Thor Bridge.*

1

TO JEFFERY, it was somehow symbolic that the cottage of Miss Katharine Knowles, on the outskirts of Kensington, should have a high wall surrounding it. He drew the Bentley to a stop, climbed out and surveyed the place.

This wall might very well have been constructed, not so much of tangible bricks and mortar as of imagery from the mind of the novelist herself. It was the apotheosis of every fictional wall—mossy, crannied, yellowed by countless suns and topped with a serrated edging of rusted spikes.

Jeffery walked to where a wrought-iron gate bisected this romantic barrier, and peered through the scrollwork. The cottage was a perfect complement to the wall about it—a snuggery of twisted chimneys, creeper-covered walls, diamond-paned windows, and angled gables, set back from a smooth lawn spangled with crazy-paving and almost theatrically charming with sundial, bird-bath, and fish-pool. It was the most incongruous setting for a detective novelist, spinning scarlet dreams of murder and sudden death. One could imagine the harsher elements of life approaching that spiked wall, but never crossing it. In such surroundings as these, Oscar Wilde might have woven those delicate silver fantasies of his "House of Pomegranates", or Shakespeare captured from the environment the magic that touched his sonnets with the lyrical quality unequalled in literature. Yet it was within this sylvan frame that Katharine Knowles had produced *Design for Death, Murder Among Mummers,* and a dozen other best-selling volumes that had placed her name at the head of the popular writers.

Mr. Blackburn pushed open the gate and, making .his way between ordered beds fringed with the first white stars of spring buds, bent his head under the low doorway. He reached up and played a gentle tattoo on the fantastic knocker. Then he waited, sniffing appreciatively at the fresh green fragrance composed of a hundred scents. The garden was as some huge, odorous *potpourri* jar. Three sparrows splashed and twittered and fluttered ecstatic wings in the afternoon sun on the edge of the raised bath, and the sundial thrust a wise finger in his direction. It was so delightful, so redolent of peace, of enchantment—so much in discord with his mission, that Mr. Blackburn sighed, turned to repeat his summons and found the door open and a brown-eyed girl in uniform looking at him.

"Yes, sir?"

Jeffery touched his hat. "I'd like to see your mistress."

The girl looked uncertain. "Miss Knowles is very busy writing. I don't know—"

Jeffery smiled. "Perhaps my card . . ." He drew forth a slip of pasteboard and a thin pencil, scribbling a few words on the blank side. He handed the card across. "Would you take this to your mistress? I'll wait."

The girl departed. Mr. Blackburn drew off his gloves and flipped them idly. Within a minute, the maid returned. "My mistress will see you, sir. Will you come inside?"

Jeffery stepped down into the hall. It was bare except for a scarlet jar of straggling pussy-willow and, at one end, a van Gogh reproduction glowed like a flameburst. The girl relieved him of his hat and gloves, then, knocked gently on a door. Opening it—"Mr. Blackburn," she announced.

It was a small room, neat, precise, and orderly, yet rescued from stiffness by touches that marked the personality of the owner. The sunshine beat through windows hung with gay curtains, licked about an orange pot on an ebony stand, and winked among the scarlet, gold, and silver bindings of the books that lined one wall. Facing him was a desk on which was a portable typewriter, pushed on one side among a stack of papers. Half a dozen reference books were gaping open near by. In the centre of the desk was a sheet of manuscript half covered with spidery, old-fashioned handwriting. A pen, the nib still wet with ink, was placed across it.

At this desk, facing him, a woman sat in a steel, high-backed chair. The closed-in front of the desk revealed only the rigid set of her body as she sat turning his card over in her slender fingers. She looked up as he entered and removed a pair of spectacles from her eyes.

"Mr. Blackburn?" Her voice was level, cool. "I am Katharine Knowles. You wished to see me?"

"Yes, madam." He took the chair to which her white hand gestured.

Katharine Knowles had been grossly libelled by Mr. Nickerson, Jeffery decided. Instead of the eccentric frump that the studio manager's description had conjured in his mind, he saw a thin, tragic-faced woman in her early forties. Only a slight crêpiness about her throat, the bluish veins on those white hands, and faint crow's-feet about the corners of her tired eyes betrayed her age. She was dressed in a frock of some dark material, edged with white at collar and cuffs. But it was the face that drew Jeffery's attention: the shadowed eyes under a high, clear forehead, the faint translucence of her cheeks, the ironic set of the lips, and the strength of the chin. It was a cold, severe, yet very remarkable face, full of character and firmness, the face of a woman who has fought and been cruelly defeated, only to rise and fight anew. Yet there was gentle humour in those dark eyes, and a kindly tolerance assuaged those bitter lines about the mouth.

The woman was speaking, turning the card over in her hand.

"On this, Mr. Blackburn, you have written 'Please see me. It is desperately urgent.' " She placed the pasteboard on her desk and turned to him. "What is this urgent business?"

Jeffery pulled his chair closer. He said quietly: "It was very good of you to see me, madam, when you are so obviously busy. Believe me, I would not have intruded were the matter not of grave importance."

"Indeed?" Miss Knowles raised thin, half-mooned brows. "Go on, Mr. Blackburn."

"I have come principally to discuss your work."

"My work?"

Jeffery nodded. "Yes. I want to discuss with you the perfect plot."

Miss Knowles looked at him, her face expressing faint bewilderment. "I am afraid I don't understand you—"

Blackburn leaned forward. "Miss Knowles. May I take the liberty of saying that I am a sincere admirer of your work. Your novels are justifiably popular. The critics call you the novelist without a failure"—the woman raised a hand, but he hurried on—"and rightly, too! Your outstanding characteristic is your ability to weave brilliant though perfectly logical plots. So logical that they might be transferred to real life. So natural in their reasoning that they might happen to any of us."

Miss Knowles dropped her hand. For a brief second she frowned, then an expression of well-bred amusement crossed her face. She said pleasantly: "Coming from an authority like yourself, Mr. Blackburn, that is a compliment I should be foolish to ignore." She smiled. "However, is this tribute to my imagination your 'desperately urgent' business?"

The young man shook his head. "Unfortunately, no, madam. I have come to give you my idea of a perfect plot."

Miss Knowles' hands came to rest on the desk. Something of the hardness had returned to her face when she spoke.

"This is extremely kind of you, sir. But I am quite capable of thinking out my own plots. I am sure yours would be most interesting, but you must realize that I am a very busy woman." She turned to the desk and took up her pen. "Perhaps at some later time . . ."

"No, Miss Knowles." Jeffery's voice was very grave. "We cannot afford to wait."

Up went those arched brows. "I beg your pardon, Mr. Blackburn?"

The young man leaned forward and gripped the edge of his chair. "Miss Knowles—please believe me when I say that you must listen to me! Give me but five minutes. Listen only to the beginning of my perfect plot. Then, if you are still uninterested, I will go."

"But why should I listen to this plot of yours?"

"Because, madam, if any other person should chance to discover it, you would find yourself in an extremely awkward position!"

The woman stared at him, eyes hard, nostrils quivering. She said coldly: "Mr. Blackburn—is this some extremely vulgar joke?"

Jeffery shrugged. "Perhaps it is," he said quietly. "Only you can tell me that when I have finished."

Miss Knowles hesitated, staring at him. Then she glanced at her wrist-watch. "I can give you just five minutes, sir. Go on. I am listening."

Blackburn sat back and folded his arms. His tone had a penetrating quietness that whispered about the sunlit room.

"It was de Maupassant, I believe," began Jeffery, "who held out the premise that literature was a medium of wish-fulfilment for the author rather than the reader—that it enabled the writer to achieve certain ideals on paper that he or she was denied in real life. Now I, for some years, have had the desire to be a writer of detective stories. Perhaps it is this urge, somehow inverted, that first drew me to criminology. Consequently, you will not be at all surprised to learn that my perfect plot is the plot for a detective story—and that my principal character is a detective novelist, species feminine."

Miss Knowles glanced at her wrist-watch. "Almost a minute of your time has gone, Mr. Blackburn," she said coldly. "Might I suggest that you come to the point at once?"

"Certainly." Blackburn closed his eyes for a moment. "I am making my novelist a middle-aged woman," he continued, "and we will label her with that ubiquitous gift to anonymity—the name of Smith. I am rather proud of Miss Smith. She has courage, not only in life but also in her profession. In her early thirties, she blazes an original trail in detective fiction with her first novel. Her second and third follow in quick succession and each one has the same paramount characteristic. The plots. They are perfect plots, logical, watertight, yet mystifying to the last satisfactory page. Small wonder that the critics rave over her extraordinary imagination. Small wonder that as she continues to turn out book after book, each one more brilliant than its successor, her sales run into hundreds of thousands and publishers vie one with the other for her name on their contracts.

"But Miss Smith, my feted, successful novelist, is far from being the happy woman that the world believes. To her ears, these triumphant diapasons lauding her genius have a hollow sound. The beating of the drum of showmanship is but the celebrated tinkling cymbal. Just as man cannot live by bread alone, neither can Miss Smith exist entirely in the world between cardboard covers. How bitterly weary she is of weaving dream romances for her characters when in real life she, their creator, knows nothing of love.

"One by one her friends drop away, marry, and lose themselves in their own worlds; friends that are frankly envious of her success and never dream that she would change places with them in the twinkling of an eye if the chance but offered itself. Of course, she has men friends, for Miss Smith is a charming and cultured woman. But they are nothing more than friends; they take her to dine and dance and then they leave, while our novelist goes back to her task of creating pen-and-ink heroes and heroines, putting them through glorious adventures existing only inside her clever head. Another perfect example of de Maupassant's wish-fulfilment, you see. And so it goes on until Miss Smith, with twenty widely read novels behind her, is turning forty, that very dangerous age for any woman."

He paused and glanced across the desk. Miss Knowles, her face rigid, her eyes like two holes seared in ivory, was staring before her. She seemed to have forgotten his presence in the room.

Jeffery's voice, gentle as a priest's giving absolution, flowed on:

"Then one day, about three years ago, a wonderful event occurs in our heroine's life. A film company comes to London from Germany. They are to make short educational films here. They approach Miss Smith and ask her to write a scenario for one of their films. And it is during her association with this film company that she meets the man who is eventually to become very dear to her. He is a German chemist—I will call him Hans Trenker—and he is employed as technical adviser on the productions which the unit are making. Trenker is almost ten years older than Miss Smith, but what is age beside their glorious friendship that matures into a deep and sincere love. Unfortunately, Trenker fears that the disparity in their ages may have an injurious effect on this friendship. In order to retain his vitality, he doses himself with minute quantities of arsenic, a process which he naturally keeps secret from the woman he loves.

"Now, among the people in this unit, there is employed as his assistant a young woman whom we will call Miss Brown. Miss Brown is much younger than Trenker; moreover, she appears to be an extremely doubtful character. One day, shortly after the unit begins work, some valuable chemicals are found missing. Trenker accuses Brown, a quarrel ensues, and it is obvious that there is bitter feeling between the German chemist and his assistant. On the following day, Miss Smith picks up her newspaper to read horrifying facts! Overnight, the studio has caught fire and Hans Trenker, trapped in the building, is burnt to death!"

A sudden dry scuffling rustled through his last words.

Jeffery saw one of those blue-veined hands, lying loosely on the sheets of manuscript, clench suddenly. The woman sat as though turned to stone, but the agony in those dark eyes tore at the young man's heart. He averted his head and stared out of the window where the shadows were lengthening through the peaceful garden.

"With the first shock of discovery," he continued softly, "our Miss Smith is stunned, crushed, broken. I think it is best that we touch lightly on the horror of that terrible morning. When she recovers, she goes down to the ruined studio to see her lover's body.

"Now, we have made it clear that Miss Smith is nobody's fool. So that when she asks to see the place where the tragedy occurred, she notices several curious facts that arouse her suspicions. There is no need to go deeply into these at the moment. Sufficient to say that she writes a letter to the Home Secretary, pointing out these facts and asking that the case of the Studio Fire be reopened. Ordinarily, such a request would have been ignored, but the name of Miss Smith at the bottom of the letter carries undeniable weight. The case is reopened, with amazing results! Not only is it proved that the studio fire was deliberately started, but an autopsy of Trenker's body uncovers arsenical traces which are believed due to poison administered to the unfortunate man by his assistant Brown.

"The assistant is arrested. The trial begins. It looks as if Brown cannot possibly escape the death sentence. Then her counsel unearths the fact that Trenker is an arsenic eater and this influences the jury to such an extent that Brown is acquitted of the murder charge and is given only a short sentence for incendiarism. Unfortunately, other things also come out at the trial, among them being that Trenker is a married man with a grown family.

"As the judge delivers the sentence, Miss Smith, who is in court, becomes violently hysterical. She screams that the girl is a murderess, that she should hang, and so vehement is her behaviour that she is removed from the court-room.

"Brown goes to prison. The nine-days'-wonder of the case gradually dies down, and eventually it fades from the public mind. With one notable exception. Miss Smith, still believing the girl guilty of murdering her lover by the foulest possible means, vows she will never rest until she has made that girl pay in return.

"And that," said Jeffery, "is what we might call part one of my perfect plot."

2

A venturesome bee sailed through the open window, zoomed twice around the room and blundered out into the garden once more. That shaft of sunlight had moved past the golden pot, on past the silver and scarlet bindings of the books. Now a pale finger lingered, striking on Katharine Knowles' greying hair, forming a soft nimbus about that proud white head. Jeffery was first to break the silence.

"Can you spare me another five minutes?" he asked gently.

The woman did not look at him. She stared ahead, almost as though gazing down some winding lane, and its shadows were reflected in the alabaster mask that was her face. Something moved in her throat as she spoke, as if the words were being forced to her lips.

"I think so. I am very curious to know—the end of your plot."

Jeffery gave a little cough. "You must remember, Miss Knowles, that this is merely a discussion," he said quietly. "During the next half of my plot, I may need your help in straightening out a few points that are worrying me. That is why I came to you. I was sure that you would help me."

The woman inclined her head.

"Eighteen months pass," Jeffery continued.

"Our Miss Smith, heartbroken by the news of her lover's treachery to his wife and family and sickened by the unwholesome publicity surrounding his death, goes back to busy herself in her writing. And so sharp is the spur of sorrow that it is during this time that she turns out her finest work. Slowly, the wound heals—but life has not finished with Miss Smith yet. At the conclusion of her eighteen months' imprisonment, a bitter and vengeful Brown comes to call on Miss Smith. She has obtained certain letters—foolish, hysterical letters—written by Miss Smith to Trenker at the height of their love-affair. From a perusal of these letters, Brown guesses that it was Miss Smith who engineered the reopening of the studio business and Brown's subsequent imprisonment. She makes a proposition to Miss Smith. Blackmail. Either the novelist pays her a sum of money or she will turn these letters over to a newspaper.

"Of course, Miss Smith pays. Anything rather than have the painful affair reopened and exposed in such a sordid light. And once the first money changes hands, Miss Smith is lost. Brown becomes greedier with every demand, and this continues for six months, when the police cause her to make a break for the continent.

"As several months pass," continued Blackburn, "and no word of Brown reaches Miss Smith, she begins to breathe freely once more. Then the B.B.C. approach Miss Smith to do a radio-drama for them. As the novelist is contemplating a detective story dealing with wireless, she welcomes this opportunity of furthering her knowledge of the profession. She not only writes the script, but asks if she may play a part. This is granted, but, unfortunately, the novelist is unsuitable and the role given to a comparatively unknown actress whom we will call Miss Jones.

"A few days later, Jones calls upon Miss Smith and reveals the fact that she is Brown, renewing her demand for money. She tells Miss Smith that this time she will hand over the letters for one thousand pounds. Miss Smith is to bring this sum to Brown's flat in Bayswater on the night of the play and wait for her there. Miss Smith consents, Brown gives her a key to the flat and goes away."

Once again Jeffery paused. Katharine Knowles had settled into that high-backed chair, her sombre eyes on the desk. Her hands were pressed together on her breast and they rose and fell as she breathed. Jeffery's tone was quieter when he resumed his story.

"Now, our Miss Smith has no intention of paying that money. For one thing, it is more than she can afford. For another, she has no proof that Brown will keep her promise and hand over the original letters. It is then that the dark thought enters her mind. If Brown were dead, she would be relieved of all this anxiety." The young man paused and shook his head. "We may say that Miss Smith was not quite sane when she harboured this consideration. Gradually, it became an obsession. Not only would she be revenging herself upon the woman she believed to be the murderer of Trenker, but she would be ridding the world of a dangerous creature. From that moment, Miss Smith's mind is made up. She means to murder Brown.

"Then chance puts into her hands a remarkable opportunity. Going through her scrap-books, Miss Smith discovers the cutting of a twenty-year-old crime which occurred in Paris. An artist murdered his mistress while she was listening at a keyhole by running a hatpin through the keyhole into the girl's ear. It is characterized as the Perfect Murder, since this method leaves no mark on the body and the victim dies with all symptoms of heart failure. This is murder as our heroine—if we may still use that term—desires it: bloodless, clueless murder. If Brown is to die, this must be the method. But what about opportunity?

"Then it is that Miss Smith realizes the wonderful chance that has been put into her hands. In the play that is to be broadcast, there is a sequence in which a character listens at a keyhole. It is the character that she, Miss Smith, was to have played . . . *and the role has been given to Brown!* Moreover, because she wrote the dialogue and rehearsed the part, Miss Smith knows every word and every gesture pertaining to that part! She remembers that just before her character goes to listen, at the door, there; is a blackout. All that is necessary is that Miss Smith attends that opening ceremony at the studio, follows the dialogue that she knows so well until the sequence preceding the blackout, slip round to the dramatic studio, wait until her knowledge of the rehearsal tells that Brown has her ear at the keyhole of the door—and thrust the hatpin through the keyhole. Then she can slip out through the back door of the studio, into her car and drive away. This presents no difficulties.

Remember, our Miss Smith is perfectly *au fait* with the topography of the studio, having visited and explored the place a number of times during her rehearsals with the company.

"She goes about the preparation of this plot with the extraordinary attention to detail for which her novels are famous. Pretending to be annoyed at the change-over in the cast, she demands that her name be removed from the play and no mention of Smith associated with the business. Hence, she reasons that when the accident occurs, her personality will not be connected with the broadcast in any shape or form.

"Also, when she receives an invitation to attend the studio opening, she makes much ado about the 'unwarrantable impudence' of the gesture, publicly declaring that nothing in the world would persuade her to attend. But she keeps that invitation guarded, since it is her passport into the scheme of murder."

Shadows were gathering in that room. The face of the novelist was a white splash in the gloom that was slowly encroaching from the corners. Still she did not speak. Jeffery gave a cough to clear a throat dry with talking, and hurried on.

"And so we come to the night of the broadcast. Miss Smith, with the key of the Bayswater flat in her bag, attends the studio opening, mixes unobtrusively with the crowd, and listens to the opening scenes of her play. Remember, she knows every single word of the dialogue by heart, having rehearsed Brown's part herself. And as she listens, she is puzzled to hear Brown interpolating a certain word every now and then. She pays but little heed, having more important things to occupy her mind. And she carries out her scheme of murder, escaping by the rear door of the studio.

"From there, she hurries round to the Bayswater flat, intent on obtaining those incriminating letters and destroying them. She waits her opportunity until the landlady moves out with the policeman who breaks the news of Brown's death, then she enters the flat with the key and begins her search. All her insane rage comes to the surface as she seeks; she is ruthless in her destruction. Eventually, she finds the letters, together with other documents. She crams the whole packet into her bag.

"She has one other thing to do. If the death of Brown should be discovered as a murder, if the wrecked flat comes under their notice, she means to leave a confusing trail. So she drags the head from the hatpin with which she committed the murder and hides the pin under the carpet. She knows full well that it will be confused with the hatpin among the effects in that studio, and positive identification will be impossible because of the missing ornament.

"Then Miss Smith goes back to her own cottage and examines the documents. After she has destroyed her own incriminating letters, she peruses the other papers—and discovers a remarkable plot. In a nutshell, Brown, in league with a drug organization, was to give a code-word over the air to the gang's head man. This code-word indicated whether her partner was guilty of betraying the organization. And Miss Smith, who knew every word of that dialogue, now understands the reason for Brown's queer interpolations, which she heard but could' not understand while listening to the opening of the play. *Brown had put over the information that her partner was guilty before she died!*

"Miss Smith realizes that the documents in her possession form a perfect, water-tight case against that partner. If, by any chance, Brown's death is suspected as murder, all she has to do is to send the documents anonymously to the police and the partner will be arrested for the murder. And that is just what happens. The death of Brown *is* proved to be murder. No sooner is this fact published in the newspapers than Scotland Yard receives the documents."

He paused, his voice on a high note. The dim-seen, pale-faced shadow in the corner spoke: "So your Miss Smith is cruel enough to let an innocent man hang for the murder she committed?"

"No!" Jeffery rose to his feet. "This is where Miss Smith demonstrates the brilliance, the genius almost, of her reasoning. Remember, there is no mention made in those documents she sent to the police of the *identity* of the treacherous partner! It is the task of Scotland Yard to discover this man's identity for themselves. And by this time, the organization that desires this man's life for his treachery will have struck! Remember also that Miss Smith *knows that Brown has put over the code-word that establishes her partner's guilt!* Consequently, she reasons that as the gang will strike almost at once, the partner will be dead before he can be arrested for the murder of Brown. There are two outstanding advantages if this occurs. Firstly, she will not have the blood of an innocent man on her hands. Secondly, the partner's lips will be sealed thus making it impossible for him to prove his innocence of the death of Brown.

"That," concluded Jeffery quietly, "is my perfect plot. Reduced to the bare essentials, the formula is water-tight. Miss Smith murders Brown, and discovers that circumstances build up a splendid case against her partner. This partner, who is shot by a gang for treachery, cannot defend himself. The police consider the Brown murder finished. The shooting of the partner, a separate case altogether, is investigated outside this country and the business in England considered closed. Thus Miss Smith remains quite unsuspected. Unsuspected, that is, until her name on the credit-title of a film arouses suspicion and, link by link, the amazing case is built up against her." Jeffery paused. "Now, Miss Knowles, I want your candid criticism. What do you think of my plot?"

The vague shape blacker than the shadows of the room stirred slightly. There was a gentle sigh like a breath expelled. Something dimly seen moved among the papers on the desk. Then a voice, a voice that held a weary gentleness, spoke softly.

"Would you turn on the light, Mr. Blackburn? The switch is near the doorway."

The young man backed, one hand groping for the switch, his eyes never leaving the figure behind the desk. His fingers touched metal, there was a click that flooded the room' with light. Katharine Knowles raised her head slowly. The thin cheeks were warm with the suggestion of a flush and the lips were moulded into a faint amusement. She spoke quietly, distinctly, each word a separate polished gem.

"You ask me what I think of your plot, Mr. Blackburn? I think it is excellent—as a plot!" A cold smile blossomed on her lips for a moment like the glint of sun on ice. Then it faded. "Now it is my turn to congratulate you on your creative ability. That is just such a plot as I myself might have evolved!"

Jeffery said slowly: "Yes, madam. It might have come straight from your own clever brain."

One white hand climbed to the woman's throat and toyed with the old-fashioned golden pendant that hung there. "Unfortunately," she said slowly, "your plot has three flaws in it."

"Indeed?"

Katharine Knowles' lips twisted ever so slightly. "Yes, Mr. Blackburn—three flaws. Firstly, I can vouch for the fact that Miss Smith did not even know that Miss Jones was Miss Brown until the news appeared in the Press. Secondly, your Miss Smith wrote no compromising letters such as you describe."

Jeffery gave a thin sigh. "And the third flaw?"

"The greatest of them all," Katharine Knowles said quietly. "Your Miss Smith may be able to prove a complete and unshakable alibi covering her movements on the night of the murder!"

"You understand, Miss Knowles," said Jeffery gravely, "that it would have to be a perfect alibi in the face of so much evidence?"

"It is a perfect alibi!" Katharine Knowles' voice rose high and clear. One hand flew to the side of that queer high-backed chair; there was a sudden mechanical whirring and the chair slid smoothly away from the desk. The seated woman propelled it to the centre of the room.

"Look, Mr. Blackburn," she cried. "This is Miss Smith's perfect alibi to your perfect plot!"

In that moment, Jeffery realized why Katharine Knowles had not risen when he entered. The chair in which she sat was an automatic invalid contraption and the lower framework supported a rigid foot and leg, a limb swollen and distended by snowy bandages.

"The one great flaw in your perfect plan," said Katharine Knowles softly. "On the morning of the murder at the studio, Miss Smith slipped on the low step of her cottage and fractured her leg! Her two maids will vouch that she has never stirred out of her cottage since that morning, and her specialist will testify that she cannot move a pace without her wheel-chair!"

3

As he steered the Bentley through the dusk in the direction of Victoria, Mr. Blackburn had cause to bless the prudent instinct that had warned him against communicating his suspicions regarding Katharine Knowles to the Chief Inspector. It was painful enough to writhe under his own bitter condemnation without any additional censure from his companion. Never had depression sat so blackly upon him as at that time. Twice he had flagellated his brain to no purpose; twice he had erected what appeared to have been a sound and stable case—and twice he had suffered the humiliation of complete and absolute failure.

"Confound it, I must be getting old," he grunted. "The intellect must be atrophying. God knows I've blundered before, but never to such inglorious depths as these! Is this to be my uncelebrated Waterloo—the one case from which Mr. Blackburn creeps away humbled and ashamed, to wince when it is mentioned and blanch at the recollection?" He trod irritably on the accelerator. "To hell with it! Why didn't I stay at Greymaster, chalking up extensions of the Newtonian formula for the edification of inky-fingered students!"

Thus it was in no pleasant frame of mind that he entered the flat. The Chief Inspector, sitting in a chair drawn up to the table, was conversing quietly with a visitor, an elderly grey-haired man wearing an old-fashioned frock-coat which fell to narrow trousers lopping over black boots. Two rather stary eyes looked out from a face purpled with meshes of tiny veins, and a brown tobacco-stained moustache drooped over a weak chin.

"Oh, there you are," grunted Read, as Jeffery entered. "Where have you been, son?" His manner was curiously repressed.

"About and about," returned the young man evasively. As he pulled off his gloves, he glanced around. There was something in the atmosphere of the room that he could not place, something in the strained attitude of his companion and the doleful aura that hung about their visitor. His eyes wandered to a small collection of articles on the table, a pocket-wallet, penknife, loose change, a pipe and tobacco-pouch and other miscellaneous objects. Read was saying.

"Jeff. This is Dr. Henry Newbolt, Miss Boycott-Smith's physician."

Blackburn nodded and took the outstretched hand. "And how is Miss Boycott-Smith?" he asked, after introductory formalities.

Dr. Newbolt blinked. "She seems a little better, I'm pleased to say," he said. "Of course, she knows nothing as yet. She's still too weak to be told, so we're delaying the bad news until she's stronger."

Jeffery frowned. "Bad news?"

The Chief Inspector drummed restless fingers on the table. "I've been trying to get you all the afternoon, son," he said quietly. "There's been another killing."

"Another?" The young man's tone leapt. "Who?"

Read spoke through tight lips. "Andrew Newland. The river police dragged his body out of the East India Dock about three o'clock this afternoon!"

A cold finger crept up Blackburn's spine and raised the short hairs on his neck. He stared at Read as a child stares at a conjurer. "Andrew Newland," he echoed. "Chief—you're sure?"

"Positive!" Read nodded heavily. "I saw the body myself. To make doubly sure, I got Dr. Newbolt down from the Towers. It's Newland, all right."

"But how . . .?" Blackburn walked unsteadily to a chair and sat down.

"He was beaten about the head with what seems to have been an iron bar. That's what the wounds look like. Conroy examined the body and said it had been immersed roughly thirty-six hours or thereabouts. We made inquiries at Newland's hotel. He left there on Friday morning early to go to the Towers. What time was it he rang you on Friday morning, son?"

"About ten o'clock," Jeffery replied. "It must have happened some time after that."

In the silence that followed, Dr. Newbolt's wheezing breath was plain. Jeffery traced a pattern on the polished table-top with his forefinger. "But why Newland?" he asked sombrely.

The Chief Inspector shrugged. "Heaven alone knows! Perhaps that lad stumbled on something that was dangerous. Although we'll probably never know just what it was." Then he paused and his eye caught the collection on the table. He swung off at a tangent. "Those are the things we took from his pockets," he explained.

Blackburn nodded and turned to Newbolt. "I wonder if you can help us in any way, Doctor? Do you know if Newland had an enemy?"

Their visitor pulled at his drooping moustache. "I'd be very surprised to hear it," he returned, moving his staring eyes to the young man. "A nicer fellow than Newland would be hard to find. He took some understanding, that's all. I'll never forget how he gave up that night of the play to sit with his aunt when she was at her lowest. You wouldn't find many young men sitting by a relative's sick-bed for close on four hours!"

"You were at the Towers?" asked Read.

Newbolt nodded. "I relieved Andrew while the play was , broadcast," he said. "I came in a few minutes before ten-thirty. When I looked into Miss Boycott-Smith's room, Andrew was sitting by the bed, his head in his hands. His aunt was asleep. He looked thoroughly worn out, poor chap. I told him that the play was due to go on in a few minutes and he glanced at his wrist-watch and nodded. He seemed too weary to speak. Then he went out into the sitting-room where the radio set stood."

"Well, good and bad go alike, I guess," muttered the Chief Inspector. "But I wish I knew why they bumped him off."

Jeffery reached across and pulled forward the articles taken from the dead man's pockets. "No indication in these, I suppose?" he asked.

"I've been through them," Read said curtly. "You'd better have a look for yourself."

Dr. Newbolt rose and pulled an old-fashioned silver watch from his pocket. "My train goes in twenty minutes," he said. "If I cannot be of further service to you gentlemen . . .?" he left the suggestion unfinished and reached for his tall black hat.

Read nodded. "Thank you, Doctor. It was very good of you to come down."

Jeffery looked up from his perusal of the articles, rose and shook the doctor's hand somewhat absently, then reseated himself while the Chief Inspector moved to the door with their visitor. When Read returned, the young man was pawing over each separate object. He tossed them aside one by one, his fingers lingering on an empty envelope addressed to Andrew Newland, care of the Winchester hotel. The envelope was soggy and the ink had run in purplish streaks across the paper. On the back, in pencil, were the words:

Call at 22, Fern Place, Battersea.

The sentence was scrawled hurriedly, as though it had been jotted down to recall an appointment. Jeffery laid the envelope on the table and tapped his fingers thoughtfully. Then he pulled a notebook from his pocket and copied the address on a blank page.

Read was watching him. "Make head or tail of it?" he grunted.

"There's very little to get your teeth into here," the young man admitted. He pushed the articles on one side with an impatient hand. "I take it that anything particularly incriminating was removed from the body before it was dumped into the water. Naturally, whoever did this thing would be unlikely to leave any visiting-cards in the pockets."

The Chief Inspector grunted again and, moving across to the sideboard, began to help himself to a drink. As he turned away, glass in hand, Jeffery called, "Mix one for me, Chief! I certainly need it after what's happened today!"

But Mr. Blackburn was destined never to taste that drink. Even as the big man turned back to the tantalus, there came the sound of running feet. The door burst open with a crash and Dennis Connolly charged into the room like a frenzied bull. Beneath his bowler hat, his face blazed like a harvest moon.

"Chief—Chief—" the words tripped and stumbled in his excitement. "Chief—we've bagged Lusinska! She was hoppin' a boat at Dover when the boys picked her up!"

Read jerked round so abruptly that his whisky described a wide arc across the carpet. "You've got her!" he cried. He took two quick paces forward. "Well—where is she now?"

"She's coming," babbled the big detective. "The boys are bringin' her along here—should come any minute now!"

Jeffery rose and, crossing to Read, took the drink from his fingers. He thrust it into the detective's hand. "Here,

Dennis, drink this," he said gravely. "Thy need is greater than mine."

Olga Lusinska said wearily:

"I did not kill that man. I went to his hotel to meet him on a business matter. What happened there I can tell you, because I saw it happen! Whether you will believe me is another matter. But I am telling you the truth when I say that I did not kill that man!"

The Russian actress slumped in a chair, the target of three pairs of eyes. The Chief Inspector stood over her, feet apart, arms folded, his favourite attitude for cross-examination. Jeffery leaned against the table, a cigarette burning away between his fingers. Dennis Connolly lounged by the window.

It was a changed Lusinska who faced them. Fear that was closely akin to panic had drawn the skin tightly across her face, narrowing those slanting eyes wickedly, emphasizing the prominent cheek-bones and setting the mouth in a thin, cruel line. The sheen had gone from her dark hair, leaving it lank and lifeless. As she sipped at the drink which Read had poured for her, the rim of the glass chattered against her teeth.

The Chief Inspector snapped. "If you were so innocent of this murder, why the hurry to get out of the country?"

Olga Lusinska's lips curled. "Would you have believed me had I told you that I saw Steinie Rodda commit suicide?"

"What's that?" Jeffery straightened. He said sharply, "What did you say?"

The woman raised her eyes to his face. "I saw Steinie Rodda shoot himself with that automatic pistol," she said steadily.

Read bared his white teeth. "Indeed? Just an entertaining parlour-trick, I suppose?"

But Jeffery had stepped to his side. "Miss Lusinska—suppose you start at the beginning," he suggested quietly. "How did you come to meet Rodda?"

Lusinska turned and placed her half-empty glass on the table. She clasped her hands on her lap and kept her eyes fixed on them as she talked.

"I met Rodda about two years ago," she began. "He was recommended to me as a specialist in perfumes. He blended a special scent for me and I went to him every month for my supply.

"I was in pictures at that time. One evening, after a particularly trying day, I almost fainted in his apartment. He was very kind and offered me a cigarette. It was a peculiar kind—smaller than the average and rolled in brown paper. Rodda lit one for me and as I inhaled the smoke it had a sweetish sickly taste that made my head swim. I wanted to throw it away, but Rodda insisted that I smoke the cigarette to the end, saying that the first effects would vanish after a while. And it was as he said. After the first few minutes, I found the cigarette marvellously soothing. Rodda then gave me a packet and told me to take them home and smoke one whenever I felt run-down. I did so."

Jeffery nodded. "You say they were different from ordinary cigarettes?"

"Yes. They were specially imported from Buenos Aires. I took them and smoked one whenever I felt tired and weary. Gradually, I found that I could not do without them. Next time I visited Rodda for my perfume, he gave me two packets; the next occasion, three. And so it went on for some six months. Until at last something horrible occurred. Those fits of wearying depression became worse and worse—and, what was more terrible, the cigarettes could not relieve me. It was during another conversation with Rodda that I told him this. I asked him the reason. Then he told me that the cigarettes were drugged with opium—that they would no longer help me and that I must have something else. By this time my mental state was so terrible that I implored him to give me something—anything to lift the depression that shadowed my life."

"And he did?" said Read through his teeth.

Lusinska nodded wearily. "Yes. He showed me a tiny cut-glass perfume jar filled with white powder. When the stopper was removed, attached to it was a small rubber tube, something like the filler of a fountain-pen. Rodda showed me how to fill the tiny tube and blow the powder up my nostrils. It was almost magical in the manner it relieved me. I bought the jar from him for fifty pounds. It was only after I had come to rely upon this white powder that I discovered it was cocaine—and that I was in the grip of the drug habit!"

The woman stopped and ran the back of her hand across her mouth. Then she reached out and took a sip of her whisky.

"Rodda continued to supply me with the drug through the months that followed. It was not until two months ago that he began to hedge. He told me that he would have to cut down my supplies, that outside influences were making the business very dangerous. But, by this time, I was far too deeply in trouble to consider consequences. I told him I had to have the drug, and for a time he went on selling it to me.

"A few days before the play at the B.B.C., however, I was again down to my last pinch of cocaine. I rang Rodda and begged for a fresh supply. He told me to wait until the morning. The same thing happened on the following day—and the day after that! On the morning of the play, I was almost frantic. I went round to his apartment and begged him again to do something to relieve my agony. He said that he had no drug with him then, but he would bring me a supply when he came to the studio opening that night. I had to be satisfied with this. All day I lived in such a hell as only a drug addict robbed of the precious powder can know. Rodda, however, kept his word. He came to the opening that night and brought me a packet of cocaine. He was to call for payment in the morning."

"So that's what brought him along to the opening?" barked the Chief Inspector. "I imagined it was something very shady!"

Jeffery was watching the actress with sombre eyes. "And you met him the following morning?"

"I did," replied Lusinska. "And so high were his charges that I had not enough money at my flat. I had to draw from my account and asked Rodda if he would drive me to Threadneedle Street. He was willing, but he said that he wished to make a call in Bayswater first. We drove to a house and he went inside. When he appeared, he was in a vile mood. I asked him if there was anything wrong—he seemed horribly afraid of something—but he just snarled a word, jumped into the car, and drove off like fury. Next day, I learnt that the house we had visited was the flat of the girl who had been killed in the play!"

Again she paused, finished her drink and placed the glass on the table. The retailing of her sordid, pitiable story seemed to alleviate the strained tenseness of her attitude. She was more relaxed now, talking more naturally.

"I did not see Rodda again until the night of his death," Lusinska continued. Her fingers writhed like snakes in her lap for a moment, and were still. "It was the old story. I had gone through my supply and had to have more. On the morning of that day, I rang him at his hotel, but he told me that he could not supply me with any more of the drug and that I was not to worry him. He hung up the receiver on my pleadings. I rang him again, but he would not answer. All that afternoon I waited, believing he would relent and call and see me—or ring me. Then about nine o'clock that night, I could wait no longer. I determined to go and see him."

Two livid spots of colour had appeared over Lusinska's cheek-bones. Hands clasped, head thrust forward on hunched shoulders, she stared ahead. Her voice had dropped to a husky whisper.

"I went into his hotel and up to his rooms. The door was locked. Returning, I approached the desk-clerk and asked him to put a call through to the rooms. He did so, but there was no answer. I was frantic with worry. I went out of the hotel, climbed the fire escape, and was surprised to find the windows of Rodda's apartment open. There was a little table near the window and on this was an automatic pistol.

"I was debating with myself whether to go in and wait for him to return when a man who had been watching me by the window called to ask if he could help me. I was terrified and, covering my face, ran down the fire escape and into the garden. There I waited until the man had gone."

"How long did you wait?" asked Jeffery as she paused.

"About half an hour," Lusinska told him. "Then I returned and climbed the fire escape again, halting outside the open window. I was just about to climb inside when there was the sound of a key fumbling in the lock of the door. I waited. The door opened and Rodda entered. He was swaying from side to side. He reached up for the light-switch, clicked it on, but no light came. Then Rodda swayed across the room to the table. He was muttering something that I could not catch. I was about to call to him when he did a most amazing thing. Quite naturally, he picked up the automatic from the table, pointed it at himself and pulled the trigger. There was a report—and he gave a queer choking cough and dropped to the floor. He was bleeding from a wound in his chest.

"I was horrified, stunned! The whole thing had been so—so casual, so unpremeditated! I tell you Rodda walked across to that table, picked up the gun, turned it on himself and pulled the trigger. It was the most terrible thing I have ever seen!

"For a few seconds, I crouched outside the window, petrified with horror. Then the sound of running footsteps broke the spell and some people rushed into the room. They clicked the light as Rodda had done, then one of them—a man—called something. I didn't wait to hear anything else—I rushed down the escape and out into the street. I realized that I was deeply involved in this fearful business and that, if I were questioned, everything would have to be told." She raised her dark eyes to her audience. "I was mad to run away, but one does not think rationally at such times. All yesterday I hid in a cheap hotel and this afternoon determined to make for the Continent." She shrugged. "And the rest you know."

There was a silence when Olga Lusinska paused. The Chief Inspector stood plucking at his moustache, his face grim. Jeffery remained staring at the actress with corrugated brow. Connolly moved heavy feet near the window. The clock chimed ten times. Then Read cleared his throat.

"You'll have to make that statement at headquarters," he said gruffly. "After that, we'll see . . ." He swung round. "Connolly—I'll leave this woman in your hands. You know what to do."

Connolly nodded and lumbered forward. He laid a paw on the actress' shoulder. She shook it off with a gesture almost of disdain. "There's no need for that," she said quietly. "I'll not make trouble. I'm ready to go with you." She stood and turned a haggard face toward the other men. "You do believe me, don't you, when I say that Rodda committed suicide?"

It was Blackburn who answered. He gave her a long searching look. "Miss Lusinska," he said gravely, "I am almost afraid to believe you!"

William Read was in a broadcasting studio. William Read was supremely happy, for he was about to give the first of his talks on criminology. He glanced at the notes in his hand then raised his eyes to the hanging microphone suspended above his head. But it was not a microphone; it was a long steel hatpin, a Brobdingnagian pin, magnified to the dimensions of a lance, and its cruel point was dropping directly toward him. He tried to move, but some living growth constricted arms and legs. He was bound with miles of cinematograph film that writhed and crawled about his body. Steinie Rodda, the feature announcer, was gesticulating for him to start—couldn't the fool see what was wrong? As the pin descended lower, Rodda became frantically angry. He pulled from his pocket a tiny automatic, waved it threateningly in the Chief Inspector's face, then turned it on himself and pulled the trigger. There was a deafening report and Rodda dropped, materializing into Carl von Bethke as he fell. And now Isabelle Simms was by his side, tearing at the binding celluloid with impotent hands, jerking him from side to side, shaking him . . . shaking him. . . .

"Hey!" screamed Read and woke to find Jeffery jerking at his shoulders.

The big man blinked and shook a drowsy head, "What the . . .?" he mumbled. Then recognizing the disturber: "What the devil's the matter with you, son?"

"Shake off this downy sleep, death's counterfeit!" Jeffery was crying. In the reflected light from the sitting-room, Read could see his face ablaze with excitement: "Chief! I've stumbled on the truth at last! The whole complete answer! How . . . why . . . and who? The entire blinking, stinking triangle! And I know it all!"

The Chief Inspector stared at his companion's fully clothed figure then jerked his head to the night-clock. "Haven't you been to bed? It's past four o'clock!"

"Who cares?" cried Blackburn. "For lo, the winter is past, the rain is over and gone; the flowers appear on the earth; the time of singing birds is come and the voice of the turtle is heard in our land!"

"The voice of the imbecile is heard in my bedroom," snapped Read. "What's all this about the eternal triangle? Another bright idea?"

"A bright idea—and the right idea!" Jeffery clasped ecstatic hands. "It must be true, Chief—it must be! The whole *amazing* plan fits together perfectly. I've been stewing in that room ever since you went to bed, flogging the old brain over the reason why Rodda should have committed suicide! And now, by God, I've got it!"

Read sat upright. "You mean—you know who the criminal is?"

"I do! And why the murders were committed! There's one other link in the chain . . . and that I can get from an address in Battersea tomorrow night—"

"You mean tonight!"

"Tonight, then!" Jeffery sat down on the edge of the bed and his manner sobered. "You've got to help me, Chief! I'm going to play a highly dangerous game, so listen carefully. I'll tell you the truth about the whole amazing business and then outline your part in the affair!"

V

CURTAIN-CALL FOR CAIN

Justice, though moving with tardy pace, has seldom failed to overtake the wicked in their flight.

HORACE.

I

MR. BLACKBURN glanced at his wrist-watch, noted that it needed but two minutes to nine o'clock, then turned to survey his destination.

The house in Fern Place presented a façade that was' faded and shabby even under the soft light of a gibbous moon. A six-foot strip of lawn separated it from the pavement and it would have taken more than a buoyant spring to rejuvenate the creeper which clung with a stubborn death-grip to the wall and hung rustling brown leaves limp across the windows. From the fan-light over the door, a steady radiance glowed. Otherwise the house was in darkness.

Jeffery advanced across the pavement, pushed open the gate and moved to the door. He knocked once, then paused with his hand in mid-air. The movement of the knocker had caused the door to swing open. It described a slow quarter arc and halted half ajar. The young man stared into a lighted carpeted hall which terminated in a door at the far end.

His hand in his pocket, Jeffery advanced. On the thick pile, he moved noiselessly. From an old-fashioned shade of coloured segments of glass, the light shone down blandly. He walked half a dozen paces and paused, listening. But throughout that house was the silence of things unborn. A click made him spin around and he saw that the door had swung to behind him. His body tensed.

"Is anyone here?" he called softly. "Is anyone about?"

No answer. The silence in that house was like the silence of a tomb. Something, perhaps the sound of his voice, caused the polychromatic lamp-shade to swing slightly and colours flickered and danced about his head. Jeffery waited for almost a minute, standing with head thrust slightly forward, every nerve in his body tingling and alert. Then he stepped forward to the door at the end of the hall. Reaching it, he turned the knob and pushed it open cautiously. The room was in darkness. He stepped inside and listened.

"Anyone here?" he called again.

Nothing broke that all-enveloping silence. He glanced about. With one exception, the darkness swamped everything. Some distance away he picked out the faint glitter of starshine through a curtained window. Otherwise, this room had an opacity that was as blinding as the dropping of eyelids. Then suddenly he stiffened and his fingers tightened about the object in his coat pocket. For a second that glint of starshine had been blotted out—to reappear again. There was someone in that room with him . . . someone who had crept stealthily past the window . . . and was creeping as stealthily toward him. His hand flew from his pocket, fingers grasping the butt of a black snub-nosed automatic. Then Jeffery spoke and his voice was cold and inflexible as a steel blade.

"Stay where you are, my friend!"

From the shadows, a soft voice spoke: "Mr. Blackburn. So you did come?"

"As you see," replied Jeffery, "I am here."

"And," continued that soft mocking voice, "what do you want with me?"

Jeffery took a step forward. Dark as the shadows about him was his tone.

"You are a clever artist, my friend, but now your mask is off! I know you as the murderer of Isabelle Simms, of Steinie Rodda . . . and of Allan Thompson, whose body was dragged out of the East India Dock yesterday afternoon." His voice snapped like a whip-crack.

"Put up your hands, Andrew Newland!" There was a soft movement in the darkness, a hissing breath of air close by his ear. Jeffery Blackburn squirmed just too late. A loaded sandbag crashed down on his head. His knees crumpled under him and he dropped down . . . down into the red mists of oblivion.

With every condition ministering to the individual's comfort, the pathway from insensibility is invariably painful. But when one is tied hand and foot in a stiff-backed chair, soaked with water and bleeding from a wound in the head, the return can be agony to the most excruciating degree. Mr. Blackburn experienced all the tortures of the damned as his stirring consciousness groped to the surface some twenty minutes later.

He raised a buzzing head heavy as a mill-stone, dragged up eyelids that weighed like iron, and the million gleaming spears flung at his eyes from the brilliantly lit room were like needles in a raw wound. He groaned and dropped his head. Vaguely he was conscious of the sharp sting of cold water flung in his face. He raised his head again, opened his eyes slowly, and through a swirling scarlet mist a figure shifted and danced. Gradually the mists cleared, the figure ceased its lunatic swaying. Details solidified.

Andrew Newland, a half-empty glass of water in his hand, stood looking down at him. Even as Jeffery had said, the mask was put aside. Newland's heavy face, robbed of that stolid veneer, was animal; the expression dangerous and ferine. His thick lips hung open in a leer and little eyes glittered cruelly under black brows. He gave a coarse throaty chuckle as Jeffery stirred, and flung the last of the water into his face. Then he reached forward and jerked up Blackburn's head, glaring down into his eyes.

"So, Mr. Clever Blackburn," he snarled. "You know!"

Jeffery licked his lips. There was the acrid taste of blood in his mouth. His voice grated horribly. "Yes, Newland. I know it all."

"Ach!" The other flung the limp head back and turned away. He lit a cigarette, gulping the smoke in great puffs so that the cords on his thick neck appeared and vanished. It gave Blackburn the few minutes' respite that he craved. With an effort, he gathered his wandering senses. A sudden movement from Newland caught his attention. The man wheeled on him and came closer. His voice had sunk to a confidential gloating.

"You say that I have committed three murders, Blackburn? You're wrong. I've committed four! True, the last murder has been committed merely in theory so far—but I assure you that it will be an actuality before half an hour is past." He thrust his face close to the bound man. "Understand?"

"Perfectly," replied Jeffery quietly. "I am to be the fourth."

Newland stepped back a pace. He nodded slowly. "I am going to blow your brains out with your own automatic," he said levelly.

Jeffery drew a deep breath. "Then why go to all this trouble?" His eyes indicated the ropes that bound him.

"Oh, that?" Newland puffed at his cigarette. "You see, I don't want you to die before I find out exactly how much you really do know. Because, unless you're a wizard, you can't possibly have the whole story, nor can you be aware of the cleverness of my planning. It wouldn't be fair to kill you, Blackburn, until you were given an opportunity of beholding the workings of a mind more brilliant than your own!"

There was fanaticism in that voice, in the gleam of those little eyes with their trace of blood at the corners, in the workings of that loose mouth. Then Newland chuckled and it was a sound that was not good to hear.

"I wonder if I can make you realize the intense amusement I had from this glorious game? Poor old Andy Newland, people would say! Just a good-natured old mutton-head—a cheerful, unimaginative clod! Of course they said that! Didn't I do everything in my power to make them believe it?" His lips drooped and the fire died out of his eyes. "What a pitiful shame that they can never know the truth!"

He squinted at Blackburn. "I've always been interested in detective stories. Always! But how they bored me with their feeble, trite plots. Always I said to myself: 'One day I shall plan a perfect plot—the crime of the century. But I shall write my detective story in blood! Not for me the moving of pale pen-and-ink characters—I should plan with living people! I will take human beings and bend them to the shape of my plot!' That was my ambition, Blackburn—to achieve a perfect detective story of which I alone knew the answer . . . and to use as my characters men and women instead of people created in the brain. I longed to set my plan in action, to gently insinuate a twist here, a tangle there, a cross-current in another direction . . . to stand off in my role of dumb clod and watch the poor helpless puppets moving like mechanical mice along paths my clever brain had plotted for them!"

Newland paused, tossed his half-smoked cigarette away and lit another.

"I might as well admit that it has long been my ambition to murder my aunt," he continued. "I bear the old dear no particular animosity, except for her ridiculous and open-handed generosity. She used to give fortunes to every charity that wrote her a begging letter! So that each month my aunt lived meant less money falling into my hands at her death. So I determined that she should die.

"I read up accounts of various crimes. Among them, I came across details of the hatpin murder which had occurred in Paris during the war. But I felt that, although this method appealed to me, the execution was not at all simple. It was during this time that I happened to meet the girl I then knew as Mary Marlowe. We became friendly—she made the advances because, as was proved later, she used my influence to get her into that radio play."

"Did you know anything of her past?" Blackburn asked.

"Not until some time later," chuckled Newland. "One night she gave a private screening of a film she had, dealing with Solanine, an alkaloid poison. The film demonstrated how it could bring about death with the symptoms of gastro-enteritis. Now my aunt suffered rather severely from gastritis and I determined to use this poison to bring about her end. I asked Marlowe where I could get it, telling her I wanted to make some experiments. Marlowe told me that she had studied chemistry and could probably get me a supply. She did so. I used to take the poison to the Towers and dope my aunt's food. When she began to sicken, I sent for the family physician, a doddering old fool named Newbolt, and, as I expected, he told my aunt she was suffering from gastro-enteritis."

Jeffery stared at the man. That he was mentally unbalanced seemed the only possible explanation for this amazing recital, delivered with a cheerful candour that was horrifying. Now Newland had begun to pace the room, illustrating his terrible confession with quick nervous movements of his hands.

"All went well for two months. Then, when I went to get my usual supply of the poison from Marlowe, she refused to give it to me. She said that she had learnt' that I was dosing my aunt and that unless I paid her one hundred pounds she would give the information to the police, together with certain letters I had written her asking for the poison.

"Of course, she had read of my aunt's illness in the newspapers and guessed the truth. What could I do? I paid the money. She gave me more poison. But if I had imagined that she would be satisfied with this one sum, I was to be sadly mistaken. She held the whip over my head in every way. That was how she forced me to get her that part in the radio play. And then came her final outrageous request. She said that I must make her my wife!"

Jeffery said grimly: "That girl realized that if your murder was successful, you would be a wealthy man!"

"Of course," grunted Newland. "And as my wife, she could have a respectable cut of that money. But I bucked at this. She said she would give me twenty-four hours to make up my mind. If we were not engaged within that time, those letters and the information against me would be in the hands of the police!

"It was, of course, a huge bluff on her part. Mixed in the crooked business as she was, she would not have dared go near the police. But I knew nothing of her past or of the drug racket, at that time. All I knew was the fact that she held those letters and information against me, the information I had *admitted* to be true by paying her hush money! So there was only one alternative left to me. Mary Marlowe had to die!"

"When was this ultimatum delivered?"

"On the morning of the radio play," Newland said. His tone was savage. "I drove about London in my car, trying to evolve some scheme. Then it was that my mind recurred to the hatpin murder. I remembered how the murderer had thrust a pin through the keyhole of a door at which a woman had been listening. And then the recollection of those rehearsals I had attended with Marlowe came back to me. I could have shouted for joy! For in the play a character was called upon to listen at the keyhole of a door, and Marlowe was playing that part! Surely this was a chance too good to miss! I drove back to my hotel with my plan half-formed and there chance put another wonderful opportunity in my way. There was a telegram from old Newbolt, telling me that Aunt had had a relapse during the night and that I was requested to come to the Towers at once."

Jeffery shifted restlessly in the ropes that were biting into his flesh. "When did you get in touch with Thompson?" he asked.

"As soon as I had formulated my plan," Newland explained. "Thompson, as you know, used to work as my double in those films I made for that crooked company. He was employed to do all the dangerous stunts that might have injured me. He resembled me closely in face and figure and a few touches of make-up here and there completed the illusion. He had been out of work for some time and would be willing to earn a hundred pounds and ask no questions. I got in touch with him at once through an agency. Then I drove out to his lodgings and told him what I wanted. He was desperately hard up and was eager to earn the money."

Newland halted in front of Jeffery and rubbed his hands. "And this was how we worked the scheme," he said. "I took Thompson back with me and left him, with my car, in the village. I went on to the Towers. I had dinner and then announced that I was walking into the village to send a telegram to Nickerson wishing him luck on the opening of the studio. I went down to the village, sent the telegram, changed clothes with Thompson who had made himself up to resemble me as closely as possible, sent him back to the Towers and drove down to London.

"There was little danger for Thompson so long as he kept his head. Most of the servants were going to a masquerade ball in the village and the Towers would be almost deserted. I instructed Thompson to speak as little as possible. He had to listen in to the play and, if anything happened, he was to go to the telephone, put a call through to the studio and ask the reason. As hundreds of other people would likewise do this, the call would not seem at all out of place, while it would definitely prove that I had never left the Towers on that night. Then Thompson was to make some excuse to get out of the house, go down into the village and wait for me. There I was to meet him, change clothes again, and he was to take the first train to London in the morning.

"There's no need for me to go into lengthy explanations of my movements," continued Newland imperturbably. "I drove down to the studio, slipped in the rear entrance, went into the rehearsal room and took one of the two keys of Marlowe's flat from her handbag, waited in there listening to the dialogue of the play which was coming from the speaker in the small studio where you and the Chief Inspector were standing. When the play reached that darkened sequence, I moved to the door, jabbed the hatpin through the keyhole and fled for my life. I believe that you heard me click the door behind me and drive away in my car."

"But the risk," said Blackburn, interested in spite of himself. "What if you had been seen?"

"The risk wasn't as great as you might imagine," was the reply. "For one thing, the only people who knew me by sight in that place were Nickerson and the people inside the dramatic studio. I had only to keep out of Nickerson's way. Also, I was dressed so that if any stray person had noticed me, they would have naturally assumed that I was one of the guests prowling about. The actual risk occurred only during the sixty seconds it took me to thrust that pin through the keyhole and get out of the studio.

"I stopped my car some little distance from the studio and pulled on a big coat and dragged my hat over my eyes. Then, synchronizing nearly as possible with the time I reckoned Thompson would be calling from the Towers, I went into a telephone-box and rang Nickerson. That was a really clever move on my part! Who would guess that the call from the Towers went no farther than the studio switchboard, which was at that time jammed with similar inquiries?"

"I guessed it," said Jeffery coldly. "Unfortunately, it was too late!"

Anger blazed in Newland's face. "Then, since you're such a damned Clever Dick," he snarled, "perhaps you can tell me what happened next?"

"Certainly," replied Blackburn steadily. "You drove around to a flat in Bayswater, waited your opportunity until the landlady and a police officer had gone, then slipped into the flat and searched for those letters. Among them you found other interesting documents."

Newland glared at him for a moment, then shrugged.

"You're right," he admitted. "I went through the flat pretty thoroughly. Not only did I want my letters, but also that can of film concerning the Solanine. I meant to destroy every possible trace of my plan. I set about picking one of the locks with the hatpin, but half-way through the operation, the end came off and the hatpin shot away somewhere. I didn't have time to look for it. I read that you found it in the flat on the following afternoon.

"I came upon a whole sheaf of documents hidden in a false bottom of the wardrobe in Marlowe's bedroom. I waited just long enough to make sure that my letters were among them, then I left. I could not risk another search for the film, since the landlady might return at any moment.

"I got back to the Towers and spent some time looking over those documents. And I had my eyes opened very thoroughly regarding the girl who called herself Mary Marlowe. Apart from her instructions from this Viardin man, she kept a sort of diary, in which she recorded the story of everything that had happened to her since the studio fire and the business of the chemist, Gallasch. It began with that and ended with the evidence she had obtained proving Steinie Rodda had betrayed the drug organization.

"As I sat turning over these pages, it came to me what wonderful sport I could have if Simms' death—we'll call that girl by her right name now—was ever proved to be murder. On the table before me was a water-tight case against her partner! And here was the greatest advantage—if Simms had succeeded in putting over that code-word telling of Rodda's guilt, the gang would probably have finished him off before the police could touch him. But you know all this, Blackburn. You figured it out in front of me that night at your flat—and that, incidentally, was the first time I realized that you were dangerous to my safety. You reasoned that business out very cleverly, the only mistake being in your thinking that I had been mixed up in the drug business myself, when I knew nothing of that plot until I read the details in Simms' diary.

"I came down to London next morning, as I had promised Nickerson—came down in the role of heartbroken suitor," continued Newland gleefully. "On the way I bought a newspaper and, to my delight, read that the doctor who examined Simms' body had given the verdict of heart failure. And then it was that I decided to have a game with the police, to try a little judicious nose-leading. It would be interesting to pit my brains against yours—and if you did outwit me, if you discovered the death of Simms to be murder, then I had only to post those documents down to you, and you would set off hot-foot to arrest Rodda. And if

Rodda, as was probable, had been murdered by the drug organization, you would be left in a bewildering maze that would "trick you at every turn!"

Newland paused. He reached for a chair, pulled it forward and sat down opposite the bound Jeffery.

"Well, I played the part to perfection, I believe," he said with relish. "I told you just enough to make you suspicious. I never dreamt, however, that you'd prove Simms' death to be murder, and it was a surprise to me when the Chief Inspector rang me last Thursday to tell me that they'd proved that girl's death a homicide.

"Meanwhile, however, other complications had set in to worry me. Simms, wily little devil that she was, had attempted to safeguard herself by telling Steinie Rodda about the business of my aunt. She had given the film into his keeping, but fortunately had held back my letters. She had told Rodda that if anything happened to her, he was to take his information, together with the film, to the police. Rodda, of course, had no idea that Simms was working against him for the drug gang.

"But Rodda saw a neat little fortune in his information. He came to me and demanded blackmail that almost took my breath away. Had he not possessed that film, I would have dared him to go to the police, since the word of an ex-gaolbird would never have been taken against mine. He had, to be sure, tried to get hold of those letters almost as soon as the morning papers published Simms' death. He went round to her flat in his car, only to find that I had been there first. Then it was that Rodda knew I had murdered Simms to close her mouth.

"When Rodda came to me, I deliberated on the best course to take. I had half a mind to let him know about Simms' treachery in betraying him to the gang (provided that she did put that code-word over before I killed her), then I realized that this would not stop him blackmailing me. He would probably fly from England and hide until the search for him died down, then return and demand his hush-money again. But while he remained in ignorance of the business, there was a good chance (again provided the gang knew of his treachery) that they would wipe him out and thus relieve me of a very considerable thorn in my flesh!

"And if this happened, there was no reason why I should not pin Simms' murder on to Rodda by sending those documents to Scotland Yard. Of course, I had no intention of allowing the police to arrest Rodda, because he knew too much about me. If they did discover his identity before the gang struck, then I would kill him myself. Thus the police would never know—never be sure whether it was the gang vengeance or another killing by Simms' murderer. And so the documents came to you, outlining a complete case against Rodda, telling everything but his name. I judged that by the time you had discovered the identity of this mysterious partner, the gang would have struck and I would be relieved of his murder. But I made two mistakes. I did not know that the Chief Inspector would get his information so quickly—nor did I guess that you, Blackburn, would reason out the situation so cleverly!"

Jeffery said quietly: "You murdered Rodda by substituting a loaded automatic for that trick cigarette-gun of his, I know that."

Newland looked at him, his expression a mixture of hatred and admiration. "You don't miss much, do you, Blackburn?" he said, his tone quieter. "Well, you're right! When the Chief Inspector called me on that Thursday afternoon and told me he wanted me at your flat that night, I guessed he was on the trail of the partner's identity. The gang had not struck so far and I could not afford to wait. Rodda had to die before the police arrested him.

"I had already made my plans and they centred about that trick cigarette-gun that Rodda owned. Often when I saw him pointing the barrel at himself and shooting cigarettes into his mouth, I had thought of how amusing it would be to substitute a real automatic for that toy. It was exactly the same size and nearly the same weight as the genuine article. I had already obtained an automatic closely resembling the toy and, with this loaded in my pocket, I went around to his hotel. I made a last plea for that can of film, but Rodda said that it was in a safe deposit and there it would remain until I paid up or he gave the key to the police. I pretended to get angry, then finally admitted that he had me cornered. If, I said, he would come around to my hotel, I would give him his cheque there and then. Rodda was delighted. He went into the bedroom to get his hat and coat. While he was gone, I took up his cigarette-gun from the small table by the window and put the loaded automatic in its place. I also removed the electric globe from the socket of the light.

"Rodda came back with me to the Winchester and we bargained until it was almost dark. Then when we had agreed on the sum, I made out the cheque and gave it to him. Then I suggested a drink. Rodda was willing. I dropped some dope which Simms had given me into his glass and he passed out cold almost as soon as he had drunk. I went through his pockets, took back my cheque and searched for the key of that safe deposit. But it wasn't on him. This was a disappointment! It meant that I would have to search his rooms. But there was no time now, for I had promised to be at your flat at eight o'clock and it was getting close to that hour then. So I walked the doped Rodda downstairs and bundled him into my car. I drove round to the Splendide and left him in the garden near the side entrance. I judged that he would go up to his room.

"But my plans miscarried badly. Because the fool must have fallen asleep again and stayed out in that garden for well over an hour. As I guessed, he went to his room, fumbled for what he thought was the cigarette-gun, and shot himself through the heart. But I had arranged that his body would not be found until the morning, giving me a chance to search his rooms for the key on my way home. But your detectives prevented that move, to say nothing of the unforeseen contingency of that Russian actress being on the spot.

"I'll admit I got a pretty bad fright when I heard that she was at the hotel at the time of the shooting. For all I knew, she may have talked with Rodda . . . he may have told her everything. Again, if she had seen the shooting, she knew that the bullet was self-inflicted, which didn't fit in with my plans at all. Because I wanted it to appear as though the gang had murdered Rodda.

"When I saw you and the detective coming out of that Chancery Lane safe deposit with the can of film, I lost my head completely. I imagined that Rodda had talked and that the police were eager to screen that film in proof of his story. And if they did screen it, I was as good as caught! In a moment of panic, I tried to run your friend down. When that failed, I made an attempt on your flat, thinking that the film might have been left there. But that was ruined by some other fool blundering in. That was my narrowest escape."

There was a silence as Newland paused. He rose and pushed his chair away. That queer light had died from his eyes, leaving them sombre as a cloud-shadowed tarn. His voice was quiet, almost restrained as he continued.

"Remember that proverb from the Arabian Nights, Blackburn? 'Only a fool tries to catch the moon in a net and harness the winds of chance.' That was where I made my greatest mistake. I was clever, but not clever enough to foresee the way in which the winds of chance would blow. And from the time I manipulated the killing of Rodda, they blew against me. And you can't fight an opponent as intangible as chance. If chance hadn't brought you to that studio on the night of Simms' broadcast, her death would never have been suspected as murder. If chance hadn't sent Olga Lusinska to the window of Rodda's room on the night of his death, you would still believe that the drug organization was responsible for his killing. It was after this that I began to be afraid. I had set certain mechanism working and now it had got out of control." He looked up. "Not that I regret the deaths of Simms or Rodda! They were both so much scum on the face of humanity. They deserved to be wiped off!"

Jeffery said harshly: "What about Thompson? He had done nothing to deserve his death!"

Newland shrugged. "Thompson's murder was on his own head," he said simply. "If he had kept out of the business, he would have been alive today. But no. His sense of righteousness was too strong for him. Alive, he would have indirectly caused my own death. Dead, he was powerless. Therefore, he had to go. It was his life or mine and I was too deeply involved to stop at a small detail like Thompson's life.

"He was waiting for me when I returned to my hotel after the attempt on your flat. He had come to return my hundred pounds. He told me that unless I gave him a satisfactory explanation regarding the masquerade of Monday night, he was going to the police with the story. I called his bluff. I told him I had nothing to hide and, if he wished, would drive down to the nearest police-station with him. That rather took the wind out of his sails. But I insisted, saying that it was only fair to me. You see, I had to get him into my car somehow. When I did, I used a spanner on him."

Newland clasped his hands behind his back and recommenced his pacing of the floor.

"I drove around London for almost an hour with the, unconscious man in the back seat of my car, considering the best means of hiding the body. Because I could not afford to let Thompson's body be discovered. His likeness to me was too great—it might have revealed the whole plan. I was somewhere in the vicinity of Canning Town before the brilliant idea burst upon me. Why not let Thompson's body be found . . . as *Andrew Newland!* Not only would it be a perfect method of hiding the body's true identity, but it would add another confusing factor to the case and leave me a genuine avenue of escape."

"Just a moment," interrupted Blackburn. "If the body was found as yours, surely you realized that it would be impossible to return as Andrew Newland and claim your aunt's wealth?"

"Naturally," returned Newland sullenly. "But I wasn't worrying about my aunt's money. I was more concerned with saving my own skin. I realized that I'd played a dangerous game—and that I'd lost! And since Rodda's death, it has been impossible for me to get supplies of the poison—that's why Aunt's condition has improved over the past few days. She will probably live to a hale and hearty old age. There was nothing I could do about it except make the best of a bad job. Because not only had I lost the chance to get my aunt's fortune, but I also stood a good chance of ending my life on the gallows.

"Therefore, I decided to effect this substitution of bodies and, with Andrew Newland dead, get away and start all over again somewhere else. I'd had my fun. If I lost the game, there it was! I've always been a good sportsman, Blackburn, if a rather bungling murderer. Or perhaps I shouldn't say a bungling murderer so much as an unfortunate victim of chance.

"Anyhow, I drove down to Poplar and ran my car behind the wall of a disused warehouse. There I took the spanner and altered Thompson's face so that it would pass as mine after some hours in the water. Then I changed the body into my clothes."

"And you scribbled an address on an envelope to trap me," added Blackburn.

"I did!" All the savage fury welled into Newland's face, so that it was blotched with scarlet. He took a step forward and almost hissed the words in the other's face.

"I'll tell you why, Blackburn! You see me now—a man who has lost everything that makes life worth living! But for you, I might be living in luxury. Instead, I am a hunted man with three murders on my conscience. And you are responsible! You have baulked, hindered, and hampered at every turn, you alone are responsible! If you had kept out of the way, I would be free, wealthy, unsuspected. Through your inquisitive busybodying, I am a suspected murderer! Even as I tipped Thompson's body into the East India Dock, I determined that, come what may, I would kill you. I realized that if Thompson's body was picked out of the water, identified as myself, and that envelope was found in his pocket, it was inevitable that your prying nose would lead you here." He stepped back, and his tone was heavy, each word weighted. "If it is the last thing I do upon this earth, Blackburn, I'm going to put you where you'll do no more of your damned investigating!"

Very deliberately, he took off his coat and laid it on the table. "I never like blood upon my clothes," he explained levelly. "And this promises to be extremely messy. Bloodstains are such awkward things to explain." He began to roll up his sleeve, exposing a muscular, hairy forearm. "It is perhaps as well that this house is empty, and that—" He broke off abruptly and his stocky body tensed. Then he wheeled like a goaded bull. "What was that?" he cried.

The scream of a police whistle answered him. Half a dozen others took up the eldritch wailing. Jeffery tugged at his ropes, then relaxed. He forced his cold lips into a ghastly semblance of a smile. "The Chief Inspector remains faithful to the tradition of his radio thrillers," he croaked. "This, Newland, is the last-minute rescue!"

And now, the bellowing of William Read echoed through the empty corridors, and there was a crash as heavy shoulders thudded against the locked door. Newland stared with dropping jaw, then he gave a high-pitched scream in which rage, fear, and madness were blended. He strode forward, fingers dragging at his hip pocket.

"You bloody inquisitive swine! They've heard every word—have they? You worked it out this way, did you? By God, it's the last thing you'll ever do! If I burn in hell, you'll burn with me!"

Out flew his hand, the fingers crooked about the butt of that small black automatic. Newland gave a crooning chuckle and stepped forward. He thrust the barrel within six inches of the bound man's forehead. Jeffery closed his eyes.

"Wriggle out of this, Mister Clever Blackburn," Newland snarled. Viciously, his finger tightened on the trigger. There was a click . . . and from the barrel of that black automatic a fat cigarette popped, smacked Jeffery squarely between the eyes, and fell to the carpet. Andrew Newland stood staring at the gun with foolish gaping eyes. And in that moment, Blackburn acted.

He tensed his muscles. Lowering his head, he flung himself forward, chair and all. His hard skull caught Newland in the pit of the stomach and the man went down like a pole-axed ox. He lay gasping and winded on the floor. Jeffery surveyed him with twisted lips.

"Steinie Rodda wasn't the only person who couldn't tell the difference between a genuine automatic and a toy," he said grimly.

With a final rending grind of woodwork and metal, the door gave. Chief Inspector Read, with Connolly and Donlin on his heels, almost fell into the room.

VI

CLOSE DOWN

"I will explain," said Dupin, "and that you may comprehend more clearly, we will retrace the course of your meditations. . . ."

POE, *Murders in the Rue Morgue.*

ANDREW NEWLAND'S boast that he was a good sportsman received a grim indictment on the following morning. The young policeman who brought him breakfast noticed that the prisoner sat very still and quiet on his bed against the wall. There was a glassy film over the dark eyes, and the heavy jaw hung loosely. Believing him to be ill, the policeman had first spoken and then, getting no answer, had crossed and shaken the broad shoulders. The body of Andrew Newland swayed, over-balanced, and fell sprawling across the floor of his cell. When the horrified policeman bent over him, he noticed a faint odour of bitter almonds rising from the parted lips.

Thus, the compositors in the vaults of Fleet Street had no sooner screwed into position the page giving details of Newland's life, than they were called upon to pull the frame apart and reassemble new lines of type regarding the criminal's death. And while radio, newspaper, and telephone carried the news to the four corners of the British Isles, Jeffery and the Chief Inspector were closeted in the latter's office at Scotland Yard.

William Read, a cigar stuck between large white teeth, a pair of horn-rimmed spectacles on that arrogant beak of a nose, was leaning back in his swivel-chair. He was scanning a typewritten account of Newland's confession, taken down word for word by Carter, as he crouched with his ear to the locked door of 22 Fern Place on the previous night. At length, Read turned the last page, placed the sheets on his desk, and removed his spectacles. He turned to Jeffery, who stood smoking by the window overlooking the Embankment.

"Gad, son—but that's amazing!" the elder man exclaimed. "How do you account for it all? Here's this chap Newland, to all outward appearances a thoroughly good sort. And behind the mask he's working this kind of thing!" His stubby fingers tapped the papers.

Jeffery removed the cigarette from his lips and turned. "Do you remember Holmes' explanation of the twisted streak in Colonel Moran, Chief? He drew an analogy by pointing out that there are some trees which grow to a certain height, and then develop some unsightly eccentricity. Holmes held the interesting theory that the individual represents in his development the whole procession of his ancestors—and that such a sudden turn to good or evil stands for some strong influence which came into the line of his pedigree. The person becomes, as it were, the epitome of the history of his own family."

The Chief Inspector grunted. "Bit far-fetched, I should say!"

Jeffery smiled. "Watson made a similar remark, although more politely expressed." He sobered. "In Newland's case, of course, there was a broad streak of insanity running through his strain. I've since discovered that his father died in a mental home, and the shock of it killed his mother. All knowledge of this was kept from Newland, but Nature has an unhappy way of asserting herself."

The Chief Inspector blew a smoke-ring and watched it float upward. "When did you first come to suspect Newland?" he asked.

Jeffery moved to the desk, pulled up a chair and seated himself. "It wasn't until Lusinska told us about Rodda's apparent suicide that the first suspicion entered my mind," he said. "After Connolly had taken the actress away and you had gone to bed, I sat down to figure out why on earth Rodda should shoot himself in such a casual manner.

"Recall Lusinska's description of the act. She said that Rodda walked to the table and quite calmly and unconcernedly picked up the automatic and turned it on himself. And my whole reasoning mind screamed . . . *Why?* No normal man commits suicide like that! It was absurd—ridiculous! Then the obvious answer was that Rodda had not meant to commit suicide! Then why in the name of reason should a man point a loaded revolver at himself, pull the trigger, and expect nothing to happen . . . unless . . ."

Jeffery leaned forward and tapped the desk. "*Unless he was in the habit of doing that action and knew that there could be no fatal results!* And in that moment, I could have kicked myself from here to Wormwood Scrubs for my stupidity! Woolly-brained mutton-head that I was—it wasn't until then that I recalled that trick automatic cigarette-case that Rodda carried—the cigarette-case that was so like an automatic that when he drew it that night at the radio studio, both of us had taken it for a genuine weapon. Here then was the explanation for Rodda's seemingly incomprehensible action. He had come into that darkened room, his mind still doped with the drug, and his first thought had been a cigarette. He had gone over to the table, picked up what he thought was his case, turned it toward his body and pulled the trigger! Here, too, was an explanation of that battered left hand with its powder-blackening! When using that cigarette-case, it was Rodda's procedure to press the trigger with his right hand and reach for the emerging cigarette with his left. But as some person had substituted a real loaded automatic for the case, it was a bullet instead of a cigarette that emerged, a bullet that shattered the groping hand and buried itself in Rodda's chest. Also, it explained why there were no finger-prints found on the automatic. Rodda, if you remember, was wearing gloves when he handled the gun."

Blackburn rocked back on his chair and puffed at his cigarette. He closed his eyes.

"Now this discovery opened up a number of remarkable conjectures," he went on. "It was not only the question of who had effected the substitution of the genuine weapon for the toy, but *why was it done?* Why hadn't the murderer gone into Rodda's room, waited for him to return, and shot him down there and then? There was only one logical answer—*the murderer couldn't do that!* For some reason, he had to be away from the scene of the crime when Rodda turned that automatic on himself.

"This brought me to the problem of why he had to be away. The only logical conclusion to this question was that he had to be somewhere else—probably establishing an alibi for the time of Rodda's murder. And keeping this thought in mind, I settled down to some close concentration.

"I had to determine the people who would need an alibi for the time covering Rodda's murder. I dismissed as unlikely the people who were in the locked dramatic studio on the night of Simms' killing, since we had proved that to be an outside job. Who else connected with the case remained? Only Katharine Knowles and the mysterious Monsieur Viardin. But Miss Knowles had been confined to her home with a fractured leg since the morning of the broadcast. She must be eliminated.

"And what of M. Viardin? Since we had no proof that this man actually was in London at the time of Rodda's killing, it seemed absurd that he should go to all this trouble to prove an alibi. Who else remained? It was some time before I remembered Andrew Newland!

"At first thought, the idea seemed absurd. Then came the conviction that it might not be quite as ridiculous as it first appeared. For had not Andrew Newland the strongest and the most water-tight alibi of everyone in London. *He was with us, sitting talking in our flat, when Rodda's murder occurred!* No matter which way I looked at the problem, I was brought back to the inevitable conclusion that if Rodda's shooting had been manipulated to provide someone with a cast-iron alibi—*Andrew Newland was the only person who would gain the most benefit from it!*"

The Chief Inspector frowned. "But we had checked up on Newland's movements through Dr. Newbolt," he objected. "We were, then, quite satisfied beyond all doubt that he was at the Towers when Simms was murdered."

"Of course." Jeffery opened his eyes. "That was what made the whole thing so incomprehensible! That was why I rejected it at first as impossible. I told myself that no man could be in two places at once. Also, we had the evidence of the telegram and the telephone-call.

"Still, I was ready to clutch at even weaker straws. And so I set myself to go over every small detail in connection with Newland. I concentrated on our entire association with him from the moment he came into this room on the morning following Simms' murder to the visit of Dr. Newbolt. And just when my head was splitting, I remembered something that almost shot me out of my seat!"

Jeffery's chair rocked forward. He leaned his arms on the desk and looked at the Chief Inspector, his grey eyes gleaming faintly.

"Chief," he said quietly, "do you remember that morning when Newland called to ask us to investigate Simms' death, do you remember casually asking him the time? Newland pulled back his cuff, revealed his bare wrist and muttered something about smashing his wrist-watch three days previous and leaving it with the jewellers for repairs." He cocked an eyebrow. "Remember it, Chief?"

Read nodded. "Yes. And you supplied the time."

"That's so. Now!" Jeffery dropped his voice and one finger tapped the desk to give emphasis to his words. "Now, when Dr. Newbolt was talking to us last night, he mentioned how Newland was sitting by his aunt's bed on the night of the broadcast. Newbolt came in to relieve him, saying that the play was to go on the air within a few minutes.

"And in the doctor's own words . . . *Newland glanced at his wrist-watch* and nodded. He seemed too weary to speak!"

Read sat bolt upright. "I'll be a pink-toed prophet!" he exclaimed. "Of course, son! Why didn't I wake up to that?"

Jeffery grinned. "I deserve spanking myself," he said wryly. "In our defence, of course, was the fact that almost a week had passed—a pretty hectic week that wiped everything else from our minds.

"When I realized this inconsistency, the old head-piece started to buzz. The simple facts were these: On the night of the murder, Andrew Newland wore a wrist-watch on his arm. Twelve hours later, he made a statement to us that he possessed no wrist-watch nor had he possessed one for three days! What did it mean? A wrist-watch isn't like a tiepin or a collar-stud; you can't wear it and forget the fact. The average person glances at his wrist-watch a hundred times a day. You don't realize how much you rely on a wrist-watch until it goes bung on you. Therefore, it was no lapse of memory on Newland's part. One conclusive fact stood out. Regarding the incident of the wrist-watch, either Dr. Newbolt or Andrew Newland was telling a deliberate lie!

"Now, there seemed no logical reason why Newbolt should lie. Especially over such an infinitesimal detail as the wearing of a watch. Then it was Andrew Newland! But why should he tell such a ridiculous falsehood? If Newland was our man, he had built up a cunning, carefully premeditated plot. He had spent months in perfecting every small item.

Why, then, should he ruin the whole thing by bringing himself under suspicion with such a paltry inconsistency?

"Then the other aspect of the case occurred to me. Andrew Newland could not possibly be our man, for Dr. Newbolt had vouched for the fact that he was at the Towers at the time of the first murder. As I said, it was impossible that he could be in two places at the one time. But wait—what if Newland had not been at the Towers? Then who was it that Newbolt had seen by the bed? Who was the man who had glanced at his wrist-watch *and had been, apparently, too weary to talk?* Could it be that Newland had employed someone else to take his place while he went about his dark business? The more I thought over it, the more likely it seemed!

"If this had happened, here was an explanation of the inconsistency of the wrist-watch! Newland had overlooked the fact that the masquerader was wearing one. It also explained why the man by the bed had been too weary to speak. He might resemble Newland in appearance, but not in voice. Here, also, was the explanation of the telephone-call which we checked up. Everything fitted perfectly!"

Jeffery crushed out his cigarette and lit another.

The Chief Inspector did not speak. He merely nodded to his companion to continue.

"But who was this impersonator?" Blackburn went on. "It would need to be someone who resembled Newland very closely, since a disguise might easily be penetrated. Could it be a twin brother? But Newland was the only relative. Did he have a double in London? I was about to dismiss this as too fantastic when I recalled Newland's film experience. Remember what Nickerson had said regarding those productions in which Newland played the lead? The studio manager described them as being wild and woolly adventures with Newland playing a kind of sporting Buffalo Bill! Was it inconceivable that this film company should employ a double to do the dangerous stunts which might injure their leading man? Certainly not! The practice is common among film companies. Then, if Newland had a double, that man would be trained to impersonate Newland in every way—his walk, his gestures, everything about him. He would be the ideal person to masquerade as Newland on this particular night!"

The Chief Inspector deposited an inch of grey ash in the tray and gave a little grunt. "Didn't the fact that Newland was supposedly dead worry you, son?"

"Worry me?" cried Jeffery. "The term is mild! It mocked at me for almost an hour! If Newland had killed Simms and Rodda, who in the name of Euclid had killed him? Did it mean that I was again on the wrong track, and that the real murderer was some shadowy figure with whom we were yet to contact? But that theory seemed absurd! Yet it was no more absurd than the premise that Newland had committed the first two murders—for was he not dead?

"I went back over Newland's supposed death step by step. I said to myself: 'There can be no doubt that that man taken out of the water is Newland. Both Newbolt and the Chief identified him.' Identity! That was what it hinged upon. But then—glorious thought—Dr. Newbolt had identified the man at the Towers as Newland when everything pointed to that individual being his double! Could it—was it possible that the man taken from the water was *Newland's double?*

"And the more I considered it," said Jeffery, "the more likely the possibility became. There was absolutely no reason why Newland should be murdered—but there was the strongest reason in the world why his double should' die! Because that double knew too much for Newland's peace of mind! I was certain, then, that Newland was still alive and planning fresh mischief!

"Then there was that detail of the envelope. If it was the double who was killed, why was that envelope left in the pocket with the scribbled address? Was it a trap—a trap for me? If so, I meant to spring it on Newland's own head. Because, Chief, I was still groping for the *motive* of all these killings! Why had Newland spawned this elaborate plan? There was only one way to discover that—to pretend to walk into his trap and pump the truth out of him." Jeffery paused and grinned again. "Then it was that I raced into your bedroom whooping Callooh! Callay!" He rose and stretched himself. "And the rest you know, Chief."

"You picked up the name of Allan Thompson from that actors' agency in Wardour Street, I suppose?" asked Read.

"Yes." Jeffery crossed to the window and flicked his cigarette end into the blue. "After I arranged with you to stand by at Fern Place, I reckoned that if anyone would know of the existence of Newland's film double, it would be Wardour Street. I went down there on Sunday morning and looked through about five hundred photographs. That's how I found Thompson's name."

The Chief Inspector nodded. He took his cigar from between his lips and tugged at his moustache. "Looks as if I've got to hand it to you again, son," he said gruffly. "But I still consider you a damned young fool to take the risk of going into that house with a toy cigarette-case in your pocket!"

Jeffery gave his characteristic shrug. "Perhaps it was childish," he admitted. " But I was keen to show Newland that he wasn't the only person who could plan surprises. You see, I felt very bitter about the manner in which he'd led me by the nose—my ego was bruised and it smarted no end! Also I wanted to let him know that I was aware of the manner in which he had arranged Rodda's death."

"But the risk . . .?"

"The risk wasn't so great," returned the young man. "That trick case was specially prepared for weight and size to correspond with a genuine automatic, and after all, I knew that the forces of Scotland Yard were outside that door all the time. Newland made it plain at the beginning that he was going to use my own gun on me. If he hadn't said that, I might have felt a few quavers. In which case, I would have yelled for you at once."

"I still think it was foolish," growled Read.

"Someone had to get into that house," Jeffery pointed out. "It was our only way of getting the proof we needed. And I had to be that one, since the trap was laid for me and the arrival of any other person would have made Newland suspicious of the trap!"

"I suppose so," the Chief Inspector admitted. "Anyhow, it's a nasty business and thank God it's over. And, as is usual with these things, the innocent suffer almost as much as the guilty. Heaven only knows how Miss Boycott-Smith will take it all."

"Newbolt hasn't told her yet?" asked Jeffery quietly.

Read shook his head. "No. He's keeping it from her until she's strong enough to bear the shock. At the moment, he's spun her a story about Newland going away on a trip and it's keeping her quiet for a time." He shifted and the swivel-chair creaked under him. "If anyone tries to tell you that money brings happiness, you can trot them out the tale of the Boycott-Smith wealth!"

There was a silence. Read dropped his cigar end into the tray and began to fiddle with the papers on his desk. Jeffery spoke after a pause. "Carter tells me that they've arrested Viardin in Vienna?"

Read nodded. "Late last night," he replied. "He denied everything, of course, so until he decides to open his mouth, we'll never know whether Simms got that code-word over the air. Not that it matters, but it would have cleaned up the case nicely to have had that point straightened out."

Jeffery walked across from the window and stood before the desk. The big man was fumbling with the typewritten sheaf of papers, removing the wire clip and re-fastening it. There was something in his attitude, a slight hesitancy, that puzzled Blackburn. Presently the Chief Inspector gave tongue, but he did not look up.

"Er—talking of radio, son," he said gruffly, "you—well—I take it you're not too keen on that wireless in the flat? So,"—and Read gnawed at his moustache—"well, I've decided to get rid of it!"

Surprise lifted Jeffery's tone. "But, Chief—you can't do that—"

"Oh yes, I can!" Read grunted. He worried the papers with irritable fingers. "I don't mind. As a matter of fact—I've had rather a belly-full of wireless myself lately. I'll see about selling that contraption in the morning."

Blackburn thrust his hands in his pockets and walked to the door. Then he turned. "It's a magnificent gesture, Chief," he said gravely, "and one that I appreciate. Unfortunately, it's a gesture I can't let you make!"

"And why not?" snapped the Chief Inspector.

"Because you'd finish up behind bars yourself," retorted Jeffery. "There's a law against selling other people's property. And that wireless set doesn't belong to you any more." He paused and chuckled at the rich colour that spread across William Read's face. "You see, Chief, I sold that wireless set after you left the flat this morning!"

THE END

RAMBLE HOUSE's

HARRY STEPHEN KEELER WEBWORK MYSTERIES

(RH) indicates the title is available ONLY in the RAMBLE HOUSE edition

The Ace of Spades Murder
The Affair of the Bottled Deuce (RH)
The Amazing Web
The Barking Clock
Behind That Mask
The Book with the Orange Leaves
The Bottle with the Green Wax Seal
The Box from Japan
The Case of the Canny Killer
The Case of the Crazy Corpse (RH)
The Case of the Flying Hands (RH)
The Case of the Ivory Arrow
The Case of the Jeweled Ragpicker
The Case of the Lavender Gripsack
The Case of the Mysterious Moll
The Case of the 16 Beans
The Case of the Transparent Nude (RH)
The Case of the Transposed Legs
The Case of the Two-Headed Idiot (RH)
The Case of the Two Strange Ladies
The Circus Stealers (RH)
Cleopatra's Tears
A Copy of Beowulf (RH)
The Crimson Cube (RH)
The Face of the Man From Saturn
Find the Clock
The Five Silver Buddhas
The 4th King
The Gallows Waits, My Lord! (RH)
The Green Jade Hand
Finger! Finger!
Hangman's Nights (RH)
I, Chameleon (RH)
I Killed Lincoln at 10:13! (RH)
The Iron Ring
The Man Who Changed His Skin (RH)
The Man with the Crimson Box
The Man with the Magic Eardrums
The Man with the Wooden Spectacles
The Marceau Case
The Matilda Hunter Murder
The Monocled Monster
The Murder of London Lew
The Murdered Mathematician
The Mysterious Card (RH)
The Mysterious Ivory Ball of Wong Shing Li (RH)
The Mystery of the Fiddling Cracksman
The Peacock Fan
The Photo of Lady X (RH)
The Portrait of Jirjohn Cobb
Report on Vanessa Hewstone (RH)

Riddle of the Travelling Skull
Riddle of the Wooden Parrakeet (RH)
The Scarlet Mummy (RH)
The Search for X-Y-Z
The Sharkskin Book
Sing Sing Nights
The Six From Nowhere (RH)
The Skull of the Waltzing Clown
The Spectacles of Mr. Cagliostro
Stand By—London Calling!
The Steeltown Strangler
The Stolen Gravestone (RH)
Strange Journey (RH)
The Strange Will
The Straw Hat Murders (RH)
The Street of 1000 Eyes (RH)
Thieves' Nights
Three Novellos (RH)
The Tiger Snake
The Trap (RH)
Vagabond Nights (Defrauded Yeggman)
Vagabond Nights 2 (10 Hours)
The Vanishing Gold Truck
The Voice of the Seven Sparrows
The Washington Square Enigma
When Thief Meets Thief
The White Circle (RH)
The Wonderful Scheme of Mr. Christopher Thorne
X. Jones—of Scotland Yard
Y. Cheung, Business Detective

Keeler Related Works

A To Izzard: A Harry Stephen Keeler Companion by Fender Tucker — Articles and stories about Harry, by Harry, and in his style. Included is a compleat Keeler bibliography.

Wild About Harry: Reviews of Keeler Novels — Edited by Richard Polt & Fender Tucker — 22 reviews of works by Harry Stephen Keeler from *Keeler News.* A perfect introduction to the author.

The Keeler Keyhole Collection: Annotated newsletter rants from Harry Stephen Keeler, edited by Francis M. Nevins

Fakealoo — Pastiches of the style of Harry Stephen Keeler by selected demented members of the HSK Society.

RAMBLE HOUSE's OTHER LOONS

Slammer Days — Two full-length prison memoirs: *Men into Beasts* (1952) by George Sylvester Viereck and *Home Away From Home* (1962) by Jack Woodford

The Organ Reader — A huge compilation of just about everything published in the 1971-1972 radical bay-area newspaper, THE ORGAN.

Dr. Odin — Douglas Newton's 1933 potboiler comes back to life.

The Chinese Jar Mystery — Murder in the manor by John Stephen Strange, 1934

The Julius Caesar Murder Case — A classic 1935 re-telling of the assassination by Wallace Irwin

The Contested Earth and Other SF Stories — A never-before published space opera and seven short stories by Jim Harmon.

Freaks and Fantasies — Eerie tales by Tod Robbins, collaborator of Tod Browning on the film FREAKS.

Vixen Scandal — Two sleaze masterpieces from the 60s by Jim Harmon: *Vixen Hollow* and *Celluloid Scandal.*

Maniac Siren — Two more sleaze marvels by Jim Harmon: *The Man Who Made Maniacs* and *Silent Siren*

West Texas War and Other Western Stories — by Gary Lovisi

Marblehead: A Novel of H.P. Lovecraft — A long-lost masterpiece from Richard A. Lupoff. Published for the first time!

The Secret Adventures of Sherlock Holmes — Three Sherlockian pastiches by the Brooklyn author/publisher, Gary Lovisi.

The Universal Holmes — Richard A. Lupoff's 2007 collection of five Holmesian pastiches and a recipe for giant rat stew.

Tales of the Macabre and Ordinary — Modern twisted horror by Chris Mikul, author of the *Bizarrism* series.

The Gold Star Line — Seaboard adventure from L.T. Reade and Robert Eustace.

The Werewolf vs the Vampire Woman — Hard to believe ultraviolence by either Arthur M. Scarm or Arthur M. Scram.

Black Hogan Strikes Again — Australia's Peter Renwick pens a tale of the outback.

Four Joel Townsley Rogers Novels — By the author of *The Red Right Hand: Once In a Red Moon, Lady With the Dice, The Stopped Clock, Never Leave My Bed*

Killing Time — New collection of short novels by Joel Townsley Rogers

Night of Horror — A short story collection of Joel Townsley Rogers

Twenty Norman Berrow Novels — *The Bishop's Sword, Ghost House, Don't Go Out After Dark, Claws of the Cougar, The Smokers of Hashish, The Secret Dancer, Don't Jump Mr. Boland!, The Footprints of Satan, Fingers for Ransom, The Three Tiers of Fantasy, The Spaniard's Thumb, The Eleventh Plague, Words Have Wings, One Thrilling Night, The Lady's in Danger, It Howls at Night, The Terror in the Fog, Oil Under the Window, Murder in the Melody, The Singing Room*

The N. R. De Mexico Novels — Robert Bragg presents *Marijuana Girl, Madman on a Drum, Private Chauffeur* in one volume.

Two Hake Talbot Novels — *Rim of the Pit, The Hangman's Handyman.* Classic locked room mysteries.

Two Alexander Laing Novels — *The Motives of Nicholas Holtz* and *Dr. Scarlett,* stories of medical mayhem and intrigue from the 30s.

Two Wade Wright Novels (and counting) — *Echo of Fear* and *Death At Nostalgia Street*, with more to come!

Three Rupert Penny Novels — *Policeman's Holiday, Policeman's Evidence* and *Sealed Room Murder,* classic impossible mysteries.

Five Jack Mann Novels — Strange murder in the English countryside. *Gees' First Case, Nightmare Farm, Grey Shapes, The Ninth Life, The Glass Too Many.*

Four Max Afford Novels — *Owl of Darkness, Death's Mannikins, Blood on His Hands* and *The Dead Are Blind* by One of Australia's finest novelists.

Five Joseph Shallit Novels — *The Case of the Billion Dollar Body, Lady Don't Die on My Doorstep, Kiss the Killer, Yell Bloody Murder, Take Your Last Look.* One of America's best 50's authors.

The Best of 10-Story Book — edited by Chris Mikul, over 35 stories from the literary magazine Harry Stephen Keeler edited.

The Anthony Boucher Chronicles — edited by Francis M. Nevins
Book reviews by Anthony Boucher written for the *San Francisco Chronicle,* 1942 – 1947. Essential and fascinating reading.

A Young Man's Heart — A forgotten early classic by Cornell Woolrich

Muddled Mind: Complete Works of Ed Wood, Jr. — David Hayes and Hayden Davis deconstruct the life and works of a mad genius.

My First Time: The One Experience You Never Forget — Michael Birchwood — 64 true first-person narratives of how they lost it.

The Incredible Adventures of Rowland Hern — Rousing 1928 impossible crimes by Nicholas Olde.

Don Diablo: Book of a Lost Film — Two-volume treatment of a western by Paul Landres, with diagrams. Intro by Francis M. Nevins.

The Charlie Chaplin Murder Mystery — Movie hijinks by Wes D. Gehring

The Koky Comics — A collection of all of the 1978-1981 Sunday and daily comic strips by Richard O'Brien and Mort Gerberg, in two volumes.

Gamefinger — Incredible 1966 sado-sleaze from Clyde Allison (William Knoles).

Dime Novels: Ramble House's 10-Cent Books — *Knife in the Dark* by Robert Leslie Bellem, *Hot Lead* and *Song of Death* by Ed Earl Repp, *A Hashish House in New York* by H.H. Kane, and five more.

Stakeout on Millennium Drive — Indianapolis Noir — Ian Woollen.

Dope Tales #1 — Two dope-riddled classics; *Dope Runners* by Gerald Grantham and *Death Takes the Joystick* by Phillip Condé.

Dope Tales #2 — Two more narco-classics; *The Invisible Hand* by Rex Dark and *The Smokers of Hashish* by Norman Berrow.

Dope Tales #3 — Two enchanting novels of opium by the master, Sax Rohmer. *Dope* and *The Yellow Claw.*

Tenebrae — Ernest G. Henham's 1898 horror tale brought back.

The Singular Problem of the Stygian House-Boat — Two classic tales by John Kendrick Bangs about the denizens of Hades.

The One After Snelling — Kickass modern noir from Richard O'Brien.

The Sign of the Scorpion — 1935 Edmund Snell tale of oriental evil.

The House of the Vampire — 1907 thriller by George S. Viereck.

An Angel in the Street — Modern hardboiled noir by Peter Genovese.

The Devil's Mistress — Scottish gothic tale by J. W. Brodie-Innes.

The Lord of Terror — 1925 mystery with master-criminal, Fantômas.

The Lady of the Terraces — 1925 adventure by E. Charles Vivian.

My Deadly Angel — 1955 Cold War drama by John Chelton

Prose Bowl — Futuristic satire — Bill Pronzini & Barry N. Malzberg .

Satan's Den Exposed — True crime in TorC New Mexico — Award-winning journalism by the Desert Journal.

The Amorous Intrigues & Adventures of Aaron Burr — by Anonymous — Hot historical action.

I Stole $16,000,000 — True story by cracksman Herbert E. Wilson.

The Black Dark Murders — Vintage 50s college murder yarn by Milt Ozaki, writing as Robert O. Saber.

Sex Slave — Potboiler of lust in the days of Cleopatra — Dion Leclerq.

You'll Die Laughing — Bruce Elliott's 1945 novel of murder at a practical joker's English countryside manor.

The Private Journal & Diary of John H. Surratt — The memoirs of the man who conspired to assassinate President Lincoln.

Dead Man Talks Too Much — Hollywood boozer by Weed Dickenson

Red Light — History of legal prostitution in Shreveport Louisiana by Eric Brock. Includes wonderful photos of the houses and the ladies.

Gadsby — A lipogram (a novel without the letter E). Ernest Vincent Wright's last work, published in 1939 right before his death.

A Snark Selection — Lewis Carroll's *The Hunting of the Snark* with two Snarkian chapters by Harry Stephen Keeler — Illustrated by Gavin L. O'Keefe.

Ripped from the Headlines! — The Jack the Ripper story as told in the newspaper articles in the *New York* and *London Times.*

Geronimo — S. M. Barrett's 1905 autobiography of a noble American.

The Compleat Calhoon — All of Fender Tucker's works: Includes *The Totah Trilogy, Weed, Women and Song* and *Tales from the Tower,* plus a CD of all of his songs.

The Naked Trocar with **The Best Revenge** — Two misdemeanors by Fender Tucker from 2007

DID3210436
L - #2229 - 291121 - C0 - 229/152/14 - PB - DID3210436